# RECYCLED

*Robert O'Brien*

# Foreword

Albert Einstein once said, "There are only two ways to live your life. One is as though nothing is a miracle. The other is as though everything is a miracle." I guess I did not understand the meaning of the phrase until now. It is about how we choose to look at life.

We either view things like the rising of the sun or the seasons perfect timing as miracles or we take them for granted and consider them automatically normal and go about our day believing that miracles are extraordinary events with unlikely timing or results. I believe each one of us at some point midway through our life evaluates our choices regarding career, relationships, decisions, and the choices we made to justify our contribution to the greater good.

We all want to be remembered and many are elevated in our memories more than others based on their life's accomplishments. We all live our lives in the way it suits us best, albeit knowing that it ends at our death, and we move on to whatever version of the afterlife in which we hold belief. Or so it would seem.

Someone once said, "You can't go back and change the beginning, but you can start where you are and change the ending." Meaning that your future is not indelibly written, and you have the power to change that future. That is where my story begins, at what I thought was the end of the life I had led up to that fateful evening. My name is Alexander Jones, and this is my story.

# The light

The doors to the emergency room's trauma bay at New York's General Hospital burst open with a deafening clatter. The shrill wail of an ambulance's siren pierced the air, almost drowning out the cacophony of medical machinery and hushed conversations. Two paramedics frantically pushed a gurney through the entrance. A cluster of doctors and nurses in scrubs and facemasks sprang into action, their faces a blend of concern and urgency.

I lay on the gurney, staring up at the fluorescent lights that dotted the ceiling like cold, sterile stars. I was acutely conscious, my eyes wide open, but it was as if my body was held captive, confined by invisible chains. My limbs were unresponsive; my voice, an inaudible murmur.

"White male, approximately 50 years old, involved in a vehicular collision," one of the paramedics rattled off as they wheeled me deeper into the trauma bay. "Blood pressure is 80 over 50 and dropping. Pulse is at 51. Shallow breathing. We've got blunt force trauma to the right region of his skull, potential spinal injuries, fractured ribs, internal bleeding, and lower limb fractures. Administered 2.5mg of epinephrine and morphine en route."

The information swirled around me, a storm of medical jargon and numbers. A car accident? My mind raced to recall the past events. The last memory I had was swirling a glass of red wine at an art gallery opening, marveling at the abstract beauty of life captured in oil and canvas.

"Move him into Trauma Room #2 and prep the crash cart, STAT! He's deteriorating," barked Dr. Johnson, the attending physician, as I was moved from the gurney onto a surgical table. Nurses scrambled to comply.

"Crash cart's ready, Dr. Johnson," Nurse Emily confirmed, her voice tinged with worry.

No sooner had they transferred me onto the operating table than the electrocardiogram emitted a long, high-pitched tone. It was a sound I'd only heard in movies, a harbinger of impending doom: a flatline. To my surreal amazement, I found myself suddenly standing next to Nurse Emily. I reached out to touch her, but my hand went right through her as if she were a mere apparition.

"Charge to two hundred. Clear!" Dr. Johnson's voice rang out as he administered a defibrillating shock. My physical body jerked from the electrical pulse, but it remained a lifeless shell. Staff members paused and looked at each other, their faces a tableau of defeat. A nurse solemnly draped a white sheet over my face.

"Time of death: 11:40 PM, Saturday, July 16th, 2023," Dr. Johnson announced, his voice tinged with a weariness that seemed to echo through the room.

As the last nurse exited and the trauma room door closed behind her, a melodious chime rang through the air. Before me materialized a celestial escalator, illuminated in a soft, divine light that stood in sharp contrast to the harsh fluorescence of the hospital.

"Please ascend," a mysterious voice beckoned, tinged with otherworldly wisdom. "It's time for your life's adjudication and journey to the next realm."

As the escalator hummed beneath me, my body tensed with a blend of trepidation and incredulity. This was unlike any conveyance I had ever known. I couldn't shift my feet; they were immobilized as the escalator ascended through the ceiling of the hospital trauma room. It then pierced the hospital's outer wall and soared into a night sky embellished with stars and bathed in the lunar glow of a full moon. The metallic pathway flattened at an incline, reminding me vaguely of people movers in airports or the escalators at Caesar's Palace in Las Vegas.

The ride spanned what felt like minutes, a tranquil interlude in which the earthly realm below gradually blurred into an indistinct tapestry. Parallel to my own route, other pathways—each replete with its circled arrows—emerged into view. On them were other souls, each ensconced in identical white gowns. A complex network materialized as these paths converged, eerily resembling the assembly lines of an Amazon warehouse—each soul maintaining a respectful distance, standing like uniquely packaged goods on a conveyor belt. In the far distance, the multiplicity of pathways narrowed, funneling down to a mere dozen for the final stretch.

A synthetic voice broke my reverie. "Welcome to the Transfer Portal System. Shortly, you will arrive at the Assessment Station to undergo your life's adjudication."

While engrossed in the mysterious message, my ears picked up echoes in Spanish, French, and Arabic. People of diverse ethnicities and backgrounds were receiving the same revelation, their facial expressions a blend of awe and perplexity. Although I could hear my own voice when I muttered under my breath, I could not discern the speech of those around me.

"Please refrain from attempting to communicate with other souls. Focus on your monitor for a life cycle review," the voice continued, more imperative this time.

A small holographic screen materialized near my left shoulder, angled for easy viewing yet unobtrusive to my forward gaze. A rapid montage of life events unfurled—some triumphant, many regrettable. I flinched at the recapitulation of my follies, wondering why I hadn't sought redemption when I had the chance. A quick glance revealed a spectrum of reactions on the adjacent conveyors: smiles of satisfaction, faces buried in tears, futile struggles against the invisible bonds holding us all.

As we approached a colossal, floating platform with a distinct pale-white border, a luminous aura radiated from its rear, reminiscent of a dawn breaking. The conveyors entered onto this celestial stage, encircling it in a semi-loop. A closer inspection clarified that this massive structure rested atop a gargantuan pyramid. Twelve distinct pathways—corresponding to the twelve facets of the pyramid—fed into this surreal arena.

Stepping onto the platform, my ears caught another announcement. "Welcome to Transfer Portal Terminal 5. Prepare for interlink exchange, transformation, and transfer to your afterlife destination."

The conveyor advanced steadily, leading me closer to the interlink exchange that the omnipresent voice had mentioned. Each conveyor belt terminated at an archway crowned with a circle. The spacing of individuals on the conveyors now made sense: it was meticulously calculated to allow the archway enough time to display a directional signal while maintaining a constant flow.

As each person reached the archway, a circular transparent tube enveloped them, spinning briefly before the circle at the apex of the arch displayed an arrow. Beyond the arch, the conveyor branched into three divergent paths—left and downward, right, and upward, and straight ahead. A momentary glimpse allowed me to see the green, purple, and red arrows, each pointing the travelers in different directions. The green arrow displayed the word "Heaven," red signified "Hell," and purple indicated "Recycle."

It intrigued me that 'recycle' was part of this celestial decision-making. I noticed that the terms for heaven and hell varied on each arch, symbolizing a multicultural acknowledgment of the afterlife. Heaven was sometimes Valhalla, Nirvana, or Shangri-La; Hell was alternatively Folkvangr, Naraka, or Gehenna.

Attendants awaited beyond each archway, clothed in robes that matched the color of the path. On a neighboring conveyor, an elderly man received a green arrow. He was given a golden shield and sword by an attendant in a gold robe as he embarked on his journey to Valhalla. Trumpets heralded his ascension, and he roared,

"Velkommen meg Valhalla," a phrase I inexplicably understood as "Welcome me, Valhalla," despite not knowing any foreign languages.

My attention returned just in time to witness a young woman receiving a green arrow. A halo appeared over her head, and her robe transformed as magnificent wings sprouted from her back. A chorus of "Hallelujah" accompanied her blissful ascent.

To my left, a Middle Eastern man, bound for Paradise, found himself surrounded by seventy-two ugly women dressed in golden robes. "Hey, Allah promised me seventy-two virgins upon my martyrdom in his name," he protested. The attendant clarified, "He never said they would be beautiful."

On another path labeled "Nirvana," a man with a purple arrow was handed a numbered ticket and guided towards a central tower with a sign reading, "Transfer to Recycling Center."

Just as I braced for my own judgment, an ominous bell tolled. I watched, heart pounding, as a man ahead of me received a red arrow and was guided down towards Hell, his soul disappearing into a pit of rising flames and echoing screams.

Doubt seized me; the monitor had only displayed the darker chapters of my life. Was this a harbinger of my own fate? Finally, my turn arrived. The tube encased me, spun momentarily, and then I heard the chilling bell tones. Fear gnawed at my guts as I approached an attendant dressed in red, holding a glass of ice water.

"Beep, beep, beep," an alarm blared suddenly.

"Hold on, Mr. Jones," said the attendant. "There has been a motion filed in your adjudication. You're being rerouted to the Recycling Center."

Confused, I asked, "What does that mean?"

"All will become clear at the Recycling Center," he assured, as the conveyor reversed direction.

Soon, I met another attendant in a white robe, who handed me a voucher. "Everything will be explained by your case worker. Have a great after-life," he said, ushering me into the tower marked for recycling.

Relief washed over me as I contemplated my unexpected reprieve from Hell. What had altered my fate? As I entered the tower beneath the starlit sky, I could only wonder what awaited me in the nebulous realm of the Recycling Center.

Emerging from an engulfing darkness, I found myself disoriented, standing inside a chamber shaped like a cylinder. Its structure was unfamiliar, unlike anything I'd encountered before. An attendant, draped in an ethereal purple robe that almost glowed in the soft light, greeted me. Adjacent to her was an object that caught my eye: a chair, its whiteness stark against the backdrop. A series of metal rods gave it the appearance of a gyroscope, and it was cocooned inside a transparent, bubble-like enclosure, complete with a door and a handle.

"Welcome to the Recycling Center Transit Station," she announced, her voice echoing with an unsettling blend of warmth and authority. Her words stirred a labyrinth of questions within me, but before I could articulate any, she continued, "Please make your way into the transport device. Secure yourself with the shoulder restraints. We cannot afford any deviations from the designated route."

I hesitated, my thoughts racing. What sort of place was this? What exactly was a "Recycling Center"? And why did it sound so final? Before I could voice these questions, the attendant intervened.

"There's no need for questions now. You'll find all your answers soon enough. Your case worker will be responsible for that. Have a pleasant journey," she said, with an air of finality that seemed to close the door on any further interaction.

Reluctantly, I complied. As I seated myself in the chair, I noticed how it perfectly accommodated the contours of my body. The shoulder harnesses felt secure but not restraining, giving me an odd sense of comfort despite the looming unknown. I was still grasping the ticket in my hand, its purpose a mystery, when a pedestal rose from the floor. It harbored a control panel, which the attendant began operating with practiced ease.

With a series of button presses followed by a hauntingly long tone, a transparent tube began its descent from above, encapsulating me within this curious contraption. I was suspended in air, levitating slowly toward the ceiling. My eyes caught sight of a small hatch swinging open above, unveiling an endless expanse of night sky. My mind toggled between awe and apprehension.

Once I reached the apex, a metallic 'clank' signaled the sealing of the floor below. I now found myself in a transparent sphere, seemingly floating in a celestial void. Below me were dual rails, much like the ones you'd find at amusement parks, albeit far more advanced and undoubtedly serving a different purpose.

Suddenly, I felt a mechanical jolt. A plunger mechanism, akin to those in pinball machines, catapulted me forward. The rails twisted and spiraled in seemingly impossible configurations—yet, thanks to the gyroscopic nature of my chair, my orientation remained stable. I zoomed through a surreal sky, a celestial universe of stars, moons, and nebulae adorning the backdrop. I was in a different realm, far from anything Earthly, my senses intoxicated by the visual symphony around me.

As I propelled forward, I saw it: a city of astonishing dimensions, where towers of white jutted into the sky, encircled by buildings of myriad colors. The city's nerve center appeared to be a grand, dome-shaped edifice that shimmered in a rhythmic dance of kaleidoscopic lights. I was awestruck. Translucent tubes interconnected buildings in a web-like pattern, all emanating from the spires that circled the city's periphery.

This must be the Recycling Center, I thought, a mixture of awe and trepidation filling me. My transport was now gliding over what seemed like the city's outskirts, providing a panoramic view of its labyrinthine complexity. I saw locals in colorful robes engaging in activities that, for now, remained beyond my comprehension. Buildings bore signs like "Robes 'R Us" and "Halo's and Wings," lending an unsettlingly commercial air to this cosmic realm.

My transport aligned itself with one of the towering spires ahead. As I neared, a grid of pulsating light materialized between the rails. I felt a deceleration, gentle yet abrupt. The next thing I knew, I was inside a glass elevator, still ensconced in my gyroscopic seat. It initiated its vertical trek, ascending higher until I found myself in a room at the pinnacle of this towering edifice. With a soft click, the journey reached its conclusion, setting the stage for yet more questions, wrapped in an enigma, cocooned in wonder and trepidation.

The translucent sphere encapsulating my seat dissolved into nothingness, and I found myself within the expanse of a vast circular chamber. Directly ahead, a semi-circular window unveiled a staggering view down into the awe-inspiring, domed edifice I'd glimpsed during my transit. Along one wall, a constellation of monitors blinked, overseen by a complex control panel situated beneath them.

Opposite the bank of monitors stood a sophisticated circular chamber. A tangle of cords and tubes fed into it, a partially open sliding door offering a glimpse inside. Above the entrance, the sign "Re-Animator" loomed, casting a long shadow over additional pedestal control panels, reminiscent of those I'd encountered at the Recycling Center Portal.

As I unbuckled the harness that held me to the seat and rose to my feet, I was interrupted by the soft "shoosh" of a sliding door behind me. An elderly man with a halo of white hair and a beard that could rival Father Time's stepped through, garbed in a robe of regal purple.

"Hello, Mr. Jones. My name is Max, short for Maximilian. I'm your afterlife caseworker. Welcome to Recycling Center Tower #9 in Soul City," he introduced himself.

"Soul City?" The words escaped my lips almost involuntarily.

"Yes, Soul City—the cradle of existence, the continuum of universal life on Earth," Max elaborated. He moved toward the control panel and lifted a clipboard. "Your original judgment from the adjudication process was, ah yes, 2000 years in Hell, punishment code #167-219543."

The weight of his words hit me like a ton of bricks. "2000 years in Hell?" I gasped.

Max continued, "Each soul is judged on Earth according to a set of standards and rules laid out by the Supreme Being. These encompass behaviors, morals, actions, and so on. You earn a score based on your life's contribution to the greater good, and from that, your afterlife fate is decided."

"Ah, much like Earth's legal system. I was an attorney, you see," I offered.

"Perhaps there's some similarity, but caution," Max replied, "our system here has its own nuances. Those ascending to realms like Heaven or Valhalla are there for eternity, possibly gaining roles like guardian angels. Those descending into Hell or other dark realms serve a sentence dictated by a precise set of codes, with a minimum sentence of one thousand years and a maximum of eternity. The latter is reserved for aberrations—glitches in the system, if you will."

"Aberrations? Glitches?" My curiosity piqued.

"Let's approach the window," Max suggested. I complied, and what lay before me in the dome was nothing short of breathtaking.

Beneath the transparent panels of the massive dome, an enormous, radiant orb spun at incredible speed. Every few seconds, it emitted a bright flash, propelling a ball of light through an opening in the ceiling. Around it, twelve stations operated with workers in yellow robes. Other personnel, clothed in blue, green, and orange robes, attended to various tasks.

"This is the Soul Reactor," Max explained, "the origin of all souls across time. It's an automated system, creating unique souls for each newborn. These souls' journey to Earth at the moment a child's heart and brain function. Occasionally, errors—outages, power surges—result in the creation of purely evil souls. These too have a right to exist, and it's the duty of the good to keep them in check, though they often fail."

We crossed the expanse of the room to approach a bank of screens that adorned the wall. Max deftly manipulated a series of controls, and abruptly, the monitors came alive with vignettes from my past—a tableau of my life's misdeeds, some of which I'd already been forced to confront on my trek to the Assessment Station.

"Observe," Max intoned. "Here in the Recycling Center, we zero in on your ethical lapses. You were originally slated for two millennia in Hell under penalty code #167-219543."

"Penalty code #167-219543?" My voice edged towards incredulity.

"We'll elucidate that shortly," Max replied. "For now, turn your gaze to the monitors."

I did, and I felt a surge of shame as I witnessed my own malevolence on display.

"We have cataloged approximately a thousand instances of morally reprehensible conduct or actions detrimental to societal welfare," Max began. "For instance, you amass your wealth by exploiting the financial markets through insider trading. Earthly laws never caught up to you, but our oversight is omniscient. Now, witness the innocent investors who lost everything. Some were rendered homeless, others took their own lives—all while you reveled aboard your yacht, humiliating your employees and partaking in disreputable activities."

He proceeded to unveil one sordid event after another. Max showcased the charity events where my presence added nothing, and corporate volunteer initiatives I intentionally evaded. He highlighted judicial proceedings where I used legal trickery to absolve criminals. The numerous hearts I shattered due to my wealth and status were revealed as well. Time stretched infinitely as my shame deepened, and when he finally discerned my profound remorse, he terminated the display.

"Code #167-219543," Max said, consulting a ledger on the control console, "involved you trudging on superheated shards of glass for two thousand years, burdened by a fifty-pound iron weight. Additionally, your hands would be crushed daily as retribution for not extending them in aid."

"I understand," I stammered. "I was vile, manipulative, and avaricious. The life I led was ignominious. I accept culpability."

"Then why have I been spared from Hell?" I queried. "Why evade the penalty you just delineated?"

"A solitary act of kindness," Max revealed, "an anomaly that had far-reaching implications."

He queued a memory from my early twenties, a seemingly inconsequential moment when I renewed my driver's license and consented to organ donation.

"This act, whether premeditated or spontaneous, may have redeemed your soul," Max noted. "Your eyes were harvested posthumously and granted sight to a young girl who subsequently prayed for your salvation."

That prayer, it appeared, had altered my cosmic judgment, diverting me to this Recycling Center.

"What does 'recycling' entail?" I wondered aloud.

"Mr. Jones," Max began, "the Recycling Center offers souls in limbo an opportunity for redemption or damnation, governed by their deeds during re-embodiment."

He elaborated on the possible fates that await in the afterlife. The ultimate choices ranged from eternal torment to celestial bliss, with some souls perpetually stagnating in between.

"That," he gestured to a circular chamber, "is the soul recycling generator. Your subsequent earthly form will reflect our assessment of your moral progression or regression. You may die and be re-animated in the same form, progress to a higher form of life as your moral progression advances or regress if you exhibit the same behaviors that brought you here in the first place.

Many creatures on Earth are recycled souls, inching their way through an eternal cycle. If your moral and social progression reaches a point where you have satisfied the requirements, you will be allowed into, which for you, is Heaven. If you regress more than three times, you will serve out your original punishment, or for those who did not have one assigned on entry, be assigned an appropriate adjudication."

He warned me of escaped souls, those who avoided this cycle and now roam Earth as restless spirits. They were to be avoided as they are partially the cause of soul regression. They escaped by not ever entering the process upon their death, unable to accept the reality, they wandered off and haunt their previous life for eternity.

"Once recycled, your past life will be forgotten. The goal is to be the epitome of your new form. Let's proceed."

I entered the chamber. As its door slid shut, I watched Max engage the controls. The chamber whirred, faster and faster, until my vision was nothing but a blur. Alarms sounded, the world whitened into a blind haze. Panicked, I shouted, but the dark swallowed me whole. Consciousness slipped away.

# new life

The room reverberated with the siren's relentless wail as Max grappled with the controls to halt the recycling sequence. With a swift sequence of inputs, he managed to quell both the process and the alarm. No sooner had he done so than the sliding door whirred open, admitting three attendants garbed in luminescent yellow robes. They burst into the room, arms laden with emergency apparatus: a fire extinguisher, an axe, and hydraulic rescue tools colloquially known as the "jaws of life."

A dense mist of white smoke swirled within the glass chamber, obscuring the contents.

"Code 422, unaccounted soul, Code 422!" bellowed an attendant, his voice tinged with panic. "Re-animator malfunction in Tower Nine. Potential lost soul situation!"

"Pry the chamber open—there's still a chance," Max ordered, urgency lacing his words.

Engaging the jaws of life to the chamber's small access point, the attendants pulled the starter cord. The tool roared to life. Minutes seemed like hours, but finally, the chamber's door groaned open, releasing a plume of smoke that filled the room. When it cleared, it was evident that Alexander Jones had vanished.

One attendant began inspecting the chamber's external mechanisms. Fumbling with a pair of pliers, he removed a fuse and held it up.

"Here lies the crux of our malfunction," he declared. "The primary fuse to the memory sanitizer blew."

"Where could he have gone?" wondered another attendant aloud.

"Disintegrated? Vanished? Phased out of existence?" quipped the third.

"This isn't a time for levity," Max snapped, his brows furrowing. "If my monitor readings are accurate, Jones was successfully reanimated before the electrical failure. That likely means we have a Code 451: a compromised memory sanitizer."

"How can you be certain?" one of the attendants inquired.

"Here's the conundrum: we can't be," Max explained. "Suffice it to say, if the memory sanitizer malfunctioned, he could retain recollections across multiple lifecycles. Proceed with the chamber's repairs. My shift isn't getting any shorter."

Ascending to the 100th floor of the Central Tower, Max pondered Jones's inexplicable fate. The elevator dinged, and he stepped into the austere office of Agnes, the shift supervisor. A person saved from eternal damnation thanks to an unexpected act of kindness, Agnes had her own complicated history with the adjudication process.

"What summons you, Max?" she queried. "Is it a social call or a procedural one?"

"We had a malfunction," Max began, outlining the situation. "Given the circumstances, it's safe to assume Alexander Jones is now an anomaly. He may still possess his original memories."

Agnes sighed. "I'll alert the Adjudication Council. This could make his next review a complicated affair."

As Max returned to his workstation, he found the attendants completing their task. "All set for the next client," one announced. Max nodded his acknowledgment, his thoughts still entwined with the strange case of Alexander Jones. For souls with retained memories had a disconcerting tendency: a proclivity to seek the past, often sabotaging their chances for heavenly afterlife in the process.

Meanwhile, I awakened from my momentary blackout. My vantage point was high, amidst the branches of a towering tree. For a heartbeat, I believed myself a bird, enthralled by my newfound freedom as I took to the skies.

But as I took stock of my form, I came to a jarring realization. "A mosquito?" I yelled into the emptiness. "Max, what on Earth?"

And then it dawned upon me: I remembered. I remembered everything. Max had promised a clean slate, but the chamber's fizzling and sparking suggested otherwise. A malfunction, perhaps?

Either way, I was now a mosquito, one of the lowest insect lifeforms on the planet—with a lifetime of human memories.

Fully aware of my identity, I hovered around, reveling in my new mosquito abilities. "Well, if life gives you lemons," I thought, preparing to dive down for my first blood meal.

Just as I was marveling at my speed and agility, a car windshield loomed from nowhere.

"Wait, no!" I shrieked, but it was too late. A loud "SPLAT" echoed, and my newly acquired mosquito life came to a swift and unceremonious end.

"Ah, not again," I muttered, finding myself reanimated in the same mosquito form. This time, I noticed another mosquito hovering next to me, vibrating its wings in what appeared to be mosquito laughter.

"Heh heh heh! Oh, man, you've got a lot to learn, newbie! First day on the job, eh?" The voice was squeaky yet raspy, resembling that of comedian Bobcat Goldthwait.

"I suppose so," I replied. "The name's Alexander, but you can call me Alex. And you are?"

"Spiffy! Yeah, that's right, Spiffy. You look confused, Alex. What's eating you? Besides windshields, I mean."

"It's a long story, but I'm not supposed to be a mosquito. I'm human. There was a malfunction in the re-animator and—"

"Heh, sounds like an opening line at 'Mosquitoes Anonymous.' Look, doesn't matter what you were, it's what you are now that counts. And right now, you gotta watch out for three things, my man: cars, spiderwebs, and bats!"

"Bats?"

"Yeah, bats! Vicious critters, they are. Fly around like they own the place. Swallow you whole if you're not careful."

"And cars?"

"Ah, the dreaded metal beasts! Always gotta watch your back, or your front, or, heck, every side! You don't want to end up as a smudge on a family's holiday photo, trust me!"

"I already did," I admitted, still trying to adjust to Spiffy's energy levels.

"Heh heh! Well, that's the cycle of life, or should I say, the cycle of afterlife," said Spiffy. "I don't remember nothing, all I know is when you die, you remember everything until you turn into something else."

"What about spiderwebs?"

"Ah, those are the worst! They're like the casinos of the insect world: once you get in, you're stuck, and you're definitely going to lose."

"Thanks for the tips, Spiffy."

"Anytime, pal! Stick with me, and you'll be sucking blood for centuries, or, you know, at least a week! Then you die anyway, and come right back, unless you get upgraded."

"Upgraded?" I inquired.

"Yea," said Spiffy, "Like this one friend of mine died, and I swear he turned into grasshopper, same voice, same stupid smile, but he never tried to find his old friends."

"Interesting"

As we buzzed around, Spiffy guiding me through the aerial intricacies of mosquito life, I couldn't help but feel a strange sense of friendship. It was bizarre, humorous, and downright absurd. Yet here I was, a mosquito with human memories, being coached by a mosquito that sounded like a stand-up comedian from the '80s.

It dawned on me then: if I had to endure this farcical sequence of lives, I might as well find the humor in it. After all, Spiffy had a point—it wasn't about what I was before but what I am now.

And so, we darted off in the direction of Central Park.

"Follow me, Alex! We're going to Central Park, the buffet of the skies!" Spiffy chortled, leading the way.

Central Park came into view, a sprawling green canvas teeming with life. Spiffy navigated us through the labyrinth of towering trees and picturesque ponds until we reached a lively gathering of mosquitoes.

"Ah, family!" Spiffy exclaimed. "Meet my brothers, sisters, and first to fourth cousins, twice removed!"

I was greeted with an enthusiastic cacophony of mosquito greetings. "Hello," they buzzed in various pitches, sounding like a broken synthesizer.

Then, a few members broke off from the buzzing mass to introduce themselves. First was Sally, a cheery female mosquito with a particularly high-pitched buzz. "Oh, it's so nice to meet another sentient one! Most just buzz around aimlessly, you know?"

Mortimer, a drab, and slightly morose male mosquito hovered over. "Well, 'aimlessly' is pretty much all we do, Sally. That and getting squashed by humans."

"And this," Spiffy interrupted, "is my cousin Dale. Dashing, daring, and always buzzing for an adventure!"

Dale spun around in a loop-to-loop before greeting me. "Pleasure, Alex. If you're ever up for dodging some frog tongues or playing chicken with a zapper, I'm your guy!"

"Now listen up, Alex," Spiffy said, pulling me aside. "The key to a good blood meal is picking the right target. You see that dachshund over there?"

I spotted the short-legged dog, prancing around a tree like it owned the place.

"Watch and learn," he added, diving down like a kamikaze pilot.

Just as we were about to pierce the dachshund's skin, Spiffy pulled up sharply. "Woah, woah, woah! Abort mission! That's a Labrador, not a dachshund!"

"What's wrong with Labradors?" I asked.

"Nothing, usually. But this one's got flea powder. Ah, poor Larry... he didn't sniff it in time. Lost him to a Labrador 2 days ago," said Spiffy.

I couldn't tell if Spiffy was joking or not as he recounted this tragic tale with the vocal quivers of a seasoned soap opera actor.

"Alright, let's try again," said Spiffy. There's our dachshund!"

We darted down, this time successfully making contact. "Quick draw, Alex! In and out!" Spiffy coached. I felt the blood rush into me, a mosquito's version of a fast-food drive-through. We quickly flew off when the dog stopped to itch itself.

"Success!" Spiffy and I high winged each other, then darted back into the sky to avoid a chasing toddler wielding a plastic shovel. "Toddlers, the guardians of the park!" Spiffy quipped. "I had another cousin whacked by one of those red shovels last week in the sand box. The mother then sprayed some stinky liquid on the toddler, and you couldn't get anywhere near it without choking."

As the sun dipped below the horizon, painting the sky with hues of orange and pink, Spiffy turned to me.

"Alright, buddy, it's getting late. You can bunk with me and the family. We've got a cozy hole in an oak tree by the pond."

"You mean you don't have your own room or home?" I asked.

"No, we share," said Spiffy. "Strength in numbers."

As we settled into our tree hole, surrounded by Spiffy's buzzing family, I reflected on the absurdity of my situation. From a successful attorney with wealth and status to a man pondering eternal damnation to a mosquito sharing a tree hole with a family that included someone who sounded like he'd spent too much time inhaling helium, life—afterlife? —was nothing if not unpredictable.

"Nighty-night, Alex! If you wake up in the middle of the night and you're hungry, feel free to snack on any spiders that stray in. They're the midnight snack that snacks back!" Spiffy chortled before dozing off.

My eyes widened at his comment, how will I ever get any sleep knowing I could end up a snack by morning. As I nestled in, my new reality sinking in, a thought flitted through my mind: "If this is the afterlife's idea of a joke, I can't wait to hear the punchline."

And with that thought, I closed my compound eyes, enveloped by the warmth of Spiffy's buzzing family and the utter weirdness that was now my existence. I was angry, angry that my success if life didn't warrant me a better opportunity for happiness in the afterlife. I was amongst the salt of the earth, a group of souls I had long felt were beneath me. Now, dependent on them for guidance in this world of uncertainty and the path forward, undetermined.

Spiffy's characteristic buzz jolted me awake. "Rise and shine, buddy! It's time for breakfast, and I know just the spot: the dog park on the west side of Central Park."

"Dog park?" I asked, rubbing my compound eyes as if I'd just woken from a very bad dream—though, in this case, the dream was my new reality.

"Oh, you're gonna love it," Spiffy said, his voice trembling with excitement. "Dogs are like buffets on legs!"

We buzzed our way to the park, darting through trees and narrowly avoiding a couple of spiderwebs. "So, what's the strategy here?" I asked.

"Ah, the art of the blood draw," Spiffy lectured. "You always wanna aim for the back. Sure, you gotta get through that thicket of fur, but it's better than getting squashed like a bug when you go for the underbelly."

"And what about people?" I inquired.

"Morning's not the time for humans. They're all over the place, running around in their underwear."

"Underwear?"

"You know, yoga pants and running shorts," he clarified.

As we approached our breakfast buffet—a golden retriever blissfully ignorant of our plans—I positioned myself for the perfect landing. "Ready?" Spiffy quizzed.

"Ready as I'll ever be."

We descended onto the dog's back, weaving our way through the dense fur. I couldn't help but feel like an explorer venturing through a dense jungle. My proboscis finally found skin, and I began to feed.

"Ah, I'm as fat as a tick," I gloated after my meal, wiping my mouth with my wing.

"Did you just call me fat?" a voice bellowed from my right. I turned to see a tick removing its head from the dog's skin. Its eyes—or whatever those were—narrowed at me.

"I didn't mean any offense," I stuttered, caught off guard by the tick's hostility.

"You better not have," the tick grumbled, "or I'd have sucked you dry."

"Sorry, it's his first day," Spiffy interjected, defusing the tension. "He doesn't know the etiquette around here."

"Well, he better learn quick," the tick huffed before plunging its head back into the dog's skin.

"As you can see," Spiffy whispered to me, "breakfast around here is a community affair, and you really don't want to offend the locals."

"Actually, that's Ralph," Spiffy leaned in and whispered to me as Ralph the tick reattached himself to the golden retriever's back. "He considers himself a bit of a blood sommelier. Used to be all about Rottweilers, said their blood had an 'earthy, robust texture with a hint of game.'"

"A blood sommelier?" I asked incredulously. The layers of this new world continued to unfold in the most bizarre ways.

"Hey Ralph," Spiffy called over, "still sticking to Rottweilers?"

Ralph detached his head once more and swiveled in our direction. "Ah, Spiffy, my dear buzzing sommelier-in-training! I've recently moved over to golden retrievers. Their blood has a delightful, sunny bouquet, much like a Chardonnay—hints of grass and open fields, with a playful undertone."

Spiffy chuckled. "Well, well, expanding the palate, eh?"

"Indeed," Ralph grinned, if a tick could grin. "One must diversify to truly appreciate the richness of life's offerings."

Spiffy turned to me and winked, "See, Alex, even in this new world of yours, there's complexity, culture, and—believe it or not—connoisseurs."

My compound eyes blinked in disbelief. Sommeliers of blood, social etiquettes among ticks and mosquitos, familial ties in an oak tree hole—my old life seemed so simple in comparison. Yet, in a strange way, understanding the sophistication of this tiny world made me more at ease, more willing to embrace the unknown ahead. If blood-sucking bugs could find nuance in life, then perhaps so could I, in whatever life—or afterlife—this was...

With breakfast over, Spiffy, Sally, and I took to the skies, leaving Central Park far behind as we headed towards Battery Park. "It's a good trek," Sally buzzed, "but it's worth it. People are always munching something outside those coffee shops and eateries. You know, easy pickings."

As we flew over Lower Manhattan, the towering skyscrapers evoked a sense of nostalgia in me. "I used to work down here," I said, taking a sudden detour from our path. "Hoffman, Jones & Drake Associates, LLP. I was a partner there. I'd like to see it."

"Really? You remember your past?" Spiffy looked both surprised and intrigued. "That's rare among us bugs. We were told we would only remember human activity but not who we were or what we did."

"Yup, I remember every annoying client and every late night," I retorted as I led them towards the iconic building that once served as my professional home.

We landed on a windowsill, and I peered inside. Familiar humans in suits, the intense atmosphere—it all seemed eerily familiar yet distant. My eyes darted to a nameplate on the wall, and it read: Hoffman, Smith & Drake Associates, LLP.

"Smith? Daniel Smith is a partner now. And in my office?" I buzzed incredulously. The man was a junior associate when I was around. "I can't believe they'd make him a partner! The man could barely draft a motion!"

As I was buzzing in disbelief, something caught my compound eye— the date displayed on Daniel Smith's computer screen. I did a quick calculation. It had been two years since my death, since the art fundraiser, though it felt like no time had passed at all in while at the recycling center and in my new mosquito form. The afterlife had a funny way of distorting time.

I felt a torrent of emotions rising within me—anger, jealousy, and a sense of unfairness. I shouted at the window, "Hey Daniel, it's me, Alex, Alex Jones," without a response. Just as I was about to lose myself in this vortex, Spiffy buzzed urgently in my ear.

"Hey, hey, cool your jets, Alex! You're not a lawyer anymore; you're a mosquito! They can't hear you, not a word, only a buzz when you get close. That's no longer your life. Get your proboscis out of the past and back into the present. We got livin' and eating to do!"

Sally chimed in, "He's right, Alex. You're among us now. No partnerships, no corner offices—just the open sky and the next meal."

For a moment, their words clashed with the storm of my thoughts. I was kind of hungry. Then, slowly, I pulled myself together. "You're right," I sighed. "It's just hard to let go of what you were when you see a piece of it right before your eyes. And to think, so much has changed in just two years—or what feels like moments to me."

Spiffy, ever the wise cracker, piped up, "Well, think of it this way, the only mergers and acquisitions you need to worry about now are mergers with a blood vessel and acquisitions of a nice, plump meal!"

I laughed, snapping out of my trance. Putting on a face. "You have a point, Spiffy. A very good point."

Leaving my former life, and all its illusions of grandeur behind, I flew away with Spiffy and Sally, towards whatever adventures awaited us next. For the first time since my transformation, I felt almost ready to embrace my new existence, in all its uncertainty and strangeness, but I had a feeling I might go back to that office another day.

# Spiffy's Return

As we soared over the maze of buildings that was Manhattan, Sally kept a steady pace ahead, guiding us towards Battery Park. I looked down to see humans strolling, hustling, arguing, and laughing. Each one engrossed in their own world, oblivious to the buzzing drama above them.

"Here we are, the crème de la crème of bug meet-ups," Spiffy announced, as we descended onto a bush frequented by various insects. An entire ecosystem coexisted here: ants marching in line, butterflies flaunting their vivid colors, and even a stink bug or two sulking in the corners. "Ladies and gentlebugs, may I introduce Alex, our new compatriot!"

A resounding chorus of insect greetings filled the air, each one as different as the bugs themselves. I was quickly introduced to characters like Zara the butterfly, who was the epitome of grace, and Morty the ant, a diligent worker forever fretting about food supplies for winter.

"You remember my cousin Dale?" Spiffy nudged me toward a daring-looking mosquito with an air of confidence. "He's the Indiana Jones of the mosquito world."

"Pleasure, again," Dale buzzed, extending a leg in a mosquito version of a handshake. "Since you're new to this life. Ever go on a midnight raid over a barbecue party?"

I chuckled nervously. "Uh, can't say that I have."

"You haven't lived until you've tried a well-marinated human, my friend," Dale winked, flying off to join a buzzing discussion about the best types of blood.

Sally nudged me. "Come on, let's grab a table." We settled onto a leaf, which in the bug world was as good as a five-star restaurant.

"So, Alex," Sally began, "what's it like remembering your past life? Most of us don't have that privilege."

Before I could answer, my compound eyes caught sight of a news ticker on a building in the distance. It displayed the date and reminding me again it had been two years since my death.

"Two years," I mumbled, a bit shocked. "I've been gone for two years. Daniel Smith made partner in two years."

Sally and Spiffy exchanged glances. "Time moves differently in the afterlife, you see," Spiffy said. "We all lose track. But you've got a chance at a second...well, existence. Don't let the past shackle you."

"Right, I understand, and Sally, it's distracting and painful" I finally spoke, my eyes drifting back from the distant skyline to Spiffy and Sally. Hiding my emotions of jealousy and regret I said, "Thanks for grounding me. So, what's next on the bug agenda?"

Sally smirked, "Well, usually after a meet-up, we like to—"

Her words were cut short by a sudden gust of wind. The leaves around us shuddered, and all the bugs instinctively hunkered down. "Looks like a human's coming," Spiffy observed, his eyes narrowing as he peered out from our leafy hideaway.

And sure enough, footsteps approached, growing louder, and a couple stopped right by our bush. The man pulled a small box from his pocket, lowering himself onto one knee, and my mosquito heart would've skipped a beat if it could. He was proposing.

"We should probably give them their moment," Spiffy whispered, but I was already engrossed in the spectacle, my previous life flashing before me. I had been too caught up in my work, my ambitions, to ever propose. Another stab of regret twisted within me, but I pushed it aside. "New life, new priorities," I murmured to myself.

After the woman's joyful "Yes!" and a brief kiss, the couple moved on, and we took that as our cue to leave as well. "You're awfully quiet," Sally noted, flying alongside me. "Penny for your thoughts?"

"I was just realizing that even if I can't propose or get promoted, I can still experience life—or, well, afterlife—in meaningful ways."

Sally grinned, "That's the spirit! Or should I say, that's the proboscis!"

"Alright, you two lovebugs, cut it out," Spiffy interrupted, his voice tinged with feigned irritation. "We've got a moonlight gathering to attend tonight at the Great Lawn. Word around the bush is that there's going to be a film screening, which means plenty of distracted humans."

A moonlight gathering? It sounded absurd, yet oddly intriguing. "A film screening, you say. What's playing? 'Gone with the Wing' or 'Citizen Cocoon'?" I joked.

Spiffy erupted into a high-pitched mosquito laugh. "Oh, you're getting the hang of this, Alex! But really, it's an action flick, so the humans will be engrossed, and we can feast without fuss."

As we veered north toward the Great Lawn, my thoughts strayed again. A film screening meant a large gathering of people, warmth, and laughter—emblems of a life I once knew but, in a context, so profoundly different. It was disorienting and fascinating, and I felt a strange sense of anticipation.

I began to realize that the mosquito life wasn't just about surviving; it was about thriving in the strangest of circumstances and enjoying a life that was so short, living in the moment. I can't say I ever did that as a human being.

We took off, our wings humming in the dusk, leaving Battery Park behind as we ascended towards the Great Lawn. The sun had already taken its leave, and the first stars began to wink into existence. City lights filled in for the lost daylight, casting their amber glow over Manhattan. I kept pace with Sally, Spiffy, and Dale, each of us occasionally twisting and turning to avoid the sudden gusts that swept between the towering skyscrapers.

"You guys ever wonder where you'll end up in your next life?" I asked, intrigued by this whole notion of continual existence, albeit in a different form.

Dale chuckled first. "Ah, the grand question of reincarnation. You're talking to someone who's actually made it a couple of levels up the food chain. I was a sparrow in one life, a house cat in another. But let me tell you, flying too close to a hawk or climbing up an unstable tree, and—bam! —you're back to square one. Or, in my case, back to square mosquito. I guess my daring nature got the better of me. It wasn't that I died that regressed me, a friend of mine who is now a dog, told me it was because I wasn't thoughtful of others or endangered their lives with reckless behavior. That's my weak spot."

Sally interjected; her voice tinged with optimism. "I've only been a mosquito a few times, but I've got a good feeling about the next round. Every life is a lesson, you know? I think I'm ready to level up."

"And you, Spiffy?" I turned my gaze to him, curious about the backstory of our ever-entertaining guide.

"Ah, I'm what you might call a veteran in the mosquito biz," Spiffy said, a note of resignation in his buzz. "Died and come back some 20 times. Still waiting for my ticket to a higher life form. The universe seems to think I have unfinished business as a mosquito, I suppose."

We continued our journey, each lost in thought about our past and future lives, the air around us growing cooler as we approached Central Park. Finally, we reached the Great Lawn. The moon hung like a celestial spotlight over the park, illuminating clusters of humans scattered around a large movie screen.

"This is it," Spiffy declared, as if unveiling a grand spectacle. "The Great Lawn at night—a smorgasbord of human activity, and tonight, a film screening to boot!"

"And what film are the humans watching?" I asked, looking at the screen where fast-paced action sequences were unfolding, guns blazing and cars flipping in mid-air.

"Looks like one of those adrenaline-pumping shoot-'em-ups," Dale observed. "Good for us. High excitement means faster blood flow."

Sally glanced at me. "Ready for your first moonlight gathering?"

I chuckled. "Considering that it involves food and entertainment, I'd say I was born—or reborn—for this."

As we swooped down toward the crowd, avoiding a few cursory swats from distracted moviegoers, I felt a newfound sense of adventure. And as I alighted on the arm of an engrossed film fan, my proboscis sinking into a rich, satisfying meal, I couldn't help but feel grateful for this strange, buzzing life and opportunity for redemption.

The four of us were like artists at an easel, carefully choosing our subjects from the array of humans sprawled on the Great Lawn. Spiffy, who had always been a risk-taker, chose a bulky man engrossed in the high-octane car chase scene that played on the big screen.

"He looks like a double cheeseburger and fries, with an extra-large soda on the side," Spiffy chuckled as he prepared for his approach.

Sally, Dale, and I watched as Spiffy skillfully navigated the air currents and descended toward the man's exposed forearm. Just as Spiffy's proboscis pierced the skin, the man suddenly jolted—perhaps a moment of on-screen suspense had grabbed his attention—and his hand slapped down hard.

"Whack!"

Spiffy was sent spiraling through the air, finally landing with a soft thud on the grass. The human, visibly irritated, flicked Spiffy off his arm and grumbled, "Damn mosquitoes," before refocusing on the movie.

Sally and I rushed to Spiffy's side, dodging the flailing arms and legs of moviegoers as Dale hovered above, playing the role of an aerial lookout. "Clear on the left, but there's a couple of ankle-biters on the right—human children with quick reflexes. Be cautious!"

As we reached Spiffy, it was clear he was at the end of this particular life cycle. One of his wings was crushed, and his eyes seemed to be losing their characteristic sparkle.

"Hey guys," he wheezed, "Looks like I'm getting an early ticket to my next life. Maybe the universe finally decided it's time for me to move up."

Sally nuzzled against him. "You'll always be top tier in our books, Spiffy."

Spiffy chuckled, then grimaced as a jolt of pain coursed through him. "If you find a mosquito buzzing unusually well to Sinatra songs in the next week, you'll know it's me. Remember, the tree near the Alice in Wonderland statue in Central Park—that's our meeting point each next life."

"And what should we bring to this reunion?" I asked, trying to lighten the mood.

"A vial of O-negative would be perfect!" Spiffy laughed, then coughed. "Just kidding. Bring yourselves, and maybe some fresh stories to share."

He looked up at Dale, who was still keeping watch above. "Dale, no risky stunts, okay? We can't lose two of us in one night."

Dale buzzed down a quick salute. "I'll be extra cautious, promise!"

Spiffy started singing, "Fly me to the moon, let me play among the stars, let me see what spring is like, on a-Jupiter and ......"

As we watched, Spiffy's eyes slowly glazed over, his wings sagged, and his singing stopped right before his tiny body went limp.

Dale landed next to us, his voice a mixture of sadness and humor. "Well, he went out as he lived—making us laugh and taking risks. Didn't we go through this with him last week at that backyard BBQ in the Bronx?"

Sally and I looked at each other, laughed and then back at Spiffy.

"Yes, I think his singing was a bit better this time," said Sally. "Don't you think?"

Though we were creatures of short lifespans and even shorter memories, we knew some moments were eternal.

"Let's go," I said softly. "We want to be there tomorrow when he shows up again."

As we lifted off, I felt a blend of sorrow and anticipation. Mourning a friend, yet excited about possibly seeing him again. With a final glance at the Great Lawn and its engrossed human audience, we winged our way into the night.

As the three of us—Sally, Dale, and myself—made our way back to our cozy hideout among the leaves of an old oak, the absence of Spiffy felt like an empty space in our formation. Dale yawned, a surprisingly endearing sound for a mosquito.

"I can't believe I'm saying this, but I'm zonked. Emotional rollercoasters really take it out of you," he said.

Sally nestled into her leaf-bed, her wings folding neatly at her sides. "Let's get some sleep. We've got a morning appointment at the Alice in Wonderland statue. Maybe, just maybe, we'll find Spiffy reborn."

We dozed off, each lost in dreams informed by our recent and past lives—buzzing melodies of Sinatra included.

Morning came, and we found ourselves by the iconic Alice in Wonderland statue in Central Park, the agreed-upon meeting point. The sun was shining, but Spiffy was nowhere to be seen—or heard. As we hovered, the grumbling in our bellies became increasingly hard to ignore.

"Alright, I'm starving," Sally admitted, "I say we grab a quick bite and come back. If Spiffy's coming, he'll be here."

Just as she finished her sentence, a small brown chihuahua pranced onto the scene, tail wagging, seemingly unattended.

"Perfect timing!" Dale exclaimed, "A walking, yapping breakfast special!"

We swooped down in formation, choosing our spots and sinking our proboscises into the chihuahua's skin. No sooner had we started our feast than the dog let out a Yelp that was less 'bark' and more 'indignant gentleman.'

"Hey! What's the big idea? Do I look like a buffet to you?"

We jumped back, startled. That voice sounded eerily familiar.

"Dale, Sally, is that you guys? It's me, Spiffy! Well, I go by Taco now."

Sally was the first to break into a joyful laugh. "Taco? You've got to be kidding me!"

Taco, formerly known as Spiffy, looked as sheepish as a chihuahua could. "Hey, I didn't choose the name, okay? Besides, I had to slip away from my owner just to come find you guys. Do you know how hard it is to shake off a human when you have tiny legs? I sure miss flying."

Dale hovered a bit closer, "Well, it's good to see you again, even if you're a four-legged snack this time around."

Spiffy chuckled, "Don't you mean, a four-legged friend?"

We all laughed at the reunion, amazed by life's capacity for surprise, even in its tiniest, furriest forms. With everyone now gathered around Taco, the dog formerly known as Spiffy, a palpable curiosity filled the air. Dale, hovering an inch above Spiffy's head, spoke up.

"So, Spiffy—ahem, I mean, Taco—why a chihuahua? Last I heard, you were ruminating about leveling up to something exotic, like an eagle or a dolphin."

Spiffy grinned, his tongue flopping out a little. "You won't believe it! After I kicked the bucket—again—I woke up to the smell of wet dog fur and kibble. There I was, at the 'Forever Tails Animal Shelter,' sandwiched between a poodle with an attitude and a bulldog that snored like a freight train."

Dale couldn't help but chuckle. "That sounds like the Ritz-Carlton of reincarnations."

"Trust me, it was more like the sitcom of animal lives. At mealtime, we had this tabby cat named Whiskers who'd stroll in like he owned the place, only to trip over his own feet. Every. Single. Time!"

Sally laughed heartily. "Sounds like Whiskers needed a few more lifetimes to get the walking thing down!"

Alex, taking it all in, wondered aloud, "So, how'd you end up with the name Taco?"

Spiffy's ears perked up. "Ah, that's the best part. This incredible young Hispanic couple adopted me—Miguel and Sofia. They were debating names, going back and forth between 'Coco' and 'Salsa.' But then Miguel dropped a taco during dinner last night. I snatched it up faster than you could say 'Fido,' and well, the name stuck! Funny, I no longer wanted a blood meal, kibble and regular food was my new craving."

Dale quipped, "A name and a snack, huh? You've always known how to make the best of every life."

Spiffy wagged his tail. "I like to think I got the dog gig this time because the universe figured I needed to learn loyalty and companionship. You know, as a mosquito, you're more of a lone ranger, always buzzing off after a quick bite."

Sally hovered closer to Spiffy's snout, teasing, "Well, it's nice to know that even in your furrier form, you're still food driven."

Spiffy gave a doggy chuckle. "Some things never change. But I've got a human family who loves me, feeds me, and gives me belly rubs. Plus, I have you guys. I'd say that's a double win."

Alex, still in his mosquito form, was buzzing with curiosity. "Wait, so you remembered us even after you were reincarnated?"

Spiffy looked up; his eyes almost misty. "How could I forget? I may have a new name, a new form, and a new life, but some things, like friendship, transcend all boundaries. Besides, do you know how many lamp posts and fire hydrants I had to sniff on my way to Central Park?"

Dale cut in, "I can only imagine the olfactory adventure you've been on."

"And don't forget the dogs I met along the way," Spiffy added. "Some were friendly, some tried to mark me as their territory. I had to dodge more than one overzealous sprinkler system, I'll tell you that."

Sally was smiling, her wings still for a moment. "It sounds like you've had quite a journey, Spiffy—or should I say, Taco."

Spiffy wagged his tail. "Both names work, as long as it's you guys calling me."

The evening felt like one of those magical moments where time stands still. Under the watchful gaze of the Alice statue, our little circle felt complete again. Spiffy may have left us for a brief period, but his return, even in a drastically different form, was like the missing piece of a puzzle clicking back into place.

"So, how do we make sure we all find each other again?" Dale asked, breaking the comfortable silence that had settled over us. "Even after we've all moved on to our next lives?"

Spiffy barked softly, "Well, we've always got the statue, and that was always the rule, right?

"We'll meet here, by this statue, no matter what we become," Alex stated with resolve. "In this rapidly changing circle of life, it's the one constant we can rely on."

We all nodded, or in Spiffy's case, wagged. It was a pact, a promise that wherever life—or the afterlife—took us, we would always find our way back to each other. And so, under the afternoon sky, with the Central Park as our silent witness, we agreed to always meet by the Alice statue. No matter what form we took next, we would search, sniff, fly, or crawl our way back to this meeting point. After all, when you've been a mosquito, becoming sentimental about the little things seems perfectly appropriate.

Just then, a distant call reverberated through the park. "Taco! Taco, where are you?"

Spiffy's ears twitched, his furry tail wagging less vigorously. "Ah, that's Miguel. They be looking for me."

Dale floated up a bit, amused. "Guess it's time for you to be the loyal pet?"

"Yeah," Spiffy sighed, "as much as I'd love to hang out more, I better get back before they think I am lost. Hopefully returning to them convinces them I was just playing. I am supposed to be on a leash, unless inside the fence of the dog park."

Sally chuckled. "Go, be the good dog, but know this: you're still our favorite mosquito at heart."

Spiffy stood up, stretching his little legs. "By the way, you guys, they live on East 71st near 5th Avenue. There's a small door at the back of the house. They usually head out to work around 9 am. If I can slip away, I'll try to meet you all here."

Alex interjected, "And if you can't make it?"

Spiffy gave a doggy smile. "Let's just say I'll leave some unmistakable signs on the nearest fire hydrant, so you know I've been there."

Alex nodded, grateful for the connection that seemed to defy even the most extreme changes. "Fair enough. Until then, Spiffy, stay safe."

"Will do!" Spiffy barked, before sprinting off toward the sound of his name, his tiny legs kicking up tufts of grass in his wake."

As we watched our four-legged friend disappear into the horizon, Dale broke the silence. "So, what's the plan? It's getting close to lunchtime, and I don't know about you guys, but I'm starving."

Sally piped up, "Well, we could try that pond over by the boathouse. Lots of picnickers there."

Dale chuckled, Let's go!"

Alex sighed, deep in thought, "It's strange, isn't it? Here we are, wondering about our next meal, while Spiffy goes back to his loving home. Makes you really think about the afterlife's sense of irony."

Dale buzzed closer to Alex. "Ah, the eternal question of 'Why?' Guess we'll keep asking until we're back here, maybe as dogs, maybe as something else entirely."

Sally nudged them both. "Well, whatever we become, wherever we end up, let's not forget our pact. Alice's statue, every single day."

And with that renewed vow echoing in our wings, we set off toward the pond to find some lunch. We were content in our mosquito forms, united by friendship and driven by curiosity but we aspired to be something more, like Spiffy.

The pond by the boathouse was teeming with life. A family of ducks swam lazily near the reeds, dragonflies hovered above the water, and tourists snapped photos on their smartphones. Even for mosquitoes like us, the pond offered a smorgasbord of choices. Yet, as we feasted on some unsuspecting picnickers, our minds were elsewhere. Spiffy's transformation and the pact we had made were still fresh in our thoughts.

Dale was the first to break the silence. "You know, ever since we met Spiffy again, I've been feeling different. Like there's a ripple in the air or something."

Sally hummed in agreement. "It's like an itch I can't scratch. I know we're due for another transformation, but this time it feels... different."

Alex found himself nodding. "I've noticed it too. Ever since Taco, I mean Spiffy returned, it's as if the universe is preparing us for something significant. A change that's not just about form but perhaps about purpose as well."

The trio fell silent, each absorbed in their own thoughts.

A few days had passed, and the itching grew stronger, more insistent. It was no longer just an abstract sense of impending change; it was a physical sensation that each of them could no longer ignore. But unlike earlier transformations, which felt like life's roulette wheel spinning out of control, this one seemed more deliberate—as if they were being gently steered rather than randomly tossed.

One morning, Sally, while waiting for the others to arrive, found a feather lying next to the Alice statue. It was a delicate thing, iridescent and light as air. She showed it to Alex and Dale when they met later that morning.

"Feathers, huh?" Dale quipped. "Maybe we're going to turn into birds next."

Alex chuckled, "Birds or not, I'm prepared for anything. But what I've started to understand is that our transformations aren't just random events. They're learning experiences, ways to evolve our souls."

Sally nodded, holding the feather gently in her proboscis. "I agree, and maybe this feather is a sign, a symbol of freedom and the possibility of flight beyond our current existence."

Alex, Sally, and Dale continued their conversation by the pond, each holding onto their own thoughts and interpretations about the future. As they were discussing the significance of the feather and what it could mean for their next lives, a blur of blue suddenly darted into their midst. Before they knew it, Dale was snatched up in slender, iridescent jaws. The force of the grab tossed Alex and Sally into a frenzied spin.

"Dale! Alex! Sally!" The cries emerged from all sides, a discord of confusion and terror.

Just as suddenly, Dale was spat out, landing softly on a lily pad in a pile of thick stringy saliva. The blur of blue settled, revealing itself as a damselfly, its wings like sapphire-tinted glass.

"Mortimer?" Sally was the first to recognize him.

The damselfly looked down at his own slender form, as if confirming his identity. "Oh, my stars! Sally, Dale, Alex, is that you? I'm so, so sorry!"

"You tried to eat me!" Dale buzzed, clearly agitated, and dripping with saliva, but relieved.

Mortimer looked ashamed, his slender antennae drooping. "You'll have to forgive me. My instincts got the better of me. Ever since I transformed into this damselfly, I've been eating mosquitoes without a second thought. The transformation was disorienting. I spent a week in a cocoon and woke up to this new body, new cravings. I even ate my friend Frank."

Mortimer his blue wings losing some of their vibrancy for a moment. "You should've seen it—there I was, hovering over the pond, and my eyes catch this mosquito that looked particularly juicy. I swooped down, grabbed it with my legs and—gulp! —it was gone. A single meal on the great carousel of life."

"That must have been traumatic," Alex said, hovering closer to get a better look at Mortimer's new form.

"You have no idea! So, the very next day, I was minding my own business near some lily pads, and who do you think shows up? Frank! Except, he wasn't Frank the mosquito anymore; he had turned into Frank the bird. The tables were dramatically turned, my friends. A shadow loomed over me, and before I knew what hit me, I was lunch."

"The cycle of life and death, it seems, can be quite vengeful and ironic," Mortimer sighed, his wings shimmering in the sunlight as if revitalized by the very act of sharing his story. "And here I am, back in the same blue damselfly body, pondering the cosmic lessons in it all." The group was silent for a moment, each contemplating Mortimer's revelation.

As Sally floated in the air, her antenna raised, she finally piped up. "So, you're saying you've got, like, a cosmic case of FOMO? Afraid of munching others?"

Mortimer's wings drooped a little. "Exactly! I feel like I'm trapped in the bug version of a daytime soap opera. 'As the Wing Turns' or something. One day I'm the eater, the next I'm the eaten. And the worst part? No popcorn to watch it all unfold!"

Dale interjected with comedic timing, "Well, just so you know, you're not nominated for Best Supporting Bug in a Drama Series. Your eating-me act needs some work!"

Mortimer chuckled, his blue hue brightening like a neon sign in a comedy club. "You guys crack me up. But seriously, maybe this 'eat or be eaten' merry-go-round is my master class in Bug Philosophy 101. You know, like an intro course before I can graduate to something cooler, like a—"

"A penguin?" Sally interjected. "I hear they get all the fish they can eat and no natural predators!"

Mortimer's compound eyes sparkled, "Or maybe a stand-up comedian! My material would kill. Get it? Kill?"

They all erupted into buzzes and wing flaps, their version of belly laughs. The group hung around the pond having their lunch—this time a little more cautious of each other's dietary habits until they decided to go back to the Alice statue to see if Spiffy (aka Taco) had arrived.

As Alex, Sally, Dale, and Mortimer chatted around the Alice statue, their laughs and musings were interrupted by a distant but unmistakable rumble.

"What's that sound?" Sally asked, her antennae twitching in agitation.

Dale's eyes widened. "I've heard that hum before! That's a mosquito control truck! Quick, scatter!"

No sooner had he spoken than a cloud of fog began to fill the air around them. Panicking, the four friends took to the skies, flying as fast as their wings could carry them. But just as they dodged one truck near the Shakespeare Garden, they found themselves trapped between another cloud of toxic mist near the Sir Walter Scott Monument.

"It's converging on us!" Alex cried out, choking on the mist. "We're trapped!"

Sally coughed, her wings faltering. "Whatever happens, meet at Alice!"

Dale added, gasping, "Never forget our pact!"

And then, the fog enveloped them entirely, their forms twitching in a final act of resistance before they fell, one by one, onto the ground below. Only Mortimer was immune, frantically trying to flap his wings to scatter the fog, but with no avail. He watched them in those last few seconds, but he knew he would see them again someday, dying today was only part of their journey.

# transformation

Alex woke up to the noise of barks, meows, and the occasional squeal of a guinea pig. The ground beneath him was hard and cold, definitely not the soil of Central Park. Alex shook his head, trying to rid himself of the dizziness that accompanied his sudden transformation. His body felt heavy, his vision clearer than ever before. But instead of wings, he now felt the weight of four legs beneath him. Shaking his newfound furry coat, he looked around.

The place was a mix of comforting and intimidating aromas: kibble, cleaner, other animals. Alex found himself in a confined space, surrounded by metal bars, and opposite to him was another dog—much older, with graying fur and an eye patch that could either mean he was wise or had seen too much.

"Where am I?" he wondered. Suddenly, he caught his reflection in a water dish to his right in the cage—fur, four legs, and a wagging tail. "I'm a dog! I made it! I'm a dog!"

"Oi, pipe down over there, will ya? Some of us are trying to nap," grumbled the older dog.

"Ah, sorry about that. The name's Alex. And you are?" Alex wagged his tail cautiously.

"Ralph," the older dog sighed, looking at Alex as if deciding whether the newcomer was worth his time.

"Ralph? As in the blood sommelier?" Alex couldn't help but let out an amused bark. In his previous mosquito life, Ralph had been renowned for his ability to choose the most nutritious and scrumptious blood types from miles away—a true connoisseur of fine dining, if you were a mosquito.

The corners of Ralph's mouth twitched upwards. "You remember. Nice to know the reputation precedes me."

Alex's ears perked up. "So, how long have you been in here, and where exactly is 'here'?"

Ralph stretched, then started to describe the space. "We're in an animal shelter, lad. It's a sort of halfway house for four-legged souls like us. We're looked after by a couple of humans—Mandy and Steve. They feed us, clean our cages, and take us to the yard out back for some sunshine and, well, 'personal business,' a few times a day."

"A yard, you say. So, we're not confined to these metal squares?" Alex wagged his tail a bit more vigorously now.

Ralph chuckled. "No, no. We get our romps. Just stay on Mandy's good side. She's the one with the ponytail and glasses. She has a soft spot for sad puppy eyes. Steve is more of the no-nonsense type, always in blue overalls, but fair enough."

"Good to know. I can't wait to explore this 'yard.' And maybe, just maybe, find our friends. We had a pact, you know—"

Before Alex could finish, the lock to their cage rattled, and the door swung open. It was Mandy, her ponytail bobbing as she approached.

"Alright, you two. Time to stretch those legs."

Mandy put a slip leash around Alex and Ralph's neck. They made their way to the yard, tails wagging and noses sniffing. Alex couldn't help but wonder what had become of his friends, and what new forms they had taken. But for now, this new world was an open book, and with the guidance of his old friend Ralph, he was ready to turn the page.

Mandy removed the leash after opening the gate to the small dog park and said, "Go take care of your business, I'll be back in half an hour to get you."

The gate swung shut behind them, and Alex and Ralph frolicked into the enclosure, enjoying the limited yet exhilarating freedom the yard provided.

"Ah, fresh air! Even if it's on a miniature scale, it's the best," Ralph said, taking an expansive sniff before stretching his legs.

"It really is liberating," Alex agreed, doing a dainty pirouette before elegantly sitting down on the grass. "By the way, Ralph, do you know what kind of dog I am? I haven't had a chance to look in a mirror yet, and it's not like I can ask Mandy."

"You, my curly-furred friend, are a Poodle. Highly intelligent, agile, and with a taste for the finer things, like gourmet kibble," Ralph said, wagging his tail.

"A Poodle, really?" Alex looked down at his paws, then back up at Ralph. "Fascinating. And what about you?"

"I'm a Border Collie—quick to learn, quicker to herd, and I've got energy to spare. Some say I should've been born with a job application in my mouth," Ralph responded with a grin.

Alex let out a chuckle. "A job application, you say? Should I be worried you'll start herding me?"

Ralph winked. "Oh, I've considered it, but you Poodles have a way of resisting authority. Plus, I don't think you'd fit well with the sheep."

Both dogs erupted into barks of laughter, enjoying the camaraderie and the humor of their new lives. As they settled in, Alex couldn't help but wonder where Sally and Dale were and what shapes they'd taken in this round of existence. Yet for now, in this slice of life, with the guidance of his wise friend Ralph, Alex felt ready to embrace whatever adventures lay ahead.

Just as Alex was about to inquire more about Ralph's thoughts on canine philosophy—because it was clear that Border Collies must have theories on almost everything—he heard a soft bark that seemed oddly familiar. He turned his head to the sound, ears perked up.

"I'm telling you, Pippa, they put me in with a Great Dane last night. I could've been an appetizer!"

The tone, the rhythm, the inherent flair of the voice—it was unmistakable. Alex's eyes widened as they landed on a snow-white

Havanese with a luscious fur coat that could only be rivaled by the fluff of a cloud.

"Sally?" Alex said, almost as if questioning the reality before him. His tail began to wag involuntarily, forming enthusiastic circles in the air.

The Havanese turned her head, and her eyes met Alex's. For a moment, time seemed to freeze.

"Alex? Is that you? Wait, are you... a Poodle?" Sally burst out, her own tail now matching the speed of Alex's in a wagging frenzy.

"In the curly-furred flesh!" Alex yelped, darting across the yard to greet her, Ralph trailing behind, intrigued by the sudden turn of events.

Sally and Alex collided in a joyous reunion, jumping, barking, and doing their best to hug with their front paws. Ralph watched the spectacle, bemused but happy for his new friend.

"So, this is Sally? The mysterious companion for which you've been pining?" Ralph asked, a grin spreading across his muzzle.

Sally disentangled from Alex and looked at Ralph. "And who's this? Your yard mate?"

"No, it's Ralph the tick, I mean Border Collie now. You remember? He's graduated from blood sommelier to philosopher, herder, and all-around stand-up dog," Alex introduced.

"Ah, a Border Collie. That explains why you look like you're contemplating the meaning of life while we're just here to celebrate our reunion," Sally joked, drawing a good-natured laugh from all three dogs.

"Okay, we have to talk about that insane mosquito sprayer back in the park," Alex said, his eyes narrowing as if just thinking about it made him uneasy.

Sally shuddered, her fluffy fur puffing out. "Ugh, don't remind me! One minute we're all having a good time, and the next, it was like a scene out of an apocalyptic movie. I've never been so terrified!"

"Yeah, it was like 'The End of Days: Insect Edition.' We barely had time to say goodbye," Alex added, his voice tinged with worry.

Both dogs paused for a moment, their tails momentarily stilling.

"You know who I'm really concerned about?" Sally finally broke the silence, her eyes clouding with concern. "Dale. He's always been the, well, you know, the not-so-fast one."

Alex nodded, his poodle ears drooping a bit. "Absolutely, I've been worrying about him too. But remember, Dale's always had a knack for landing on his feet—or legs, all six of them, in fact. So, if anyone could dodge that fog of doom, it's him."

Sally perked up, wagging her tail again. "You're right. Dale is surprisingly resourceful when it comes to dodging danger. Remember the time he almost got swatted by that kid with the fly swatter?"

Alex chuckled. "Oh, I could never forget. He dodged that thing like Neo in 'The Matrix.' So agile!"

Sally smiled, comforted by the memory. "Well, wherever he is, I just hope he's safe. And that he knows to meet us at Alice. It's our one constant, our North Star."

"Agreed," Alex replied. "Let's keep the faith. Our next rendezvous at Alice will be one for the books. Or should I say, for the script? After all, if we can survive being bugs, dogs should be a walk in the park."

Sally laughed, her tail wagging enthusiastically. "Literally!"

Ralph, overhearing the last part, interjected. "Ah, the resilience of friendships through multiple lifetimes. That's script-worthy material for sure!"

And so, amidst the new smells, sights, and experiences of doghood, Alex and Sally found comfort in the familiarity of their friendship, holding onto hope that they would see Dale again.

Steve and Mandy returned right on schedule to move the dogs back to their kennels. Leashes were clipped back on, and the small cavalcade made their way through the maze of the animal shelter, their paws clicking softly on the tiled floor.

As they passed by a corridor, Sally nudged Alex discreetly. "Hey, look there, on the windowsill of the cat room."

Alex turned his gaze to where Sally was pointing. An orange tabby was sitting on the windowsill, looking highly annoyed as it swiped a paw at the world outside. It had a tiny placard next to it that read 'Whiskers.'

"Ah, so that's the famous Whiskers that Taco mentioned, huh?" Alex quipped, trying to catch the feline's eye. But Whiskers was too engrossed in his own drama, yelling what could only be assumed were cat expletives at the pigeons that dared to perch near his window.

"Yes, that's him. Taco said he's like the Shakespearean actor of the cat world, full of sound and fury," Sally replied, letting out a soft bark of laughter.

Steve and Mandy finally led them to the kennels. Ralph and Alex were guided into one, their leashes removed, and the door securely closed behind them. Sally was placed in the neighboring kennel, sharing her space with Pippa, a majestic Husky with piercing blue eyes.

As they settled in, Alex turned to Ralph. "So, what's the sleeping arrangement like? Do we call dibs or is it like a free-for-all?"

Ralph chuckled, "Oh, it's pretty laid back. Just find a corner that suits your fancy. But let me warn you, the blanket near the water bowl—that's mine."

Sally, overhearing their conversation, chimed in from her kennel, "Oh, we have to make do with what we have here, right? Pippa's already claimed the pillow."

Pippa gave a soft 'woof' of agreement, settling herself comfortably on said pillow.

"And so, our new journey begins," Ralph mused, looking thoughtful.

"Indeed, it does," Sally agreed, "But at least, we're not navigating it alone."

Both kennels fell silent, but the air was far from somber. For in the middle of transitions and transformations, there was solace in constants—friendship being the most steadfast of them all. And as the lights dimmed in the shelter, each dog nestled into their chosen corner, hearts and minds filled with dreams of reunions and the unwritten chapters yet to come.

The next morning, the kennel came alive with a flurry of activity. It was Rabies Shot Day—a term that Sally found highly dramatic and unnecessary.

"Do they call it 'Breakfast Day' when they give us kibble? No, they do not," she remarked dryly as a vet gave her a quick jab.

Ralph simply shrugged. "Somehow the pomp and circumstance makes it seem less dreary, don't you think?"

Soon after the minor medical proceedings, Steve and Mandy began prepping the dogs for the big adoption event at the pet store on East 87th and Lexington Avenue. Ribbons were tied, coats were brushed, and there was even a mist of doggy cologne in the air.

"Goodness, they're making us smell like a department store at Christmas," Alex observed, sniffing his newly scented fur.

"Let's just hope we don't attract bargain hunters," Sally shot back.

Upon arrival at the pet store, the dogs were placed in a special cordoned-off area, replete with "Adopt Me" signs and enough chew toys to furnish a doggy palace.

Enter the potential adopters—Upper East Side dwellers ranging from Instagram influencers to semi-retired attorneys. Alex caught the eye of a lively elderly woman named Beatrice, a retired art history professor. She wore vintage horn-rimmed glasses and had an air of being cultured but relatable.

"Ah, a Poodle. The epitome of French sophistication," she declared. "You shall be my muse, cherie! Your name will be Pierre!"

Sally, on the other hand, was swooped up by the Johnsons—a family of four. Mr. Johnson, a laid-back tech guru, Mrs. Johnson, a yoga instructor, and their two high-energy kids, Emily, and Tim.

"Snowball! Snowball! Can we call her Snowball, Mommy?" Emily was practically jumping with excitement.

"Hmm, I was thinking more of a 'Bianca,' darling," Mrs. Johnson countered.

"I like that name," Mr. Johnson interjected, taking a pragmatic approach to agree with his wife.

Pippa ended up with a young professional named Clara, a marketing manager who looked like she might spend her weekends at silent discos and farmers' markets.

"Finally, a fur companion for my TikTok videos," Clara grinned, her eyes already envisioning viral fame.

One by one, the paperwork was signed, and the leashes were handed over. Before departing, each new owner ventured into the aisles of the pet store to select essential supplies—bedding, feeding bowls, and a myriad of squeaky toys.

Beatrice picked out an elegant chaise longue-styled pet bed for Alex, declaring, "Only the finest for my Parisian comrade!"

The Johnsons went for an eco-friendly, recycled material bed for Sally, along with a variety of plush toys modeled after fruits and vegetables. "Start the vegan influence young," Mrs. Johnson winked.

Sally thought to herself, "Oh dear,"

Clara picked a sleek, minimalist bed for Pippa and a collection of smart toys that could be operated via smartphone.

Ralph, unfortunately, did not get adopted, and yelled out, "I'll be along as soon as I can, takes a special person to want a mutt."

As each dog left the event, their tails wagged in a mix of anticipation and nostalgia. New beginnings awaited, just a stone's throw away from Central Park, the place that had seen their previous avatars and would hopefully reunite them in their new forms.

Barking at each other, they communicated their intentions to get to the Alice statue as soon as they could. The journey was far from over, but this felt particularly promising. And so, Alex, Sally, and Pippa ventured out to explore the streets of the Upper East Side with their new families—each one carrying the spirit of adventure, and the task of getting accommodated to their new homes.

A few sunrises and sunsets had adorned the New York sky, adorning it with hues of color, a visual spectacle that went largely unnoticed by the busy human populace but brought immense joy to our canine heroes as they acquainted themselves with the peculiar habits and rhythms of their new human families.

As the city continued its perpetual buzz, the day arrived when the trees in Central Park bore witness to a clandestine gathering of furry friends under their shade. It was a well-planned meeting, a pact formed in whispered barks and secretive glances exchanged during their brief encounters in the neighborhood. The chosen venue, as always, the Alice statue, a place familiar yet different, carrying memories of their past lives and beckoning new adventures in their present forms. Alex, Sally, and Pippa approached the iconic statue, their hearts brimming with tales and experiences that begged to be shared.

Each of them carried the vibrant energy of their newfound freedom, the curiosity to know more about the other's adventures, and the comforting knowledge that amidst the ever-changing dynamics of their lives, their friendship remained a strong, unyielding force. It was a reunion marked with spirited wagging tails and affectionate nuzzles, an undeniable proof of their deep bond that transcended time and form. It was here, amidst laughter and playful jostles, they settled down to share tales spun from days of observant eyes and wagging tails, keen on narrating their little escapades and the daily habits of their human companions.

Alex nudged Sally playfully, his curly poodle fur bouncing with each motion. "You know, Beatrice is always so lost in her art. She paints for hours, not even noticing when I slip out. It's like I have a daily pass to freedom. How about you?"

Sally laughed, her tail wagging at the speed of light. "Oh, you have no idea! The Johnson household is a whirlwind of activity. But luckily, I found my window of escape. Every day, after yoga and the kids' hustle and bustle, the house becomes eerily quiet, giving me the perfect chance to dash out unnoticed. It's almost poetic, don't you think?"

Alex nodded, clearly impressed. Pippa chimed in eagerly, her voice vibrating with excitement. "Guess what? Clara is always engrossed in her phone, doing this strange dance, and talking to it. It's during her 'TikTok hours' that I make my grand escape. I still can't wrap my head around what she finds so captivating in that little screen though."

The group erupted in laughter, the park echoing with their joyous barks and the familiar warmth of friendship rekindled. Sally looked at Alex, her eyes twinkling with mischief. "And here we are, united in our little secret haven, thanks to our unsuspecting humans and their peculiar habits. Who would have thought?"

Pippa lay down on the cool grass, her gaze drifting towards the sky. "It's kind of wonderful, isn't it? Finding this freedom and still having a loving home to return to."

The others joined her on the grass, a trio of happy conspirators under the watchful eyes of the Alice statue, sharing whispered tales of their daily adventures and dreams of countless more to come. It was a perfect snapshot of freedom, friendship, and the innocent guile that brought them together in the heart of the park.

Suddenly, in the midst of their lively exchanges, a rustling sound emerged from the bushes nearby. The trio turned their heads in unison towards the noise, bodies tensed, and ears perked up. A moment later, out popped a sprightly figure that seemed to carry a burst of sunshine with it — it was a brown Chihuahua with eyes that twinkled with mischief and delight.

"Spiffy!" Alex and Sally barked almost in harmony, their faces breaking into wide, welcoming smiles as they recognized their old friend.

Rushing towards them, Spiffy couldn't contain his enthusiasm. "You wouldn't believe it, friends! After meticulous observations and careful calculations, I have found it, the golden gateway to freedom!" he exclaimed, his tail whipping the air excitedly.

Alex cocked his head to the side, his curly fur bouncing slightly as he did so. "Do tell, Spiffy," he urged, a playful sparkle lighting up his eyes.

Spiffy pranced in a small circle before settling down, clearly enjoying the attention and the suspense he had built. "Well, my esteemed fellows, it turns out that the corner of the garden fence has a loose board. With just a bit of pushing and, let's say, tactical repositioning, I've managed to create an opening just large enough to slip through," he announced with a proud puff of his chest.

Sally bounced excitedly, "Oh that's brilliant, Spiffy! This means you don't have to wait for park time to see us. You have all the freedom to explore!"

Pippa, who had been silently observing, finally piped up with a slightly shy yet curious expression, "Um, I'm Pippa. I don't think we've met before," she said, extending a paw towards the jubilant Chihuahua.

"Oh, where are my manners! Spiffy, meet Pippa. Pippa, this is Spiffy, also known as Taco in his past life," Alex quickly introduced, facilitating a warm handshake, or rather, pawshake between the two.

Spiffy greeted Pippa with a friendly nudge and a warm, sunny smile, "Nice to meet you, Pippa. Welcome to the grand adventures of the Alice statue gang!" he exclaimed, as they all chuckled, the atmosphere light and joyous.

As the group reveled in the delight of being united, they batted around various options for their day's exploration — a nearby playground that had the most marvelous smelling sandbox, or perhaps the pond that shimmered so invitingly in the morning sun.

Just then, a flurry of movement caught their attention. They all turned to witness a squirrel scurrying behind a tree, a swish of its bushy tail visible as it darted behind the trunk. Without missing a beat, the gang erupted into a spontaneous chase, their previous plans forgotten in the exhilarating pursuit.

"Over there! By the oak!" Pippa yelled, her eyes sharp and focused.

"Cut him off near the bushes!" Alex instructed with an authoritative bark, leveraging his strategic mind to corner their furry target.

Sally followed suit, her agile body allowing her to keep up with the squirrel's erratic movements, "I'm gaining on him! I am!"

Spiffy, with a smaller but sprightly frame, darted in and out of spaces the others couldn't manage, his exuberant shouts echoing as he joined the chaotic chase.

The frantic squirrel managed to reach a tree, scampering up the trunk with astonishing speed, leaving the group of friends encircling the base, their breaths heavy but faces carrying excited smiles, the spirit of the hunt lighting up their eyes.

With everyone's eyes fixated on the little creature, they heard a series of taunts descending from above, "Haha, you couldn't catch me! Better luck next time, slowpokes!" The voice was familiar, filled with a teasing lightheartedness that was unmistakable.

Sally's ears perked up, recognizing the tone, her eyes widening as she exclaimed, "Wait, that voice... Dale, is that you? This is Sally, I am here with Alex and Spiffy."

At her words, the squirrel descended gracefully, a series of agile leaps bringing him to the ground level. Indeed, it was Dale, their lost friend, standing before them in his new squirrel avatar, his coat sleek and his eyes twinkling with mirth.

The reunion was filled with ecstatic barks and squeals as they crowded around Dale, their tails wagging furiously. Dale appeared equally thrilled, his little body vibrating with excitement. "You guys, this is amazing! I have a tail, a really bushy one!" he expressed, turning around to showcase his new appendage with evident pride.

"And the trees! Oh, you should see how I can leap from one to another. It's almost like flying again!" Dale shared, his eyes shining with the thrill of his newfound abilities, illustrating with his paws the vast jumps he could now execute.

The gang listened to Dale's experiences, their faces reflecting wonder and happiness at their friend's joyous reincarnation. Here, amidst the familiar surroundings of the park, the group felt a harmony restored with Dale's return.

The group spent the next couple of hours exploring the conservatory pond south of the statue until they decided they should return home before their presence is missed.

"With the wonderful reunion we had today, how about we gather again in two days?" Sally proposed, her eyes eager with anticipation. She paused before adding, a note of seriousness entering her tone, "We're nearly complete, just missing Ralph. We know where he is; let's make sure we remain cautious while venturing out."

A chorus of approving barks and nods met her suggestion, affirming the pact of their clandestine meetings, a tangible buzz of excitement reverberating among them at the prospect of continued adventures and the fulfillment of being in each other's presence.

With hearts full of joy and spirits buoyed by the day's adventures, they each found their ways back to their human abodes, sneaking in with a skill that spoke of a fast mastery of their environments.

Once safely inside, they sought out their favorite napping spots, the exhaustion from their eventful day overtaking them. As they lay down, they carried with them the warmth of friendship and the comforting knowledge that they were not alone in this human world.

# flashback

The early morning sun streamed through the ornate drapes of Beatrice's Upper East Side apartment, illuminating patches of the hardwood floor with a golden glow. In the tranquility of dawn, the city outside was just a soft murmur, preparing to burst into the cacophony of another busy day.

Alex, now nestled in a chaise lounge dog bed that lay on the floor near Beatrice's bedside, slowly stirred. He lifted his head, eyes blinking away the remnants of sleep. He could hear the gentle sounds of Beatrice moving about in the adjacent room.

She went about her routine with practiced grace, reminding Alex of a long-forgotten dance. The sounds of water boiling, the scent of freshly ground coffee beans, the soft shuffling of pages; it all felt uncannily familiar to Alex. He remembered those exact steps, that rhythm. It was eerily identical to how he began his mornings in his previous life.

Beatrice then settled at her favorite spot near the front window, her silhouette framed against the morning light. She sipped from her French press coffee, the aroma of which mingled with the faint scent of toasted bread and bacon. As she glanced through the morning newspaper, occasionally glancing at her phone to check the market conditions, Alex couldn't help but feel a pang of nostalgia.

He was served his breakfast, a well-balanced canine meal that was no doubt nutritious and fulfilling. But as he nibbled on it, his senses were overwhelmingly drawn to the tantalizing human breakfast just a few feet away. The rich aroma of coffee, the sizzle of bacon, even the texture of buttered toast—these were sensory memories that tugged at his very soul.

And in that moment, Alex felt a deep, wrenching ache. The life he had known, the habits and routines that once defined his every morning, seemed to be playing out right in front of him, yet just beyond his reach. It was as if he were a ghost, witnessing a life he could no longer inhabit.

He sighed, a soft, forlorn sound that went unnoticed in the backdrop of the morning's rituals. Resting his head on his paws, he allowed the weight of his emotions to settle, a blend of longing and sorrow.

Beatrice, oblivious to the emotional turmoil playing out beside her, continued with her routine, unaware of how closely her morning mirrored that of the dog watching her so intently.

The juxtaposition of their lives, one current and one remembered, played out in that sunlit room, a poignant reminder of the ephemeral nature of existence and the enduring power of memories.

Beatrice got up from her breakfast table and clipped the leash onto Alex, affectionately now known as "Pierre," and they both ventured out onto the busy streets of New York. Alex seemed to be particularly attentive today, absorbing all the scents and noises as they trotted down familiar lanes lined with tall oak trees, passing recognizable landmarks one after another.

As they neared a small park, a particular scent drifted into his nostrils, freezing him in his tracks. It was the unique blend of an old leather-bound book combined with a subtle hint of rich mahogany wood. Beatrice noticed the sudden halt and gently nudged him, but Alex was far away, his mind drifting back to a life once lived, a life clad in a human body.

As if sucked into a time vortex, Alex found himself standing in a grand library adorned with towering shelves laden with numerous ancient books. He was wearing a finely tailored suit, signifying his prosperous career as a brilliant attorney. The room reverberated with the whispers of a thousand stories, preserved in the yellowing pages of the books surrounding him.

A flurry of memories swept over him, a montage of bright and dark moments unfolding before his eyes. He could see himself, Alex, immersed in late-night research sessions, poring over colossal law books, striving tirelessly to climb up the ladder of success, a young man full of ambition and drive.

He saw flashes of joyous occasions - promotions celebrated with friends, becoming a partner, proud moments standing in courtrooms defending clients, and the inner satisfaction of a job well done. Each memory was more vivid than the last, stirring a symphony of emotions within him.

Yet, amidst the surge of joyous memories, a shadow loomed, foretelling the tragic events that led to his untimely departure from the world. Alex found himself amidst a web of complex cases, the pressures mounting as he delved deeper into the abyss to take advantage of loopholes in the justice system, an arena fraught with moral dilemmas and taxing demands. The energy and zest for life were slowly sapped out of him as the burdens grew heavier, the days longer, and the expectations higher.

As the memories continued to flow, he saw himself gradually losing the essence of what made life beautiful, replacing the vibrant hues of joy with an ever-deepening grayscale and greed. Friends and family became distant memories as work consumed his life, a relentless tide eroding the shores of his spirit.

He could feel the tight knot of anxiety in his stomach, the restless nights spent tossing and turning, the relentless hammering of his heart as it battled against a sea of stress and despair. He recalled the lonely nights in his office, the body unable to keep up with the mind's tireless churn. And then, the final, harrowing moments, the breath growing shallower, the room spinning, until finally, darkness embraced him.

Alex was brought back abruptly to the present as Beatrice shook him gently, a look of concern painted on her face. The park, the scents, and the surroundings slowly came back into focus, but a deep melancholy lingered in his eyes, a window into the profound journey through the memories of a life once lived, a life of grand dreams, remarkable successes, but also of unyielding selfishness and heart-wrenching loss.

It was a bitter-sweet moment of reunion with his human past, a poignant reminder of the complexity of life, and the delicate balance between ambition and wellbeing. As they resumed their walk, a solemn Alex moved forward, with a newfound appreciation for the simplicity of his current canine existence yet carrying the richness of human experiences woven in the depths of his soul, an existence now tinged sadness, regret, and selfishness of what could have been, of dreams unfulfilled, and a life left unfinished.

As they continued their leisurely stroll, Alex felt a storm of conflicting emotions brewing within him. He was torn between two worlds — the memories of his past life, rich and complex, filled with highs and lows, juxtaposed against the simplicity and comfort of his present canine life. An undercurrent of guilt gnawed at him as he pondered over the privileges he was enjoying, courtesy of Beatrice's love and affection, while still cherishing the precious memories of a life once led.

The pair made a stop at a pet boutique, where Beatrice decided to spoil him with a new collar. It was a stunning piece, meticulously crafted and studded with tiny shimmering fake diamonds. As Beatrice fastened the glittering collar around his neck, a strange feeling overcame him; a blend of undeserved luxury and a silent acknowledgment of his present reality enveloped him. The sparkling collar felt like a tangible link between his past opulence and his current state of bliss, albeit in a different form.

Their next stop was a sidewalk café, adorned with blooming flowerpots and bustling with vibrant energy. Beatrice settled into a seat, a sunny day on the sidewalk as the vibrant life of the city ebbed and flowed around them. A friendly waiter brought a bowl of fresh water for Alex, setting it down with a warm smile. Beatrice's graceful hands broke off tiny pieces of food, indulging him with morsels of delectable treats as she enjoyed her lunch.

With each bite, Alex experienced a symphony of flavors, and while appreciating the generous offerings, his mind couldn't help but drift back to the lunches of his past life, rare steak and a baked potato dripping with butter and melting in his mouth. Yet, as he sat there, a loved and pampered pet, he felt a strange sense of contentment, a tranquility that eluded him in his previous life.

Beatrice showered him with loving strokes, her soft hands running through his fur, a gesture that spoke volumes, a gesture that emanated pure love and affection. It was then that he realized the depth of the bond that had formed between them, a bond that was tender, simple, yet profoundly beautiful.

As they returned home, Alex felt a lingering melancholy, a deep pondering over the intricate web of lives he had been a part of. Beatrice proceeded to set up her painting easel, her eyes sparkling with the passion for her craft. Alex found a cozy spot right under her chair, curling up in a comfortable ball, his eyes oscillating between the masterful strokes of her brush and the golden rays filtering through the window.

A sense of peace enveloped him as he snuggled close to the gentle rhythm of Beatrice's movements. With each stroke of her brush, he felt as if she was painting away the jagged edges of his traumatic past, replacing them with vibrant tones of love, warmth, and acceptance.

But as he lay there, his mind drifted, wandering through the pathways of memory, grappling with the complex emotions that straddled two worlds. His heart was a battleground of acceptance and resistance, longing and satisfaction, complex memories of a human life, and the simple joys of being Beatrice's beloved pet. It was a journey of self-discovery, of reconciling with his past while embracing the present, a delicate dance between yesterday and today, as he found solace in the silent companionship and the gentle strokes of a loving hand, painting not just on the canvas but also on the canvas of his recovering, resilient spirit.

The next day as the sun climbed higher that morning, Alex made his way to the familiar rendezvous point at the Alice statue. As he approached, he noticed Sally, Pippa, and Spiffy already engaged in a jovial exchange, their tails wagging and heads bobbing animatedly. The sight of them, the familiarity of their presence, brought a semblance of warmth and comfort to Alex's conflicted heart.

Upon his arrival, he was greeted with affectionate nuzzles and friendly barks. They exchanged tales of their adventures over the past couple of days, Spiffy sharing a funny encounter with a particularly audacious squirrel, and Pippa recounting the curious antics of the young humans in her family.

After a while, the conversation took a deeper turn as Alex, with a more subdued demeanor, shared the emotional turmoil that had been brewing within him. The vivid memories resurfaced, and a complex weave of joy and sorrow spilled from him in a heartfelt confessional. He spoke of the surge of nostalgia triggered by a familiar scent, of the flood of precious memories with his former human, and the subsequent grappling with guilt and confusion as he ventured deeper into this new life.

The group listened with attentive ears and empathetic eyes, their faces reflecting understanding and gentle concern. Sally, with a wisdom that belied her youthful demeanor, offered comforting words. "Alex, it's all right to miss your past life. We all have things that we hold dear."

Pippa chimed in with her own perspective, relating her fleeting memories from her previous life as a mosquito. "I sometimes recall flashes of flying freely, feeling so light..." she mused, her eyes acquiring a distant look before returning to the present with a comforting smile towards Alex.

Spiffy joined in, encouraging Alex to find a balance, to honor the beautiful memories while still making room for the new ones that were forming with Beatrice. "Remembering can be a form of honoring, not just a source of pain," he noted sagely.

It was about that time that Dale arrived, bringing with him an energetic burst of humor and lightness that somewhat eased the heaviness that had settled around the group. Noticing the ongoing conversation, he playfully interjected his thoughts, regaling them with amusing anecdotes from his days as a mosquito, engaged in daring and dangerous moves to amuse himself.

"I reckon this life ain't so bad," he chirped, throwing a squirrelly grin at Alex. "Got yourself a fine lady pampering you, plus this glamorous circle of chums. You've got a good thing going, mate!"

The group burst into laughter, the warmth of their companionship filling the air with joyous barks and chirps. Through their collective strength and affection, they formed a vibrant support group, helping Alex to realize that while the past was a treasure trove of beautiful memories, the present held its own unique joy and opportunities for love and happiness.

Together, they sat there under the comforting shade of a tree near Alice statue, a band of friends united in their second chance at life.

Sally turned towards Alex, her gaze filled with deep understanding and a well of wisdom that came from her own experiences. She nudged him affectionately, encouraging him to look at her as she began to speak.

"Alex, you know, it might help to find something, a small memento, something that connects you to the beautiful memories of your past," she began, her voice carrying a gentle, nurturing tone.

"Something that can sit in a special place in your new home, a bridge between your past and present."

She paused, allowing the words to sink in, before sharing her own journey of blending her vivid, albeit scattered memories from her mosquito days with her vibrant present life. "In my new home, I found a cozy corner near a warm vent that reminded me of the comforting heat and the hum of summer evenings in the tree. It became my little nook of nostalgia, a place where I could reminisce yet feel secure in my current family's love."

Alex listened, his ears perked, as Sally continued to weave her story, an encouraging blueprint for harmonizing the precious threads of the past with the fresh canvas of their present lives. "It's there that I've been able to find peace, cherishing the fleeting moments of being airborne while also growing to adore the affection and cuddles my family showers upon me," she said, her eyes glistening with a harmonious blend of nostalgia and newfound joy.

She then leaned closer, her voice tender and sincere as she nudged Alex to forge a deeper connection with Beatrice. "Alex, there's a beautiful bond blossoming between you and Beatrice. It's evident in the way you talk about her that she cares for you, the love reflected in her actions," Sally said, conveying a profound understanding of the intricate dance between holding on and letting go.

She urged him to let himself fully embrace the love Beatrice offered, to find comfort and safety in her presence, encouraging him to forge a pathway of trust and affection that would allow him to blossom in his new life.

Then, with a deep breath that bore a whisper of vulnerability, Sally shared her own apprehensions about the unpredictable road that lay before them in this mystical afterlife. "We've been given this rare second chance, and none of us really knows what lies ahead in this grand, uncharted journey," she confessed, her voice tinged with a mix of wonder and uncertainty.

Yet, as she looked around at her circle of friends, a spark of hope ignited in her eyes. "But we have each other, and we have these beautiful bonds with our human families. I say we embrace the unknown, with the cherished memories in our hearts and the exciting promise of new experiences to forge," she concluded, her voice carrying a hopeful note, reverberating with the deep-seated trust in the magic of possibilities.

The group sat in a reflective silence, the resonance of Sally's words hanging in the air, weaving a thread of unity, and understanding between them. Each of them had embarked on a remarkable journey, each thread bearing testimony to the resilience of spirit and the joy of second chances.

In the midst of this profound reflection, Alex found the courage to share a discovery that had touched him deeply. His voice gentle yet tinged with a newfound strength, he began to describe an event that unfolded earlier.

"I... I found something," Alex said, his voice breaking the contemplative silence. The group turned their focus towards him, encouraging eyes and wagging tails urging him to share. "The other day, while I was fetching a ball from under Beatrice's bureau, I found a man's sock," he paused, a soft smile touching his lips as the memory embraced him.

He continued, the words flowing more freely now, "I remember the routine from my past life, putting on shoes and heading off to work every morning. It was a glimpse into my past life, but in a strange way, it comforted me." Alex's voice carried a warm resonance as he shared the delicate way he had embraced the sock, a tangible connection to a time that once was. "It's like it was there for a reason, a piece from a jigsaw puzzle of my past."

He sighed, a look of serenity washing over his face as he relayed his decision, "I placed it under my pillow. That can be my memento. It's my bridge, a special item that helps me hold on to the beautiful aspects of my previous life while being fully present and grateful for the love I have now."

"Alex, that's wonderful," Sally barked, her tone sincere and encouraging. "It's a perfect token to cherish those memories."

"When should we meet up next?" asked Spiffy.

"Tomorrow," said Pippa. "Tomorrow is Saturday, and if we are lucky, we can see Ralph during the adoption event. I hope he is ok, I kind of miss him."

The group barked in agreement and scampered off in different directions.

"Don't mind me," yelled Dale. "I'll just be here......here in my tree.... doing nothing.... uh, guys?

Dale scampered up the tree and sat on the branch. "I want to be a dog now," he said aloud. He didn't notice that Pippa was still under the tree.

"You will, or something better," replied Pippa as she started to run off. "Just keep having faith and stay out of trouble!"

# the cat caper

The day graced the city with a gentle embrace as the dragonflies hovered over the vibrant gardens surrounding the Alice statue. Saturday had awakened with a jovial spirit, painting the park as families with little ones began to trickle in.

At their designated rendezvous, the gang exchanged greetings, their tails wagging in harmony to the rhythm of anticipation. The atmosphere was alive yet charged with a pulsating undercurrent of adventure that hovered in the air.

"Alright, everyone, remember the plan," Sally initiated, as she scanned the vicinity for any potential intruders. "We've got to be quick and stealthy. We will run through The Ramble, past the museum and stop at the reservoir. From there we wait until the little human light shows on the sign and run across 5th Avenue to East 87th."

The group nodded in agreement, hearts pounding in their chests, echoing the drumbeats of a grand adventure that awaited. Even though the excitement was bubbling in their veins, they knew that leaving Dale behind was the wisest choice.

Dale twitched his little nose in understanding, a smirk stretching across his face, "You just want to ensure that I won't have all the fun chasing tails at the event, don't you?"

A collective laughter broke out among them, lightening the mood as they embarked on their mission. With a harmonious blend of agility and stealth, they maneuvered from the statue through The Ramble and over to the reservoir. They hid behind a row of parked cars, their little paws whispering secrets to the pavement as they ran across the street and closed in on their destination — the bustling adoption event at the pet store's sidewalk two blocks east of 5th Avenue.

The sight that greeted them was a whirlpool of vibrant and chaotic emotions. The air buzzed with a mixture of excited barks, curious meows, and a diverse array of humans buzzing around, creating a rich concert of sounds and scents. Amidst this exhilarating canvas of life, their eyes searched desperately for one familiar face.

Then, there he was — nestled amidst a group of puppies in a puppy pen was a medium size crate, Ralph's recognizable form appeared, his wiry-like hair distinguishing him amidst the sea of adorable faces.

"Ok," said Sally. "Wait until the people in the blue shirts go inside."

As soon as the shelter staff went into the pet store. Spiffy couldn't contain his delight, letting out a jubilant, albeit hushed, "There he is! Oh my, look at him!"

Pippa was the first to inch closer, her eyes welling up as she managed a soft, "Ralph!" That single utterance held a depth of joy and relief, a reunion they had yearned for, now blossoming into reality before their eyes.

Ralph's head turned, and as his eyes met theirs, a radiant glow of recognition, surprise, and sheer happiness danced in them. He wiggled out of the cuddle of puppies, striding over with a grace that spoke volumes of his gentle spirit.

"Hey there, everyone! Oh, it's really you!" he greeted, his voice shaking with emotion as they exchanged quick nuzzles through the bars of the crate. "Man, I am glad to see you! It's been really crazy around the shelter the past week, lots of new arrivals and a few adoptions. I didn't think they were going to bring me, but here I am."

"You look a bit different, better," said Pippa.

"Yea, they gave me a bath and then I spent some time in the salon getting groomed," said Ralph. "Guess they really wanted me to make an impression as just before you got here, a young couple took me for a short walk. They went inside with Steve and Mandy. I hope they take me home."

"That's wonderful news," said Alex. "Keeping my paws crossed for you."

"I'm so proud of you," exclaimed Pippa. "I hope if you do get adopted, your new owners are wonderful."

Spiffy walked up to the kennel and whispered, "You do remember the plan, right?"

"Plan?" inquired Ralph.

"Yea," replied Spiffy. "If you get adopted, learn their schedule, find your escape route, and meet by the Alice statue as soon as you can."

"Oh, yea, that plan," said Ralph. "If it happens, give me a few days to get settled, then I will come to the statue. We have mission to accomplish."

"What mission?" asked Spiffy.

"I'll tell you later......you might not want to join in," said Ralph.

Suddenly, the anticipated moment arrived, heralded by the sound of the sliding glass doors breaking the serene bubble of their reunion. It was a sound that carried a lot of weight; a sound that announced the culmination of a week filled with nervous anticipation and, hopefully, the start of a new chapter in Ralph's life. The conversation halted mid-sentence, replaced by a whirlpool of emotions as eyes widened and hearts clenched tight.

Like a colony of ants, the little group instinctively scattered, finding refuge behind the adjacent cars in the parking lot, their little hearts pounding in their chests, a stark contrast to the newfound silence that enveloped the area. There was a gentle swaying of leaves as they peeked through gaps and over curbs to witness the defining moment of Ralph's life.

A young couple emerged from the store, the vibrancy of youth reflected in their smiles, with a sparkle of happiness illuminating their eyes. The woman held onto a folder that undoubtedly contained Ralph's adoption paperwork, while the man carried a new leash, a symbol of their commitment and the start of their journey together.

Despite the whirlpool of emotions churning inside them, the group couldn't help but exhibit their playful nature, whispering and nudging each other, indulging in lighthearted banter that was characteristic of their bond.

"Oh, look at that, Ralph is getting himself some young, hip parents," Pippa jested, the twinkling of her eyes betraying her teasing demeanor.

"I bet they will baby-talk him to death," Sally chimed in, her voice tinged with amusement as she imitated a high-pitched cooing sound, causing a ripple of giggles to circulate among the group.

With whispered jokes and playful nudges, they exchanged grins, momentarily forgetting the gravity of the situation as they reverted to their youthful, playful selves, teasing Ralph in absentia as a means to lighten their heavy hearts.

The playful banter continued as they watched the couple approach Ralph's enclosure. The anticipation reached a height as they shared in Ralph's wonder, his nerves, and his burgeoning hope. They watched as the couple knelt down, the woman extending her hand for Ralph to sniff, a gesture of goodwill and the first step in forging a bond of trust and love.

As Ralph stepped out to greet them once again, his tail wagging slightly, his body language reflected a cocktail of excitement and apprehension, a dance between the past and the future. The group could see his hesitant steps becoming more assured as he neared the couple, a journey of trust initiated with tentative steps and hopeful wagging of tails.

There was a beautiful serenity in the way Ralph allowed the man to leash him, a silent agreement sealed with the click of the leash, an understanding forged with gentle strokes and loving gazes exchanged. It was a surreal moment, witnessing their friend embarking on this exciting new journey.

As the couple led Ralph towards a shiny new SUV parked nearby, the gang could feel their throats tightening, eyes brimming with tears of joy, pride, and a touch of melancholy, knowing that their friend was stepping into a new, loving home, yet venturing into the unknown without them.

The vehicle pulled out of the parking lot, the couple in the front with Ralph comfortably settled in the back seat, his head poking out slightly as they drove past the group's hiding spot. It was a fleeting moment of contact, a cascade of emotions conveyed through sparkling eyes, before the vehicle turned the corner, heading towards the warm embrace of the sun as it stretched across the park.

They stood there, witnessing the SUV disappear in the distance.

"A few days," said Alex. "That's what he said."

"Yes," replied Pippa. "We will be ready."

The group covertly headed back toward the reservoir near The Great Lawn in the center of Central Park to part ways and return to their respective homes. The anticipation of adding Ralph to their gang brought wags to their tails as they scattered in different directions. A banter of barks ensured as they said their goodbye for the day.

Several days later, under the gaze of the Alice statue, the group congregated once again, their faces wearing expressions of expectation and curiosity. The park echoed with the harmonious blend of whispers and rustles, punctuated by the melodic songs of birds heralding a new day full of possibilities.

Alex and the group waited with bated breath; their gaze fixed on the path that led to their meeting point. Tensions were high and the clock was ticking when finally, breaking through the bushes, Ralph appeared, a tired but triumphant smile lighting his face.

Breathing heavily, Ralph detailed his tardiness, "It was hard guys, but I made it! I have a doggy door that leads to the backyard, yet escaping was no easy feat; I had to dig a tunnel under the azalea bush. I managed to gauge my owners' schedule; they work from 8 to 5 every day."

As he caught his breath, the group gathered around him, peppering him with gentle licks and nuzzles, a gesture of unity, of being there for one another. Ralph, seemingly refreshed by the affection showered upon him, continued, "I learnt something important during my days at the new place. You remember Whiskers from the shelter, right? He has become somewhat of a permanent resident there. He is allowed to roam freely in and out of the shelter, has got his very own bed and bowls in the office. It appears to have brought tranquility to his previously frantic self."

Ralph's face then adopted a serious expression, a gravity settling in his eyes as he spoke, "But even with all these comforts, there is a sadness that clings to him, a hesitancy to venture too far from the shelter; a place that, while safe, is not a home. He needs a family, someone to give him a true home, full of warmth and love."

The group listened, rapt with attention, their hearts swelling with empathy for Whiskers. They could feel the weight of the responsibility that was slowly settling on their shoulders, a silent agreement passing between them, nodding in understanding and determination to help Whiskers find an adopter.

Alex spoke, his voice firm yet tender, "We are a team, a family. We have seen and helped each other through so much. It's our duty to ensure Whiskers finds the love and the home he deserves."

Sally chimed in, her voice carrying a determined note, "Yes, we need to help Whiskers find a loving family. It's our mission now."

It was then that they sprang into action, each member brainstorming, throwing ideas, a pool of strategies emerging as they formulated a master plan to help their friend, Whiskers find his forever home. They knew it wouldn't be easy, it would need unity, strength, and a dash of cunning ingenuity.

In a harmonized flurry of enthusiasm and determination, the group commenced their mission, their first stop being the cherished reservoir. As they trotted through the park, a mosaic of autumn hues graced their path. Pippa couldn't help but be mesmerized by a squirrel busily hoarding nuts, her tail giving away her excitement as she pointed and exclaimed, "Look at Dale's friend working hard for the winter!"

The group erupted into giggles, their laughter blending with the noises of the park. Spiffy, never one to miss a beat, chimed in, "Maybe we should recruit him for our mission, a squirrel's perspective could be invaluable!"

As the group ventured further, they approached the familiar pet store; memories of their recent joyful reunion with Ralph bloomed in their minds, a beacon of hope and testimony to their strength when united. The memory fueled their spirits, infusing them with a renewed vigor as they trotted past the six blocks, finally arriving at East 92nd and 1st Avenue, where the renowned ASPCA animal shelter stood, a haven for many animals like Whiskers, waiting for a chance at a new beginning.

Ralph couldn't help but share his recent escapades, narrating his adventures in his new home, bringing a wave of laughter and light-hearted teasing to the group. In a playful gesture, Sally teased, "So, superstar, now that you are used to the pampered life, will we see you refusing to step out unless you have a red carpet laid out?"

A round of hearty laughter followed, even as the shelter loomed in front of them, a reminder of the serious mission that lay ahead.

The group converged, their faces wearing a serious expression now as they strategized. The atmosphere buzzed with suggestions, a whirlpool of ideas flowing as they discussed the plan to find

Whiskers a loving home. This particular shelter was always open for adoption, so prospective new owners were always coming and going.

In the midst of the serious deliberation, a pair of pigeons caught Alex's attention. He paused and then announced in a mock serious tone, "I hereby appoint these pigeons as our aerial reconnaissance team!" Pointing to the seemingly engaged birds that were busy pecking at the ground, oblivious to their new titles.

The group couldn't help but burst into laughter once more, the pigeons seemingly joining in, bobbing their heads amusingly, offering a momentary release from the serious atmosphere and filling their mission with a touch of whimsy.

They regrouped, with Pippa verbalizing the plan. "Ok, we go around the side, so we are not seen and look for Whiskers. We need to work with him to change his approach to humans. So, think of the advice you would give him. Remember, he's not a dog, so keep in the character of a cat."

As the group navigated stealthily around the shelter, the gentle rustle of leaves and the soft patter of their paws formed a harmonious backdrop to their mission. As they rounded a corner, they were greeted with the sight of Whiskers, a spirited feline with a wild heart, ardently engaged in the noble pursuit of hunting a grasshopper. He was a picture of focus, his body low and eyes wide, every fiber of his being tuned to the task at hand.

They paused, admiring Whiskers' feline grace before Sally softly cleared her throat, breaking the serene tableau. Whiskers' head snapped towards them, his expression changing rapidly from surprise to a warm recognition as he bounded over, momentarily abandoning his hunt.

"Whiskers, old friend," Ralph began, his voice filled with warmth and a tinge of urgency. "We've come because we want to help you find a loving home, a family that will treasure you."

Whiskers seemed to ponder this, his green eyes reflecting a pool of deep thoughts before he finally nodded, willing to listen to what his friends had in mind.

The group gathered around, each offering pieces of advice, channeling what they believed to be the finest feline characteristics to woo a potential adopter.

Pippa was the first to share her advice rich with empathy and understanding. "Whiskers, remember, humans love it when cats show their soft and tender side. Perhaps you could try kneading on a soft blanket or purring loudly when someone shows you affection, perhaps rubbing on their leg with your body. It's a sure way to win their hearts."

Spiffy chimed in next, with a cheeky sparkle in his eye, "And don't forget the classic head-tilt! Give them a mysterious look now and then, let them wonder what's going on in that smart head of yours!"

"That's' a dog thing," explained Sally.

Alex, not to be left behind, offered, "You know, Whiskers, a playful demeanor is always a hit. Maybe bat at a few toys, show them that you're keen on having fun and being their playful companion."

Sally then leaned in, her voice gentle yet assured, "You've got this warm, glow in your eyes, Whiskers. Use it to your advantage. Lock eyes with them, draw them in with your warmth, and let them see the special heart that beats in you."

As they shared their tips, a beautiful blend of earnestness and light-hearted banter filled the air, nurturing a hope that blossomed in Whiskers' heart. It was then Sally summarized, "And Whiskers, be yourself. You have this incredible spirit, a heart that is brave and loving. Let that shine through. We believe in you."

Sally motioned towards the shelter, her eyes filled with empathy and a silent encouragement, as she said, "Alright Whiskers, it's showtime. Head back inside and find those humans peering through the cat room window. Try rubbing around their legs, giving them your most affectionate nudges. Remember, it's all about connecting; you're an actor on stage, and it's your time to shine."

Whiskers hesitated for a moment, the weight of the task before him seeming monumental. Yet, as he glanced at the sea of encouraging and loving faces around him, a surge of courage welled up within him. With a determined nod, he agreed, "Alright, I will give it my best shot." His voice trembled slightly but was laced with a firm resolve.

As Whiskers moved gracefully towards the shelter's entrance, the group found a hidden vantage point, their eyes filled with hope and anticipation as they watched their friend venture on this vital mission.

Inside, the shelter was abuzz with activity; potential adopters wandered around, their eyes scanning the various pets, each with their own story waiting to be told. Whiskers headed toward the cat room, a symphony of purrs and meows greeting him. He took a deep breath, shaking off his initial hesitations, and soon found a group of people peering into the room through a large window in the hallway. He proceeded down the hallway to where they stood.

With an agile grace that belied his previous hesitancy, Whiskers wove through the legs of the spectators, his fur brushing against them softly, his golden eyes casting enchanting glances, luring them in with his irresistible charm. It wasn't long before an older woman, with a kind yet lonely gaze, noticed him.

She turned to Mandy, who was standing nearby, her voice firm yet tinged with a hopeful curiosity as she inquired, "Oh dear, this one seems quite special. Could you tell me more about him?"

Mandy offered a hesitant smile, replying, "Oh, that's Whiskers, our resident shelter cat. He's a bit of a lunatic if I'm being honest, very independent and... well, slightly erratic at times. You might prefer a different cat."

But the older woman shook her head, her eyes still locked onto Whiskers who seemed to have staged a one-cat show just for her. She insisted firmly, yet kindly, "No, I would like to see him in a private room, there's something about him."

With a resigned nod, Mandy led the woman and Whiskers into a separate, quiet room. It was a sanctuary of soft light and warm tones, encouraging a calm demeanor in its occupants. The group, watching anxiously from their hiding spot, could feel their hearts race in tandem with Whiskers as the door closed behind them.

Inside the room, Whiskers seemed to remember every piece of advice given to him. The room echoed with the gentle sounds of purring as Whiskers rubbed affectionately against the woman, his golden eyes locking with hers in a warm, soulful gaze, sharing a connection that spoke of potential love and companionship. He displayed a playful side too, batting gently at the toys present in the room, his actions reflecting a spirit youthful and full of zest.

When they finally emerged from the room, the older woman had a radiant smile on her face, a twinkling in her eye that had not been there before. She turned to Mandy, her voice holding a newfound determination as she announced, "I will take him. He will be my companion. I live alone in a beautiful apartment on the West Side of Manhattan. It's peaceful, with large windows and plenty of sunshine; it will be perfect for him."

Mandy nodded, clearly surprised yet pleased with the unexpected turn of events as she began the necessary paperwork, while the older woman knelt down beside Whiskers, whispering softly, promises of love, warmth, and a forever home echoing between them, as tears of joy brimmed in her eyes.

Outside, the group of friends erupted into silent barks, their faces filled with happiness, pride, and a heartwarming realization that they had successfully helped Ralph's friend find a home that promised love, affection, and countless joyous moments. It was a mission accomplished, a golden day, not just for Whiskers but for the gang, a group of souls trying to earn their place in the afterlife.

As Whiskers was put into a cat carrier, a temporary box with holes, the woman exited the shelter. The gang could see one paw of Whiskers waving a hole in the side of the box. An audible, "Meow!" could be heard and interpreted as "Thanks!" The woman hailed down a taxi and the two disappeared down the avenue.

Sally said, "All right, back home. It's been a long morning; we all deserve a nap."

Sally and Pippa headed north while Ralph, Alex, and Spiffy head west, back through the park as they traveled back home, each eager to see what the next days' adventure would hold.

# new horizons

On a quiet Sunday morning, the sunlight heralding a day that promised joy and fresh beginnings. In a house adorned with warm colors and tastefully chosen artifacts, the atmosphere brimmed with light-hearted anticipation for the day ahead. A soft call echoed, ever-increasing in urgency, as Beatrice wandered through the house with Pierre's harness and leash in hand, calling out for him.

"Pierre... Pierre! Where has that little adventurer hidden himself now?" Beatrice mused aloud, her voice a gentle yet insistent melody weaving through the house as she looked in every possible nook and cranny that could harbor the elusive Pierre.

Finally, her voice reached Alex who was indulging in a tranquil nap in a sun-dappled corner. With a stretch and a yawn that displayed an exaggerated sense of disturbance, he rose to his feet. Taking a moment to smooth his coat with a few strategic licks, he made his way towards Beatrice, his tail wagging in mild amusement.

Seeing him emerge, Beatrice sighed with a mixture of relief and playfulness. "Ah, there you are, my Mon cherie. Ready for our walk?" she asked, leaning down to lovingly secure the harness around him. "It's time for our walk, I want to try a new coffee shop across the park on the Upper West Side."

As they stepped out, the neighborhood greeted them with its vibrant life. Families out for a stroll, children's laughter ringing in the air, and other canine companions excitedly exploring the day's offerings with their human counterparts. It was a painting of joy, drawn with strokes of sunlight, green leaves, and myriad colors from the blooming flowers adorning their path. Fall was coming, its scent was in the air.

They moved gracefully through the familiar lanes and across the park alongside Terrace drive to a coffee shop located just one block from the park on West 69th street called "The Magnolia". Beatrice sat down at a table out front under the green awning adoring the storefront of the coffee shop. A young woman in a white shirt and black skirt covered by a green apron took Beatrice order while Alex laid down next to the chair.

"Isn't this a nice neighborhood Pierre?" she said. "I almost moved over here after I left the university, but I couldn't leave my friends and my apartment with the art studio. It just didn't make sense. Plus, I like having the backyard garden for you to sun in."

A sight caught Alex's discerning eye. Across the street, outside a brownstone coming down the stairs from the door was a familiar looking human. Alex detected a scent and as he focused his gaze on the woman, he realized it was Lisa, his former young secretary. He noted the scent of jasmine and flowers, the familiar perfume that used to linger in his office after she delivered documents to him. Her figure, a frame from his human past, a vibrant but solitary soul who had been an important part in the fabric of his previous life's narrative.

She reached the bottom of the stairs, repositioned her purse upon her shoulder and began to walk across the street to the coffee shop where he and Beatrice were.

Lisa had always carried a quiet grace about her, a gentle spirit encased in a slender frame, adorned with a cascade of chestnut hair that shimmered in the sunlight. She had an ever-present aura of kindness in her eyes, a warmth that seemed to embrace you in a comforting hug whenever she engaged in conversation. Yet, in spite of her apparent open heartedness, there had been an unmistakable shade of loneliness that lurked in the depths of those expressive eyes. She rarely talked about the people in her life, and Alex never knew her to have someone special in her life. She was always in the office before him and often went home well after dark.

Noting that time through the adjudication and recycling center ran differently, he realized that it had been years since he had seen her. Alex noticed the way she carried herself with the same graceful demeanor, yet with a touch more confidence and an elegance that had matured over the years. The loneliness seemed to have deepened, however, finding residence in the subtle lines that marked her still youthful but ever-so-slightly weary face. She carried the solitude as a constant, silent companion, shaping her daily existence into a solitary dance of one.

Alex didn't understand how he knew, perhaps some instinct innate in animals or dogs, he just sensed the loneliness in her gait as she walked. He felt a stir in his heart, a surge of empathy mixed with a resolve as firm as steel. The vibrancy of the young woman who had once added a touch of light to his daily office life deserved to experience the full spectrum of love and companionship.

As Lisa disappeared down the street, a seed of determination took root in Alex's heart, a secret mission formed, fueled by a deep understanding of the quiet yearnings of a solitary heart. He turned to Beatrice, his eyes filled with a resolute sparkle as they continued their walk, a new purpose giving a vigorous swing to his tail. He knew what he had to do; the next chapter of his afterlife mission was clear as day. It was time for him to help Lisa, who deserved nothing less than a love story that echoed with laughter, warmth, and endless joy.

In the days that followed, Alex embarked on a meticulously planned operation rooted in the purest intentions — to sprinkle a dose of love in Lisa's solitary life. Every morning, after Beatrice went to her studio, Alex would stealthily sneak out of the house, his heart buoyed by a mission that warmed him with a tender glow of purpose. He traced Lisa's footsteps from a safe distance, becoming a silent guardian of her daily routines.

Lisa's days unfolded in a cadence of solitude yet in tune with the simple joys of life. She visited the same café near her brownstone, where she would savor her morning coffee while engrossed in a book, a serene smile gracing her face as she flipped through the pages, a beacon of grace and tranquility. She would catch an Uber or taxi downtown to the law firm and work until evening. Her evenings after work were dedicated to painting classes at a nearby art studio, or a quick workout at the local gym 3 blocks from her home.

On the weekend afternoons, she would often wander into Central Park, finding solace in the embracing arms of nature, sometimes sketching the lively scenes around her, or lost in the world of melodies as she listened to her favorite songs on her phone. Every place she visited, she carried with her an aura of soft-spoken grace, a tender reverence for the world around her, creating a mosaic of beauty through her daily rituals, yet always as a solitary figure, a solo dance in the bustling sequence of life.

As days turned into weeks, Alex was a quiet observer, carefully noting the nuances of Lisa's preferences and routines, a palette of colors that defined her in the present day. He identified her favorite spots in the park, the quiet corners she preferred for her afternoon respites, and the moments when her eyes seemed to long for something more, a deeper connection that remained just out of reach.

The planning phase materialized as a delicate set of observations and heartfelt wishes. Until that point, Alex had kept his mission secret from the group as they continue to meet at the Alice statue every several days. Alex finally enlisted the help of his trustworthy group, gathering them under the embracing boughs of their familiar meeting tree near the Alice statue in Central Park. He narrated Lisa's story, his experiences with her in the past, the glimpses of her world that he had silently witnessed and voiced his deep-seated desire to bring the colors of love into her somewhat gray palette of life.

As Alex conveyed his plan with earnest sincerity, there were discerning looks exchanged among the group, Sally expressing her concerns gently, but firmly. "Alex, you are an incredibly kind soul.

But remember, we are here to forge our paths, untethered from our past lives. You must not get entangled in the lives we left behind."

Yet, Alex stood firm, a rock amidst a stream, holding steadfast to his belief in the purity of his mission. He acknowledged the warnings but argued, "Lisa was more than just an acquaintance. She was a young woman who brought kindness and warmth into a corporate environment often too rigid and cold. I feel a deep connection and responsibility towards her, to at least try to bring a ray of sunshine into her life. Perhaps this is my moment to do something good and unselfish to help my journey."

The others were silent, pondering over Alex's words, the clear sincerity and determination resonating in his voice. Finally, it was Pippa who broke the silence, her voice tender yet supportive, "If it is to bring love and joy to a kind soul, then it is a mission worthy of our efforts."

Nods of agreement followed, a gentle consensus forming amidst the group as they rallied behind Alex, their faces reflecting a mix of worry and hopeful anticipation. And thus, with a heart brimming with resolve and a spirit buoyed by the support of his friends, Alex set forth on his new mission, a secret endeavor sparked by kindness, a silent pledge to bring warmth and companionship into Lisa's solitary life, ever hopeful that the Universe would conspire to bless her with a love as tender and true as her spirit.

"So, what's the plan," asked Spiffy. "It looks like a daunting task."

Ralph spoke up, "You know Alex, my owners Brian and Kim take me to the park every Saturday, without fail. In fact, half the time, I just got back from being with you guys."

"So, what are you saying," inquired Pippa.

"They usually take me to the fenced dog park and sit down with a friend of theirs," Ralph continued, his voice tinged with enthusiasm, "A friend who, I think, could be a perfect match for Lisa. He's around her age, kind-hearted, with a penchant for art and has a calm demeanor which might resonate well with Lisa's personality."

The group listened intently; the air thick with anticipation as they all realized that this was no longer just an idea but a feasible plan taking form before them. Every one of them knew that this mission required a balance of subtlety and careful crafting to respect Lisa's autonomy while fostering potentially beautiful connections.

They began to strategize meticulously, allocating roles based on each of their strengths and insights into human behavior. Sally, with her nurturing nature, suggested planting small, thoughtful gifts at Lisa's favorite spots — little tokens that resonated with her interests, perhaps a hand-painted bookmark or a delicately crafted pendant.

"Where would we get our hands on these items," asked Pippa. "We need to create a chance encounter between Lisa and Ralphs owners' friend."

"Ralph, where exactly does Brian and Kim sit?" asked Alex.

"They sit at the benches in the garden just outside the Theodore Roosevelt Park Dog Run, just behind the American Museum of Natural History."

"Perfect, she walks down the pathway between the dog run and the museum every Saturday. All we need now is to devise a way for them to accidentally meet."

Amid the congregation of verdant bushes and flower gardens, an atmosphere of tensed excitement and anticipation enveloped Alex, Pippa, and Spiffy as they envisioned each segment of the carefully crafted plan. Each of them, including Dale the squirrel, assumed positions that maximized their strengths, uniting for a cause as pure as facilitating a possible love connection.

Spiffy would be the heart of the operation, his agile and quick self was entrusted with the role of being the lookout, a role involving a back-and-forth sprint between The Ramble and the Dog Run. In the vast expanse of the park, his speed would be their asset, helping them track Lisa's movements and communicating them to the rest of the group with well-rehearsed signals. The dog's keen senses would maintain a vigilant watch, tuning into the surroundings with a discipline that echoed that of a seasoned scout.

In parallel, Pippa was preparing for her role, which entailed evoking sympathy and diverting Kim's attention at the critical juncture. Pippa's expressive eyes would tell a tale of pain as she feigned a limp, inching slowly yet determinedly towards Kim with an act that bespoke vulnerability. She knew the art of conjuring empathy; with her sweet demeanor, she would be impossible to ignore, thus ensuring Kim's focus would be entirely on her.

As for Spiffy, he bore a significant chunk of the responsibility, being swift to find and approach Brian and Kim's friend with a demeanor of a lost dog, his leash trailing along. The artistry in his performance would lie in striking the right balance between looking distressed yet approachable, adding an element of serendipity to the intended encounter.

Dale was entrusted with a mission that was small yet pivotal to the plan's success. With nimble movements characteristic of squirrels, Dale would maneuver with ease and precision to hook Spiffy's leash onto a convenient spot, facilitating the connection between the friend and Spiffy, and by extension, with Lisa. A task that demanded both speed and subtlety, carried on tiny but determined shoulders.

And then, there was Alex. He had sculpted this operation from scratch, integrating the thoughtful suggestions of the group into a cohesive strategy. On the day, Alex's role was crucial, being the shield that would protect their delicate plan from external disruptions. His task involved creating a delightful distraction, a vibrant whirl of energy running in circles around the tables, engaging in an almost playful dance that would enthrall onlookers, ensuring their gazes were drawn away from the orchestrated events, yet without arousing suspicion.

As they stood there in their strategic huddle, the group could feel a unique blend of nervousness and exhilaration weaving among them, each of them united in the hope and fervent desire to kindle a spark in Lisa's life, to brighten her solitary world with a splash of color, a hint of romance.

At the core of it all, their plan symbolized a profound respect for Lisa's independent spirit. They were merely facilitating a chance meeting, a beginning with endless possibilities, leaving the reins of destiny firmly in her hands, while offering a tender nudge towards the vibrant spectrum of connectedness and affection that life had to offer. This was the compromise in helping Alex to not do too much connected to his previous life.

As they broke from the huddle, a solemn yet hopeful determination marked their faces, a silent agreement that they would each play their part to perfection and provide a single circumstance for Lisa's heart to find a home.

Saturday dawned with a freshness that heralded the unfolding of something beautiful. The assembly congregated at their designated meeting point — the enchanting environs of the Alice statue that bore witness to countless whispered secrets and shared joys over the years.

Spiffy was the epitome of vibrant energy, his eyes sparkling with anticipation, wearing a radiant smile that bore no trace of the fatigue that usually clung to him. Dragging along a pink leash that stood out against his fur, he exuded an air of readiness that was almost infectious.

The sight of the pink leash quickly became the epicenter of laughter as the gang huddled around, teasing Spiffy mercilessly. "Looks like you raided a kitty's wardrobe!" chuckled Sally, her eyes twinkling with mirth. The hilarity escalated as Spiffy defensively explained that it had belonged to the family cat before him, opening up a floodgate of jokes that teased the boundaries of the age-old dogs versus cats debate.

Giggles and light-hearted banters echoed as they moved to their planned hideout amidst the vibrant foliage of the garden near the dog run. They nested there, their hearts pulsating in a harmonious rhythm of hopeful excitement, intertwining with the melodies of nature that surrounded them.

Not long after, Ralph made his appearance, flanked by Brian and Kim, instilling a sudden rush of alertness in the group. Spiffy was quick to spring into action, scouting the vicinity with a keen eye to gauge if the much-anticipated friend had accompanied them.

Spiffy returned, his face beaming with a positive report. "He's here!" he announced breathlessly. "A rather dashing fellow, around 30, by the looks of it. Overheard Brian calling him Justin, apparently, he is his brother." The group leaned in, absorbing every detail as Spiffy painted a vivid picture of Justin, a kind-hearted looking man, handsome, physically fit, and impeccably dressed.

With the details locked in, Spiffy charged forth up the path that kissed the boundaries between the dog run and the museum. Every nerve in his body was alert as he scanned the surroundings for Lisa, his heart echoing the group's shared hope, a hopeful beat in a symphony of dreams coming alive.

It wasn't long before Spiffy was darting back, eyes wide and heart pounding with adrenaline. "She is coming; I'd say in about five minutes she will be passing near the bench where Justin is seated," he relayed, his voice thick with anticipation, punctuated with short, excited breaths.

The atmosphere was electric, charged with a beautiful concoction of hope and nervous anticipation. The group exchanged quick, determined nods, each of them ready to play their well-rehearsed parts in this delicate ballet of fate. The plan was set into motion, choreographed with the kindest intentions.

As they launched into action, their intentions weaved seamlessly through the execution of the keen-eyed strategists.

Pippa was the first to move, her aged limbs gracefully portraying a subtle limp as she approached Kim. There was an art in her movements, a careful display of vulnerability that beckoned nurturing instincts to the surface. Kim's face transitioned from relaxation to concern as she noticed Pippa's hobbling figure, her hand instinctively reaching out to provide solace and support.

Almost simultaneously, Spiffy reappeared, the pink leash dangling conspicuously from his mouth, rushing towards the dashing figure, Justin, who was yet to notice the perfectly orchestrated scene gradually unfolding around him. A playful, slightly desperate whimper escaped Spiffy as he nudged Justin's hand with his nose, encouraging a touch, a connection that bore the weight of kind-hearted intentions and hopeful dreams. He reached out to grab the leash only to have Spiffy move far enough for it to fall out of his reach.

Justin stood up and bent over and Spiffy again moved as Justin moved, baiting each other until he reached the edge of the path.

The garden echoed with Dale's frantic signals from the tree above, his small form darting between branches, ready to play his role with a level of agility and precision that only a squirrel could master. Each signal he sent out was a testament to the collaboration that bridged differences in a unifying goal.

Away from the center stage yet holding an essential role in the ballet of connections was Alex, engaged in a light-hearted frolic, drawing smiles and gentle chuckles from nearby onlookers. His cheerful antics served as a radiant distraction.

The world narrowed down to a beautiful frame where Justin's face transitioned from a subtle confusion to a soft, appreciative smile as he connected with Spiffy. Unbeknownst to him, the small congregation of furry strategists and one diligent squirrel were guiding a delicate web of connections, weaving a gentle path leading to the woman slowly approaching, the solitary figure enriched with depths of beauty and layers of untold stories.

And then, time seemed to slow as Lisa approached Pippa and knelt at her side comforting her about her apparent injury. As Spiffy and Justin neared her, Spiffy suddenly turn around and ran through Justin's legs only to have him turn around, take a step, and fall over the bending Lisa who was petting Pippa.

Surprised, she stood up to see Justin laid out like a sack of potatoes on the grass. She hesitated for a moment, her eyes meeting Justin's, a connection sparked in that fragile yet potent second, birthing an interplay of shy smiles exchanged, a mirror of softness reflected in their eyes, opening a door to the realm of possibilities, of shared dreams, and beautiful tomorrows.

"I'm sorry," said Justin. "I was trying to catch the brown chihuahua with the pink leash. She looked lost."

Spiffy thought, "Great, they think I am a girl."

"No problem," said Lisa. "I was comforting this furry husky who apparently has an injury to her leg."

As Lisa held out her hand to help Justin get up off the grass, Pippa and Spiffy darted into the bushes in the garden followed closely by Alex and Sally, who was watching from behind a picnic table.

The group peered out to see Justin and Lisa seem somewhat enamored with each other. They were both smiling, and Lisa was gently brushing the hair from her eyes as Justin spoke. They sat down on a nearby bench. It wasn't important to hear the conversation. The mission was completed successfully, facilitate a chance meeting. Now, it was all up to love.

Alex felt good, his heart swelled with the knowledge that he perhaps planted the seed of love, maybe even blossoming into something more.

It was time to go, the group high fived and howled to their success and went on their separate ways, back to their homes to revel in their success and rest.

# the stand off

The air was crisp, and the vibrant colors of fall descended on the park with warm purple, amber, and ruby tones. Each leaf that twirled gracefully to the ground signified the cycle of life, a beautiful yet poignant reminder of the transient nature of existence. In this lively canvas of colors and emotions, the dog park buzzed with activity, a haven for the community to converge in a chorus of barks, laughter, and joyful chatters.

Up in a sturdy tree near the iconic Alice statue, Dale was busy orchestrating his preparations for the colder months that lay ahead. A nest, strategically located to oversee the park's activities, was under construction. Dale's tiny heart pounded with a mix of anxiety and excitement as he gathered nuts, unable to comprehend why but driven by an instinct as old as time.

Meanwhile, relationships were blossoming on the ground. There were the elderly couples leisurely strolling with their slow-paced canine companions, and the young families who sought to instill the joy of pet companionship in their little ones.

The atmosphere carried a serene joy, yet it was a fragile joy, constantly threatened by the underlying dynamics of dominance and territorial disputes, characteristic of dog parks worldwide. Within this lively mix, occasionally, sharp growls interrupted the jovial barks, a testimony to the undercurrent of volatility that existed in such communal spaces.

As the morning progressed, a ripple of unease threaded through the crowd, a subtle acknowledgment of a disruptive presence that had just entered the park. A dog of imposing stature for a medium size dog and a rough coat of dark shades marked his territory with a boldness that bordered on aggression. His powerful build and deep growls resonated with a menace that shifted the park's atmosphere from vibrant to tense.

At the other end of the leash, the dog's owner carried himself with a similar aggressive disposition, his piercing eyes scanning the surroundings critically, his towering frame speaking volumes of his domineering nature. His presence, alongside his canine companion, signaled a disruption in the park's harmonious rhythm, a prelude to an unavoidable confrontation that lay just on the horizon.

In the moments that followed, the park witnessed a palpable shift in dynamics, a tension that burgeoned with every step the man and his bully dog took. Unbeknownst to the regular park goers, this was just the beginning of a dramatic chapter that would unfold, a standoff that would draw lines of allegiance and test the strength of bonds forged in the delicate community nurtured in the dog park's environment.

The gruff man proceeded to open the gate to the dog park. His dog, a Bulldog, although smaller in stature, was packaged in a powerful looking frame. Upon removing his leash, he immediately ran in circles around the park, around the trees barking and growling as if to signal to the other dogs that he was the boss of the park.

As the morning blossomed into a full-fledged day, a notable coincidence was unfurling at the park's entrance. Unplanned yet fortuitously, Beatrice and Spiffy's owners chose this very day and hour to visit the dog park. Surprised with smiling faces, they greeted each other under the shade of a large oak tree.

With the Bulldog momentarily preoccupied at a distant corner of the park, a sense of serene normality prevailed as Alex and Spiffy were unharnessed from their leashes, granting them the freedom to explore the vibrant space brimming with life. The human chatter faded as the two friends reunited, their wagging tails displaying their happiness in the crisp air.

"I didn't expect to see you here, Spiffy," Alex articulated, his voice carrying an undertone of genuine delight.

Spiffy responded with equal fervor, "Neither did I, Alex. It feels like one of those happy coincidences, doesn't it?" His spirited reply resonated in the space between them.

As they moved further into the park, they exchanged updates, playful nudges accompanying tales of their recent adventures. Spiffy couldn't resist sharing the joyous success story of the 'chance meeting mission', and wondered if Alex had any updates.

Spiffy listened intently as Alex explained that he and Beatrice have not been back to the coffee shop recently, but he hopes they go soon. Amidst their joyous catch-up, their keen senses began to pick up on a growing tension, a wave of disruption radiating from a slowly approaching source.

Their ears tuned into a series of growls, gradually increasing in volume, breaking the rhythmic cadence of their conversation. Simultaneously, their owners, engrossed in a cheerful exchange, remained blissfully unaware of the shifting energies around them.

The Bulldog had finished his business in the corner and was now traversing the park with a purpose, a dominant stride signaling his intention to assert control over the space. The park's atmosphere started to morph, the light-hearted banter between Alex and Spiffy growing subdued, replaced by a growing sense of apprehension as the Bulldog drew near, a dark shadow inching closer in the vibrant canvas of the park.

A sudden halt in their conversation marked the onset of a tensed atmosphere as both Spiffy and Alex turned their heads, catching sight of the imposing Bulldog approaching them. The jovial atmosphere around them seemed to hang in a precarious balance as a heavy silence engulfed the space. The expressions on their faces mirrored the apprehension that was steadily brewing in their hearts.

With a strained smile trying to maintain the peace, Alex initiated a cautious greeting, his voice tinged with unease, "Hello there, it's a nice day, isn't it?"

A stern face met his gentle approach, the Bulldog's deep-set eyes carried an uncompromising sternness as he responded, his voice deep and growling, "Nice day? It was, until I saw you two taking up the best spot in this park. This area," he gestured expansively with a sweeping, powerful forelimb, "is for the ones who deserve it. Clearly, not the likes of you two."

Spiffy, albeit smaller and now clearly intimidated, mustered the courage to chime in, trying to convey a sense of comradery, "We all share this park, it is a place for friendship and..." but he was abruptly cut off by the Bulldog, who was now increasingly hostile and toxic in his demeanor.

"No, no, no, this isn't a democracy. This place obeys the laws of the jungle, and in the jungle, power rules," the Bulldog retorted, his tone harsh and derogatory, his imposing physique taking a step closer to Spiffy, forcing the smaller dog to step back, an evident fear in his eyes. The Bulldog then gestured towards the other side of the park, a clearly less appealing area with fewer amenities and almost devoid of shade, "Move there if you know what is good for you."

The Bulldog's abrasive words filled the space around them, a force of negativity that pierced through the calm and vibrant canvas of the dog park, replacing the excited meet-up with fear and hostility.

Alex felt a protective surge rise within him as he saw his friend Spiffy being bullied. He stood taller, positioning himself between the Bulldog and Spiffy, his voice firm yet maintaining a degree of calmness as he replied, "We were here first, and we have every right to enjoy this part of the park as you do. We won't move just because you say so."

For a moment, there was a tense silence, a standoff where piercing glares were exchanged, and the surrounding atmosphere thickened with a foreboding sense of a brewing storm. The Bulldog snarled, a clear sign of anger and readiness for a confrontation.

"My name is Spike, and I own this park!" he said. "If you know what's good for you, you will leave this area now."

Not wanting to start a fight, Alex and Spiffy slowly backed away and moved to the sunlight portion of the park where many other dogs who were threatened had retreated.

As they stood there, the park transformed into an arena of life's stark realities, a ground where bullying and toxic behaviors clashed with friendship and the spirit of unity.

"What right does he have to claim territory in the park?" uttered Spiffy. "It's not right."

"For the moment," Alex replied. "Let's defuse the situation by just enjoying our time together."

"No, I don't know what kind of human I was or what I did in that life, but no one bullies me or my friends around," said Spiffy.

Breathing heavily and with a resolve firming in his small chest, Spiffy turned around abruptly, breaking away from Alex. The smaller dog's determined steps echoed louder with each pace as he headed back towards the shade, his heart pounding in his chest. His determined figure caught the eyes of other dogs in the sunlit area, a ripple of whispers and nudges spreading through them, their attention shifting towards the determined figure marching courageously.

As Spiffy reached the shaded area, the crowd of dogs gathered in an impromptu circle, the atmosphere thick with anticipation. A mixture of fear and respect reflected in their eyes as they beheld Spiffy standing tall, albeit his smaller stature, facing the bully named Spike with an unwavering gaze.

In the middle of the circle, Spike wore a smirk, his massive frame leaning down towards Spiffy, a caricature of mockery drawn across his face, assuming victory was imminent due to his size and ferocity. However, Spiffy's face reflected no fear, his bright eyes lit with an inner fire of courage and determination, displaying an undying spirit that belied his small form.

The silent support from the audience ignited a braver flame in Spiffy's heart, his posture straightening as he spoke with an unwavering voice, bearing wisdom beyond his years, "Spike, a park is a place of joy, a haven of friendship. No one owns it, and certainly not through bullying and scaring others away. Your strength should be a shield for the weaker, not a weapon to harass them."

At a little distance, Alex stood paralyzed, torn between rushing to Spiffy's aid and letting his friend fight his battle. His body was taut, every muscle ready to spring into action, yet his heart ached with the pride of watching Spiffy hold his ground, an array of conflicting emotions vivid in his eyes - fear, pride, and a blossoming hope that echoed the sentiments of the hushed crowd around.

The face-off between them intensified, the stark contrast between Spiffy's stern yet calm demeanor against Spike's increasing irritation and bellicosity was evident. With each word Spiffy spoke, it seemed to strip away the facade of toughness that Spike wore, revealing an insecure soul underneath.

The dialog ebbed to a quiet lull, the crowd around held its collective breath, witnessing a battle not of physical prowess but of moral strength and courage. The air vibrated with tension, each second stretched long as both parties engaged in a silent battle of wills.

Spike replied, "You think you can......"

"I'm not finished yet," yelled Spiffy as he continued to tear down Spike's defenses. In a show of unexpected maturity and insight, Spiffy then softened his stance, his voice taking on a gentle yet firm tone, "We can all share this space and enjoy it together, Spike. There's room for everyone. You don't need to own something to enjoy it. And being the strongest also means being the kindest."

The surrounding dogs murmured in agreement, supportive barks and nods came from the crowd, a community rallying around the wisdom emanating from the small yet fearless figure standing before them.

Spike found himself cornered, not by physical force but by the truth that echoed through Spiffy's words, the sensible words reverberating around the park, reaching deep into the hearts of all present. The bully's aggressive facade faltered, his posture deflated as he found himself isolated, his brawn losing against the brave heart and wise words of Spiffy.

As the confrontation reached its peak, everyone awaited Spike's response. The heavy silence was suddenly broken as Spike hesitantly began; his tone stripped of its earlier hostility. "You see, my owner... he expects me to be this tough, ruthless dog, dominating over others. It is this image that I am supposed to maintain here," he said, with a hint of regret lacing his deep, usually intimidating voice.

The bulky bulldog continued, almost apologetically, "But that's not who I want to be. I don't want to see the world through a lens of power and antagonism, nor do I wish to be at odds with fellow dogs." His massive head lowered, breaking eye contact with Spiffy, his stance losing its aggressive rigidity. Spike seemed to wrestle inwardly before adding, "I suppose, it doesn't have to be this way."

There was an evident vulnerability in Spike, laying bare a truth that was contrary to his fierce exterior, hinting at a deep-seated desire for change, a wish to be more than what he was molded to be. It was a defining moment in their little community, a rare glimpse into the potential journey from fear to understanding, from dominance to respect, and from isolation to unity. The dog park held its collective breath as Spiffy stood small yet mightier than ever, embodying courage and wisdom, symbolizing a beacon of hope, poised to guide them toward a path of kindness and mutual respect.

In the large canvas of life where small incidences sometimes delineate profound turning points, the small assembly of dogs and their humans started to disperse slowly. The atmosphere in the dog park, once tense and charged, began to settle into a softer, more hopeful rhythm, the beauty of which accentuated by the gentle whispers of the wind rustling through the leaves of the large oak tree.

Alex and Spiffy led the way, a cadence in their steps as they moved towards a more tranquil area under the shade of the large oak tree. Remarkably, Spike followed — his earlier abrasive demeanor like a distant memory as his movements mirrored a sense of tentative curiosity and a desire for a connection that was freshly unearthed.

As they nestled comfortably in the cool, forgiving shade, an atmosphere of tentative peace enveloped them. Alex was the one to break the silence, his voice gentle yet carrying a sense of deep understanding, "Spike, we all have stories, don't we? How long have you been living this dog life?"

Spike hesitated but then seemed to find courage in the genuine warmth in Alex's inquiry. With a sigh of vulnerability, he began, "It's been three years for me." His large head lowered slightly, his voice tinged with an unspoken melancholy as he continued, "It's mostly lonely. My human spends most of his time either at the gym or a bar, and I only see him during the night and over weekends."

The conversation flowed naturally, with Spiffy chiming in with gentle encouragement, urging Spike to delve deeper into his experiences. The large Bulldog seemed to grow more comfortable as he shared, "You know, before this life, I was a mouse. Always on the edge, always feeling small... being bullied." His deep-set eyes carried the tales of his former vulnerability, the remnants of a life where he perennially lived in fear, a striking contrast to his present robust exterior. "Being a bulldog this time, it... it allowed me to feel powerful, to act out against the fears I once had. But it's just..." his voice trailed off, lost in the bittersweet irony of his own narrative.

The moment under the oak tree formed an intricate picture of unity in diversity, each dog carrying histories deep, some heavy with lessons, others light with joy.

Spiffy's voice cut through the reflective silence, carrying a note of hope, "You know, Spike, this doesn't have to be the end of your story. You can choose a different path, one filled with friendship and adventures."

Alex nodded in agreement, his expressive eyes reflecting wisdom and kindness. "Exactly," he chimed in, "Spiffy and I, we meet near the Alice statue in this park every few days with a lot of other friends. If you can find a way to join us, you're welcome to be part of our adventures."

Spike looked between the two, a hesitant hope blooming in his previously desolate landscape of loneliness and misunderstood strength. He said, "Even after the way I treated you?"

"Yes," said Spiffy, "You can be our friend, and use your strength for good things."

The words hung in the air, not just an offer, but a pathway to redemption, a chance for Spike to rewrite his narrative, transforming it from one of fear and dominance to one of friendship and understanding.

As they parted ways, a new understanding dawned in the park — one that spoke of evolving bonds and the hope for a community fostered not on the tenets of power, but on mutual respect. The large oak tree stood witness to this turn of events, its sturdy branches reaching out, as if blessing this newly formed friendship.

# the picnic intrusion

It was a brisk fall morning the next week in Central Park, Halloween was approaching, and winter's breath was beginning to touch upon the city, hinting at the cold days to come. Pippa and Sally strutted through the park, their noses attuned to the fascinating scents that danced on the crisp breeze. As they neared the meeting spot, the Alice statue, a flash of color caught Pippa's eye.

"Look, Sally!" exclaimed Pippa, picking up a brightly colored flier with her mouth that seemed to have flown away from its original post. The pair hurried towards the Alice statue where their group convened every morning. The statue stood proudly amidst the fall splendor, witnessing countless tales of friendship through its silent presence.

Alex, Spiffy, Ralph, and Spike awaited, their curious eyes fixed on the piece of paper Pippa held. As they gathered, Alex, having retained his human literacy, took charge, and began deciphering the contents for the eager audience.

Pippa laid it on the ground and placed a paw on it to keep it from blowing. "Alex, tell us what it says. It looks important," she said, her tail wagging with impatience.

Alex cleared his throat, a theatrical pause ensuing as he dramatically unfurled the edge of flier as it rolled up in the breeze. "Ladies and Gentlemen, it seems we have stumbled upon an announcement most grand," he began with a flourish, adding a sense of mystery that had everyone's tails wagging with anticipation.

"Do spill it, Alex, you have us all on curious here!" Spiffy couldn't hold back, his tiny body vibrating with excitement.

A grin stretched across Alex's face as he narrated, "Well, it seems the humans are organizing a grand picnic celebration right here in our beloved park." He emphasized the word 'grand', drawing circles in the air with his paw for effect.

Spike leaned in, his big bulldog frame a picture of expectation, "Does it say anything about food, Alex?"

"It most certainly does, my friend," Alex replied, his eyes twinkling with mischief. "There will be a veritable feast; an abundance of treats for us to enjoy if we play our cards right!"

The group erupted into enthusiastic chatter, their minds racing with the possibilities this picnic presented. Ideas flowed and laughter echoed, the statue of Alice seemingly joining in their joy with a benign presence.

Yet, amidst the bubbling excitement, they all noticed Dale's absence, a fixture in their group who hadn't been seen for more than a week. Concern tinged their joyous plotting, the joy dampened by the noticeable void.

"Where's Dale?" asked Sally.

"I don't know," exclaimed Pippa. "It's been more than a week since we last saw him."

As if on cue, a slightly disheveled Dale appeared, his breath hurried and his appearance slightly untidy. "Sorry I'm late, friends," he huffed, looking more exhausted than they had ever seen him.

"Dale, you look like you've been through a whirlwind! Where have you been?" Sally asked, a look of concern overtaking her features.

Dale gave a tired but satisfied smile, "Oh, I met someone," he began shyly, his gaze drifting as he continued, "She's wonderful but has had me busy sprucing up the nest, gathering pine nuts, acorns, you know... making it exactly right. Move it here, then over there, then here again. I'm exhausted."

The group erupted into a collective laugh then "Aww," their hearts playfully warmed by Dale's romantic endeavors, and just like that, the missing piece of their group was back, and the planning resumed with renewed vigor.

"Well Dale," Alex commented, "It looks like we have another mission, but this time just for ourselves. They are planning a picnic in the park, and......It's this Saturday!"

"We don't have much time," said Spiffy. "That is if we are going to make plans to raid to participate in the ahem," clearing his voice. "Eating of goodies!"

"You mean raiding, uh, stealing of wonderful, tasty and delicious food," replied Ralph.

As the group gathered closer, their eager eyes on Alex, he continued to relay the details mapped out on the vibrant flyer.

"There are going to be three main spots where the humans will be congregating," Alex informed, tracing invisible lines on the ground to illustrate. "The Great Lawn on one end, Bethesda Terrace in the middle, and Sheep Meadow on the south end." His nose nudged at different points as he mentioned each location, creating a makeshift map that his friends studied intensely, their tails swaying in unified rhythm.

"Our Alice statue is here, right smack in the center on the east," he continued.

A fervent brainstorming session ensued, with each dog bringing a unique perspective to their picnic intrusion strategy.

Spiffy, the smallest of them all, but undoubtedly the nimblest, was the first to offer his suggestion. He cleared his throat, standing on his hind legs to command attention. "I propose Operation Silent Paws," he declared, his tiny frame reverberating with the seriousness of his strategy. "We go in stealthily, moving from one tree to another, taking cover behind bushes... essentially being shadows, seen by none and feared by all."

There was a nod of approval, the vision of them being stealthy warriors of the park igniting a flame of exhilaration in their spirits.

However, Spike had a different perspective. The robust bulldog stood, stretching himself before laying out his plan which contrasted vastly with Spiffy's. "Spiffy, that's a fine plan," he began, nodding appreciatively before he continued, "But we are not just any group; we are a force, a presence that commands respect and, yes, a bit of fear. I say we go in bold and fearless, showing ourselves as we are!" He stomped a paw for emphasis, his eyes burning with fervent enthusiasm. "We shall call it P-Day, the Picnic Day, where we conquer and feast!"

The others exchanged looks, varying degrees of amusement and consideration dancing in their eyes as they mulled over Spike's audacious plan.

Ralph then chimed in, his wise and calm demeanor bringing a balancing note to the table. "I think we should blend in, be a part of the crowd but in a civilized manner. The humans will bring their pets making it easy for us to pass ourselves off as being in the right place. We can maybe find little costumes, imagine us going in dressed as tiny humans," he suggested, the others bursting into laughter at the mental image but also finding the idea endearing.

Pippa joined in, her inventive mind spiraling into action as she proposed a reconnaissance mission prior to the D-day. "We could do a little scouting a day before, get to know the ground, find the best spots that would have the most food and least foot traffic. Knowledge is power, my friends! These types of events, they always set up the tents and tables a couple of days ahead."

Sally endorsed Pippa's idea adding, "Great idea, we can determine the best location for us to be successful."

Dale, the romantic of the group, suggested, "And let's not forget to have fun, enjoy the music, the laughter, maybe even find a dance partner amongst the picnickers!" His eyes twinkled at the thought, a dreamy expression taking over.

"Stop getting mushy," said Spiffy. "That's your human experience taking over......we are dogs, let's act like dogs."

Laughter erupted and they agreed to conduct some reconnaissance in two days, Thursday afternoon.

The Alice statue seemed to watch over them benevolently as they talked, the group filled with an infectious energy of laughter, and the spirited exchange of ideas. Their plans ranged from the stealthy to the bold, but they all agreed with Spike, they would call it P-Day.

The meeting ended with a group howl, and they dispersed with bright eyes and wagging tails, a shared look of conspiracy and joy lighting their faces, ready to take on the picnic with zeal, strategy, and a heart full of adventure.

Thursday dawned bright and hopeful, the clear skies reflecting the burgeoning anticipation in each member of the ensemble as they congregated at their established meeting point, the Alice statue. It stood with an air of majestic serenity, overseeing the lively bunch who gathered around, their eyes filled with sparkles of adventure.

With a sense of purpose enveloping them, the group split up to cover more ground, each team responsible for scrutinizing one of the potential target spots. Pippa and Sally ventured towards the Grand Lawn, their sharp eyes scanning every nook and corner for possible hideouts and vantage points. The lawn was a haven of sprawling greens, offering ample spots for a stealthy approach. They noticed families setting up picnic spots, delineating territories with vibrant picnic blankets. The sight of children playing frisbee and couples lounging under the warm sun painted a picturesque scene that was both alluring and promising.

Off to the side alongside the path they observed men setting up the tents that would serve food. Another group of men where unloading picnic tables and benches and placing them on the lawn in long rows.

At the same time, Spiffy and Ralph directed their efforts towards scrutinizing Sheep Meadow, a location renowned for its relaxed ambiance. As they darted stealthily amongst the leisure seekers, they couldn't help but be charmed by the vibrant atmosphere.

Groups were congregated in small pockets, with an appealing amount of space in between, a layout that facilitated ease of movement without drawing too much attention. It was not lost on them that many people had brought along tasty looking snacks, the aroma wafting and tantalizing their senses. This would be the case on Saturday, without tables and chairs, people just threw down a blanket and opened a basket of food. Easy pickings.

Meanwhile, Spike and Alex embarked on a mission to assess the feasibility of Bethesda Terrace as a location for their picnic adventure. Despite the grandeur of the place, with its beautiful fountain serving as a centerpiece, it soon became clear that it was less than ideal for their operation. The open layout and the bustling activity surrounding the stage area offered little in terms of cover, and the constant flurry of activity made it challenging to move around unnoticed. They exchanged a knowing glance, their experienced eyes communicating the unanimous decision that Bethesda was a no-go for their grand plan.

As twilight descended, the group reconvened at their beloved Alice statue, a guardian of their secrets and plans. The atmosphere was abuzz with excited chatter as they shared their findings, laughter ringing out at the recounting of the comedic incidents of the day, including a moment when Spiffy had engaged in an impromptu dance with a group of children, and Pippa getting adorned with a flower crown by a group of picnicking artists.

As they distilled the experiences and observations of the day, it became clear that their focus had to narrow down to the Grand Lawn and Sheep Meadow. The latter offered a relaxed environment where people came to lounge and enjoy their self-packed meals on the expansive grassy areas, a setting ripe for mingling without raising eyebrows. The Grand Lawn, with its beautiful open spaces dotted with trees, lines of picnic tables and food tents, offered a bounty of opportunities for a stealthy advance, coupled with the prospect of a rich harvest of picnic delights.

Thus, with a spirit of unity and shared enthusiasm, they began to refine their strategy, assigning roles based on their individual strengths and deciding on the signs and signals to communicate silently on the P-day. Their plan was coming together. With the plan set, they rushed home so as not to be noticed missing by their owners.

Alex creeped back into the yard into the garden where he arrived just in time to hear Beatrice calling his name, "Pierre, it's dinner time."

Alex rambled through the tall dog door Beatrice had installed for him and did his "turnaround" to show his happiness about the meal she prepared for him. Of course, it was the same dry kibble. He thought, Saturday, I will have some real food.

Thursday's reconnaissance mission had granted the group valuable insights into the picnic ground realities. The detailed explorations paved the way for a fun day filled with a medley of experiences and the meticulous delineation of their plans. The monumental day arrived, the sky a clear azure canvass promising a day of adventures and, hopefully, a bounty of spoils. The group convened at their usual rendezvous point, the Alice statue, faces alight with a fusion of excitement and anticipation.

"Alright, team, today is P-Day!" Alex began, his voice firm and decisive as he outlined the specifics of their strategy, based on the intelligence gathered during the reconnaissance. The key targets were the Grand Lawn and Sheep Meadow, the spots promising a blend of festivity and a generous smattering of food-laden tables.

Synchronized with a level of expertise that could only be attained through years of friendship, the dogs moved out, their steps measured yet buoyant, each entering into their designated roles with an intuitive understanding of the unique contributions they brought to the table.

Spiffy took charge of the stealth division, guiding Pippa and Sally through a labyrinthine path of bushes and trees, their movements seamless and virtually undetectable, a whisper of shadows flitting through the festive grounds. Their agility and nimble footwork allowed them to approach the picnic tables undetected, orchestrating synchronized movements to lift the delectable treats from under the unsuspecting noses of the picnic-goers. The trio managed to secure a few sandwiches and a trove of sausages, their faces displaying triumphant grins as they retreated back into the foliage, a mischievous sparkle dancing in their eyes.

Meanwhile, Spike and Ralph embraced the role of minglers, a bold contrast to the stealth team. With disarming smiles and wagging tails, they interacted with the picnic-goers, each displaying their individual personalities brilliantly. Spike was the robust heartthrob, eliciting affectionate strokes from the ladies as he unabashedly played the cute card, diverting attention while Ralph skillfully extracted a piece of cheese or a bite of a sandwich here and there, his actions camouflaged under the guise of playfulness.

Dale, the romantic of the group, was tasked with the most poetic mission — to woo and win hearts through dance. As a live band began playing, Dale found himself dancing on a tree branch above the event, his nimble moves capturing attention and encouraging a crowd to gather around, entranced by his dance prowess. The delightful distraction was all his friends needed, facilitating their escapades as Dale became the star of the show, a true entertainer, lost in the joy of dance, a picture of delight that was almost human in its genuineness.

As the day progressed, the park became a canvas of hilarity and charm, a dynamic play of shadows and light as the group operated in perfect harmony, shifting between roles, merging, and diverging as the situation demanded. Their friendship was their strongest asset, their understanding of each other's strengths and weaknesses allowing them to navigate the intricacies of the mission with an admirable blend of courage, stealth, and joy.

The day was far from over, but as the group converged in a secret alcove, their stash of spoils growing impressively, they couldn't help but let out joyous barks, their faces alight with the glow of success.

And as they paused, gathering their breath for the next phase of their grand mission, the world around them echoed with laughter and music, a testimony to the joy and festivity that the day held.\

"Whew!" said Spiffy. "What a first round!"

"Yea, gonna sleep good tonight after we feast, we need a few more items to polish off our own picnic," said Sally.

"Did you see the big layout of BBQ on the table by the tree where Dale was dancing? " said Pippa.

"Yes," exclaimed Spike. "I'm gonna try and get the whole pan if Dale can distract everyone by throwing acorns down."

The group moved with cohesive unity, exploiting every opportunity presented to them. However, amidst this celebration of chaos and stolen treats, a deep undertow of emotions was about to surge in one member of their team.

As Alex maneuvered through the animated crowd, a familiar sight halted him in his tracks. There, amidst the festive crowd, were Lisa and Justin. They were sharing a tender moment, hands intertwined, eyes locked in a warm embrace of souls recognizing each other's presence with joy and love. A microcosm of past memories and shared acquaintances manifested before Alex, momentarily bridging the gap between his canine existence and his past human life.

"They are still together," he mumbled to himself. "Looks like the chance encounter actually worked."

A calm sadness rested upon him as he watched them only to be interrupted by Spike running through the tables with a pan of BBQ in his mouth, being chased by a mob of adults and children.

With his mouth, pre-occupied holding the pan, the garbled words of "I got it, I got it," could be heard as he ran off into the bushes that encircled the Great Lawn.

As the pandemonium continued, Spiffy found himself cornered by a curious little girl, no older than six, who seemed utterly fascinated by the audacious little infiltrator. With wide eyes filled with innocence and wonder, the child reached out to grab hold of Spiffy. "Gotcha, doggy!" she exclaimed, her small hands scooping Spiffy up in a gentle yet firm grip.

The rest of the pack glanced back, their eyes widening as they saw Spiffy in the little girl's grasp. However, quick-thinking Pippa swung into action. Utilizing her agility and stealth, she made her way towards them, a determined sparkle in her eye. In a calculated move, she stuck out a paw at the right moment, causing the little girl to trip and lose her grip on Spiffy. With an agile twist and a leap, Spiffy was free. "Run, Spiffy, run!" Pippa shouted, her voice resonating with urgency and camaraderie.

Spiffy wasted no time, darting towards his friends, his little heart pounding in his chest. "That was a close one!" he exclaimed, once he was safely amongst his companions. Ralph chuckled, a deep sound that vibrated warmly, "You've got more lives than a cat, Spiffy."

Their antics continued with an almost choreographed series of hilarious escapades. Alex and Sally created a diversion, pretending to have a noisy argument of barks over a sausage link, drawing the attention of a group of picnickers. This gave the others an opportunity to snatch some goodies unnoticed.

Finally, with their mission accomplished and their mouths and paws full of spoils, they retreated to their sanctuary – an alcove hidden behind the bushes, away from the prying eyes of the humans.

The space was a riot of colors, with a patch of lush green grass at the center, offering a soft bed for the victorious band.

They lay down, a circle of companionship, sharing and enjoying the fruits of their labor, conversing animatedly with their mouths full. "Ihhh wassh show fun!" Spiffy managed to say, a big chunk of burger in his mouth, his words muffled but the joy in his eyes unmistakable.

Pippa lay on her back, her stomach round and full, a joyful laugh escaping her as she recounted how she had tripped the little girl. "She was a little cutie though, wasn't she?" she giggled, her tongue hanging out in a satisfied manner.

Sally shared in the laughter, agreeing wholeheartedly, "Yes, but not cuter than Spiffy making his great escape, running like the wind with those tiny legs!" The group erupted into a fresh wave of laughter, their joy unrestrained, a band of mischievous, yet endearing warriors reveling in their success.

The afternoon sun began its journey down the eastern sky as they lay there, bodies relaxed and hearts full. The festive sounds from the picnic area became a distant hum as they shared stories of the day. It wasn't long before they heard the rumbling of bushes. The picknickers had called Animal Control. Ralph looked through a bush and saw the unmistakable white coveralls of the dog catchers. White coveralls, green baseball caps on their heads and holding a log pole with a loop on it.

"Here puppy, puppy, puppy," he heard one say.

"Quick, it's the dog catchers," shouted Ralph. "We need to leave this area right now."

The group agreed to go in all different ways to confuse the dog catchers. "You guys ready?" said Ralph. "One, two, three, go!"

The group darted out in six different directions confusing the two dog catchers so much that in the confusion and their turning around, they ran into each other and collapse in the bushes. One of them landed on the Japanese holly and screamed, "Yeow, I think I got bit!"

"No, you didn't," said the other one. "You've fallen into the holly bush you idiot."

The gang barking as they ran across the Great Lawn into The Ramble, echoing their farewells as they headed to the homes on the edge of the park. P-Day was a success and will live in memory as one of their greatest days.

# the great race

A few weeks had passed since the legendary P-Day, a day still etched vividly in the minds of the adventurous canine squad. Central Park wore a festive look, vibrant and inviting, as the locals embraced the joys of the fall season.

The gentle hum of morning activity in Central Park gradually greeted Beatrice and Alex as they embarked on their daily walk. The brisk air carried the crisp scent of fallen leaves, weaving with the distant laughter of children playing. As they ambled along, the coffee shops lining the park began to stir to life, their inviting aroma wafting into the streets, teasing the senses of early morning walkers.

But today, outside their favorite coffee shop, something different caught their eyes. A vibrant and joyous advertisement displaying an array of colorful images and letters announced the upcoming event – the Halloween Dog celebration in Central Park.

Beatrice's eyes widened with interest as she read aloud, "A day of fun-filled activities, a costume contest, games, and oh look, Alex, they even have a race to find the fastest dog in NY! Doesn't it sound exciting?"

Alex could feel the contagious enthusiasm from Beatrice as his tail began to wag involuntarily. Images of dogs dressed in all manner of fun and goofy costumes danced in his mind. Yet, what truly caught his canine imagination was the thought of racing with other dogs, feeling the rush of the wind against his fur, the pulsating energy of the crowd cheering them on. Yes, he thought, this would be another day of joyous adventures, not just for him, but for the entire group.

As they continued their walk, Beatrice started brainstorming, her mind whirling with ideas for costumes. "Perhaps you could be a superhero, Alex, with a flowing cape! Oh, but maybe something humorous would be better. A hotdog suit with you as the sausage in the middle?" she pondered aloud, chuckling at the mental image.

Alex, on his part, seemed to warm up to the idea, even if it involved being dressed as a hotdog. The joy emanating from Beatrice as she contemplated various themes was infectious. He found himself sharing in her imaginative journey, envisioning the laughter and smiles that such a costume would bring to the faces of the people in the park.

As they reached their home, Beatrice's face wore a smile of anticipation, her eyes sparkling with the adventures that awaited them. Alex shared in her excitement, his spirit lifted, his tail wagging in cheerful agreement with the joyous rhythm that had taken over Beatrice.

It wasn't just a celebration they were looking forward to; it was a celebration of community, of joy, and of the magical bond that connected them all. As Beatrice started researching costumes online, she came across a collage of ideas on a web page. She printed it out on a piece of paper, Alex lay by her feet, his heart warm with the glow of affection and anticipation, eager for the day when he would step out, not just as Alex, but as a vibrant participant in a festival of joy, friendship, and spirited competition.

And as they sat there, she placed the paper on the floor in front of Alex and said, "Alright, Pierre, what will it be, there's a whole selection of ideas to choose from."

Alex scanned the paper, there was a superhero, a hotdog, a pumpkin, various costumes of ghosts and witches and then animals. He noticed the image of a poodle painted like a Zebra. He placed his paw on the image, looked up at her, hoping that Beatrice would interpret his paw as his selection.

"You want to be a Zebra?" she asked.

Alex stood up and turned in circles in excitement, that move usually told her was happy. Beatrice looked at Alex and then the image and said, "Well, what do you know, this one is done with washable paint."

Beatrice being an artist immediately understood she could save money and do this herself, quickly researching the paints she would need to complete the task and ordering them from Amazon.

The morning before Halloween was abuzz with frantic energy as the spirited group gathered in their favorite spot, a hidden corner amidst the lush foliage of Central Park near the Alice statue. Excitement danced in the air, the sound of animated chatter rising and falling like a harmonious symphony as they shared tales of their owners' preparations for the grand celebration.

Sally started the conversation, unable to hold back her giggles as she revealed her costume, "You won't believe this, but I'm going to be a fluffy unicorn, complete with a sparkling horn!" she said, a whimsical grin lighting up her face as she envisioned herself in the enchanting attire.

The laughter that ensued was heartfelt and boisterous, filling the air with joy as others chimed in with their own revelations. Ralph said with a mock serious tone, "Well, I am going to be dressed as a lion, the king of the jungle."

Pippa couldn't resist teasing him, "Oh please, more like the king of the playground," she said, her eyes twinkling with playful mischief.

Spiffy, the smallest of the lot, proudly announced his costume with a grand gesture, "I am going to be… a fierce dinosaur!" his tiny voice attempting to sound fearsome, adding to the hilarity of the image.

"You're gonna be a lizard?" asked Sally.

"No, a dinosaur," said Spiffy.

"That's what I said!" replied Sally as laughter engulfed the entire group.

Then, it was Alex's turn, and with a grin he revealed his upcoming transformation into a zebra. The group fell into a contemplative silence, imagining the scene before bursting into affectionate laughter, everyone approving the original choice with enthusiastic nods and barks of approval.

As they joked and jeered, Spike seemed slightly detached, his eyes carrying a hint of envy. He finally spoke up, "Well, my owner is planning to go for a motorcycle ride with his buddies. I guess I'll just be watching you guys from the sidelines." His voice carried a note of disappointment, but the group rallied around him,

"We'll find something for you Spike," said Pippa.

"Any ideas of what you want to be?" asked Ralph.

"I want to be a tough guy," replied Spike.

"Oh, I know, there's a little leather jacket and sunglasses in the front window of the pet shop," said Spiffy. "I bet I could sneak in there and run off with it. What do you think?"

"As long as you don't get caught," said Alex. "We will have a hard time getting you out of the animal shelter."

"Nah, I'll be in and out before they even notice," replied Spiffy.

Their conversation naturally flowed into an eager discussion about the grand finale - the fastest dog race. Despite the uncertainty of their participation, a consensus formed among them - they had to be prepared. And so, they began to practice, setting up an impromptu racetrack. Excitement bubbled as they took turns racing, encouraging, and cheering for each other,

Ralph, the Border Collie in the group was clearly the fastest of them all. He was giving tips on how to use your tail as a stabilizer when turning, although everyone was making fun of Spiffy's short nub.

"Spiffy, you'll just have to turn your knob, Ha Ha," said Alex.

"Very funny," he replied. "I start and stop pretty quick, that's my edge."

Their practice session echoed through the park, a wonderful mixture of barks, laughter, and encouraging shouts. Ralph played the coach, shouting instructions and offering encouragement, his voice rising above the rest, "Come on, faster, faster! You can do it!"

Suddenly, Dale showed up in the tree and shouted down at the group. "What are you doing?"

"We are practicing for the dog races on Halloween," said Alex.

"Oh, that sounds like fun. I wish I were a dog. Anything I can do to help?" said Dale.

"Sure, you can help count time to see if we are improving or not," said Alec.

As the day progressed, they practiced. Dale recorded their time marking on the tree with his sharp nails. They urged each other to give their best, the spirit of competition tinged with a deep bond of friendship, the laughter resonating with the joy of shared dreams and aspirations.

They laid down on the grass, exhausted but happy. They couldn't help but envision the glorious day ahead. It wasn't just about the costumes or the race; it was about being together.

The next day, Halloween, a sea of excited faces – both human and canine – began to flock to the famous dog park, the centerpiece of the day's celebration. It was a delightful sight to behold as the park gradually filled with a kaleidoscope of colorful costumes, resonating with joyous barks and laughter, setting a lively and vibrant scene for the day's events.

Within the park, the esteemed judges took their place, two older widows who were known and revered in the community. Their devotion to the welfare of animals was legendary, their generous contributions to the animal shelter had not only fostered countless beautiful friendships between humans and their furry companions but had also facilitated the creation of this very dog park, a haven for pets and owners alike to forge precious memories. The ladies wore graceful smiles, their eyes twinkling with genuine joy as they surveyed the sea of vibrant colors and playful costumes that lay before them.

Meanwhile, the group assembled with their owners at a designated area, the air abuzz with electric excitement as they eagerly compared their costumes, their eyes wide with wonder and admiration for each other's attire. Sally's unicorn attire shimmered in the morning light, Ralph's majestic lion mane attracted curious gazes, and Pippa looked resplendent in her royal outfit. Alex stood tall and proud, his zebra stripes a testimony to Beatrice's artistic skills, drawing appreciative glances from both human and canine spectators alike.

Spike, who had believed he would be missing out, suddenly felt a tug of hope as Spiffy hurriedly barked out a secret to him through the fence separating them. "Spike, listen! Your costume is hidden in the alcove. I managed to grab it just before the pet store closed yesterday, Uh, it's not the tough guy one, it was gone, but I found a perfect one for you," Spiffy said, his face wearing a triumphant grin.

Spike's eyes lit up with surprise and joy, a whirlpool of emotions swirling in his heart as he realized the extent of the friendship that surrounded him. He made a dash to the alcove, his heart pounding in his chest. As he returned, the group erupted into cheers seeing him don a pirate costume, complete with a bandana and a faux parrot perched on his shoulder.

As the day unfolded, the park reverberated with joyous barks, laughter, and applause, creating many unforgettable moments. The costume contest was a spectacle of creativity, each presentation met with enthusiastic cheers from the crowd and affectionate nods from the benevolent judges.

Whether it was the playful prancing of the unicorn Sally or the regal strides of Pippa, every moment was golden, a testimony to the beautiful bond that united the group in joy and friendship. And amidst the vibrant and joyous chaos, the group stood united, their hearts swelling with pride and happiness, cherishing the beautiful memories being made on this magical day, a celebration of friendship, and of Halloween.

With the costume contest approaching its grand finale, the palpable excitement in the air grew. The two esteemed judges took to the podium, their faces reflecting the joy and the difficult responsibility they bore in choosing the winners amidst such a splendid display of creativity and community spirit.

Finally, the moment of announcement arrived. The entire park seemed to hold its breath as the judges exchanged warm, approving nods before addressing the anticipatory crowd. One of the judges, her voice rich with affection, announced, "In the glorious third place, we have the little Maltese, dressed impeccably as the most adorable UPS man we have ever seen!" A roar of applause broke out as the tiny contestant and his owner, a charming little girl, trotted forward, its tail wagging in euphoric circles as it accepted its ribbon with pride, the joy in its eyes sparkling like stars.

With the crowd still buzzing with excitement, the second judge took the microphone, her voice trembling slightly with the emotion of the moment. "Our runner-up has graced us with a magical appearance today, taking us to a land of dreams and fantasy. Let us give a huge round of applause to the mystical unicorn, Sally!" The crowd erupted into joyous cheers, the applause thunderous as Sally and her owners pranced forward, her unicorn attire shimmering beautifully in the sunlight, reflecting her vibrant personality.

The air vibrated with exhilaration as the judges prepared to announce the winner. The first judge returned to the microphone, her face glowing with an affectionate smile that carried the warmth of the sun. "And now, the moment we have all been waiting for. Our grand prize goes to a contestant who has exhibited remarkable creativity and spirit, embodying the adventurous essence of this festive day. Let us congratulate Alex, our magnificent zebra!"

Beatrice jumped for joy and she and Alex quickly stepped forward. The applause was deafening, a symphony of cheers and jubilant barks filling the air. Beatrice beamed with pride as she walked with Alex to receive the grand prize.

After the award ceremony, the park continued to buzz with festive activities and exhibitions. Beatrice, still reeling from the delightful victory, led Alex through the vibrant landscape of Central Park, their hearts open to the marvels awaiting them.

They wandered into a mesmerizing exhibition where a Border Collie champion leaped gracefully through the air, catching frisbees with a balletic elegance that left spectators in awe. Alex watched, his eyes wide with admiration, feeling the vibrant energy and the spirit of agility that the champion embodied.

As they proceeded further, they came upon a thrilling exhibition where a group of Whippets and Labradors were engaged in a daring competition, diving off a dock into the pond, each striving to achieve the greatest distance. Alex and Beatrice watched, their faces reflecting the awe and excitement of the breathtaking performances that unfolded before them.

After the sound of animated discussions and rustle of excited dogs and their owners settled somewhat, the park buzzed with fresh exhilaration as the attention turned towards the makeshift dog racetrack. A vibrant patchwork of colors, the space bore a testimony to the community's spirit, adorned with makeshift fencing, cheerful orange cones, and an endearing finish line that heralded the promise of friendly competition, and celebrated athleticism.

The first race for the day was announced — a race for the lightweights, the ones under 10 pounds. Dogs of various petite sizes took their places at the starting line, their tiny frames brimming with vibrant energy and determined spirits. Spiffy was a contestant in this race. Beatrice and Alex found a prime spot to watch the action, the latter perched keenly, his eyes following every little contestant with wide-eyed fascination and especially on his buddy Spiffy.

The starting signal sounded, a burst of eager yelps filled the air as the little warriors sprinted with all their might, each pint-sized athlete giving their all, their little legs a blur of speed. The crowd cheered vociferously, encouraging the little champions as they raced towards the finish line with hearts grander than their small statures. After a furious dash, Spiffy's small lead gave way to a diminutive Dachshund by the name of Fritzi who emerged victorious, her short legs having carried her swiftly and valiantly across the finish line, earning jubilant cheers and loving pets from the onlookers.

The air was thick with competitive spirit as the middleweight category was announced next. Dogs within the 10 to 25 pounds bracket assembled, a diverse array of breeds showcasing a delightful representation of size, coat, and colors. Ralph, Pippa, and Sally made up a third of the field in this race. The excitement escalated as the gun signaled the start. It was a breathtaking sight to behold, the field of dogs surging forward in a harmonious rhythm of motion with Ralph, Pippa and Sally sitting in the top three spots halfway through the race. The race was tight, with several dogs displaying remarkable closing speed and determination. The crowd watched, hearts racing as a spirited Beagle named Toby came out of nowhere and edged out in front, crossing the finish line just ahead of the gang to the thunderous applause and shouts of encouragement.

Finally, the race for the heavyweights, the contenders being those weighing over 25 pounds, brought a fresh wave of excitement. The track bore witness to an ensemble of majestic strides and powerful limbs as the larger dogs displayed their might. Amongst them, Alex stood, his eyes glistening with anticipation. The race was a marvel of power and grace, a symphony of coordination and communal joy.

Beatrice cheered Alex on as he joined his hefty companions in a display of extraordinary athleticism, their muscles rippling, hearts pounding, and spirits soaring in a remarkable ballet of motion and force. It was a sight to behold, the track a canvas of fluid poetry and rhythmic agility.

And as the heavyweights thundered towards the finish line, every heart in the park raced with them. It was a close call, every dog giving their utmost, displaying heartwarming determination and spirit. But it was Alex who showed a burst of acceleration in the final moments, breaking ahead with a furious sprint, his zebra-striped body crossing the finish line with a victorious surge, the cheers and applauds reverberating off the trees and buildings in the park.

Beatrice's heart blossomed, her beloved Pierre had taken first place in both contests. What an achievement. While well wishers were congratulating her and old friends were catching up, Alex lay on the ground, exhausted. What a set of stories they will have to tell the next time they meet at the Alice statue. He could see Spiffy walking off with his owners, 2nd place ribbon around his neck. He had a gait, a prance that warmed Alex heart.

"Psst," whispered Spike. "Great job, thank everyone for the costume, I had a blast. See ya later!"

Alex smiled at Spike, how a soul could change by just offering friendship. How indeed he thought.

# spiffy gets lost

Early November had ushered in a bristling cold that swept through Central Park, a reminder that winter was fast approaching. The trees stood bare, their naked branches reaching out to the gray sky as if in anticipation of the first snowflakes. Despite the chilly weather, a dedicated group gathered at their usual spot, each member wearing a fur coat that was nature's solution to the dropping temperatures. Alex, Pippa, Sally, Ralph, Spike, and Spiffy - a close-knit group, united by bonds stronger than the cold that sought to bite into their flesh.

As they settled in their customary circle, a noticeable void became apparent. "Isn't Dale usually here by now? You know how he likes to be the first one to find the juiciest news of the neighborhood," Pippa remarked, her brows furrowing in worry as her eyes scanned the surroundings, as though hoping to catch sight of Dale trotting towards them with his tail wagging energetically.

Spike let out a deep sigh, his breath forming a visible cloud in the frigid air, "Yeah, ever since I joined the group, he's never missed a meet. Not once." The group nodded in agreement, anxiety casting a shadow on their usually jubilant gathering.

Sally attempted to lighten the mood, her voice shaking slightly as she offered, "Maybe he found himself a cozy spot, you know? A secret hideaway to escape the cold. Dale's a clever one, after all!" Despite her efforts to sound upbeat, her eyes carried a tinge of fear, reflecting the group's collective concern.

Ralph shook his head slowly, the somber atmosphere stifling his usually lively spirit. "I passed by all his favorite spots today; there was no sign of him," he shared, his voice carrying an undertone of dread as the group's faces mirrored his concern.

Alex, who had been silent, chimed in, his voice conveying a strange mix of hope and worry, "We need to be positive. Dale is smart, and he knows this park as well as any of us. Perhaps he's simply taken a short vacation, exploring new parks, making new friends?"

As days turned into chilly nights and back into frosty mornings, with no Dale to brighten up their gatherings, the group's worry deepened, carving a permanent fixture of dread in their hearts. The park, with its empty trees and cold winds, seemed to echo their sentiment, as if mourning the absence of one of its liveliest spirits.

Every day, each member took it upon themselves to scout different parts of the park, venturing into less frequented areas, hoping each time to return with good news. Yet, each day ended the same, with shaking heads and downcast eyes, and the chilling cold biting even harder as if feeding off their growing despair.

Spiffy, the youngest of the group, could not bear the heaviness that clouded their meetings. He broke down one chilly morning, his small body shaking with sobs, "He's... He's got to be out there somewhere, scared and alone. We've got to find him; we can't just wait here and do nothing."

The group drew close, a tight knot of warmth in the cold park, their bodies leaning into one another, sharing strength and resolve. As the day's light dimmed, they sat together, their heads bowed, united in their worry and the unspoken promise that they would find their missing friend, no matter what it took. They couldn't let the cold take away one of their own. It wasn't just the weather that was cold; their world felt colder without Dale's warm and overly cheery spirit. They resolved, there in their tight, protective circle, that they would bring warmth back into their lives; they would find Dale.

In the biting cold one morning Spiffy waited until his owners went to work and then embarked on a solo mission, a determined streak lighting his eyes. The urgent need to find Dale had grown day by day, leaving a hole in the group's vibrant dynamics. Alone but resolute, Spiffy ventured farther away from the familiar paths of

Central Park, entering the lesser-known territories near Safari Park, west of the reservoir.

His senses were constantly on alert as he navigated through the unfamiliar terrain, the sounds and smells sharply different from the comforting familiarity of Central Park under the watchful gaze of the Alice statue. Spiffy's sensitive nose caught the aroma of food, and without a moment's hesitation, he followed the trail that led him to the bustling surroundings of Billy's Hot Dog Cart stationed across the street from a lively playground.

Lost in the all-enveloping smells of sizzling sausages and warm buns, Spiffy failed to notice the approach of animal control officers until it was too late. Before he could comprehend the situation, a net was cast around him, pulling him away from the aromatic haven and into the confining space of the animal control vehicle.

Desperation surged through Spiffy as he realized the gravity of his predicament and the vehicle driving off. After a few moments it stopped again, and he could hear the sound of dogs barking outside the van. His heart pounded in his chest like a frantic drummer, but deep within, a spark of bravery ignited. Harnessing every ounce of courage and agility, he managed a daring escape. Utilizing a brief moment when the door opened, he managed to open his cage, a trick taught to him by Ralph, and slip through it, darting into the labyrinth of streets that was Manhattanville.

Spiffy's heart raced as he navigated through narrow alleys and crowded streets, a whirlwind of anxiety and fear clouding his mind. Every shadow seemed a threat, and every noise echoed like a drum in his ears. The environment here was harsher, the air carrying a mix of distrust and cold wind that pierced through his fur, sending shivers down his spine.

As Spiffy ventured deeper into the rough part of town, he soon stumbled upon a group that exuded a powerful and intimidating presence. The Dawg Dominion ruled this territory, a notorious gang of stray dogs with a reputation that reached even the far corners of Central Park. They carried themselves with an air of authority, overseeing various activities with a fierce yet organized grip that resembled the operations of a mob.

The gang consisted of different breeds, each bearing a story of survival in their eyes. The leader, a muscular Rottweiler name Capo, with a scar across his face, eyed Spiffy with a scrutinizing gaze that sent shivers down his spine. A gaunt greyhound with a cunning look was whispering to a Great Dane bearing a coat that had seen better days.

Despite the fear curling in his stomach, Spiffy knew he couldn't back down now. Summoning a courage, he didn't know he possessed, he stepped forward, locking eyes with the Rottweiler. His voice wavered but held firm as he spoke," Excuse me, Sir." He gulped then continued. "I'm a bit lost, had a run in with animal control. I am looking for my friend Dale, he's a squirrel from the south part of the park."

The territory of the Dawg Dominion was notorious, but it was also extensive, holding secrets and information that could potentially lead Spiffy to Dale. But what Spiffy didn't realize was that his brave approach didn't impress Capo.

"Well, what do we have here? A 10-pound bag of meat?" said Capo.

The Greyhound, acting a bit crazy said, "Yea, yea, boss, and just in time for dinner."

The Great Dane slowly circled Spiffy, looking him over, pushing on his back with his massive paw. "Looks a little putrid to me boss," he said.

"Wrap him up, we'll take him back to the warehouse and decide what to do with him later," replied Capo.

The gang of dogs looped a few ropes around Spiffy's neck and legs, stuffed a sock in his mouth and threw him into the back of a little red wagon being pulled by an old Mastiff. As Spiffy lay in the wagon, he could see the spoils of their looting and embezzlement from the local strays.

Meanwhile, in the chilled afternoon air of Central Park, the group gathered solemnly at their regular meeting point, the comforting shadow of the Alice statue providing a silent guardian over them. As they discussed the looming uncertainty over Dale and Spiffy, their worried faces displayed the taut lines of distress, each grappling with the grave situation that unfolded in their tranquil world.

Suddenly, a scruffy figure gingerly stepped into the clearing, it was an orange and white disheveled looking cat clutching a white napkin tightly in its paw, waving it aloft in a tentative gesture of peace. The assemblage of dogs froze, their eyes widening as they took in the unfamiliar figure — a cat, their age-old adversary, yet here it stood, extending an olive branch in the most peculiar manner.

As the feline approached, a familiar voice rang out, soft yet firm, "Hello, my friends., Alex, Sally?" The group exchanged bewildered glances until realization dawned, their jaws dropping in synchronized amazement. It was Dale, somehow transformed into a scruffy but dignified cat. His fur bore the traces of hardship, yet his eyes sparkled with the same warmth and humor that had always characterized him.

With a demeanor of urgency, Dale recounted his harrowing ordeal, detailing the tragic event that led to his untimely demise at the hands of malicious teenagers armed with a BB gun. His voice choked with emotion as he narrated his miraculous rebirth in an unfamiliar feline form, waking up beside a trash can in an unfamiliar alley.

With furrowed brows and a demeanor of urgency, Dale began recounting the series of unfathomable events that led to his mysterious transformation and the distressing news about Spiffy.

The group gathered around him, their faces showing a blend of confusion, concern, and curiosity as they leaned in to hear Dale's testimony.

Taking a deep breath to steady himself, Dale began, his voice uneven but determined, "It started a few days ago... I was... I was attacked by some teenage boys in the park. They had a BB gun..." He paused, struggling to keep his composure as he fought back tears. The group exchanged horrified glances, the air thick with shock and empathy.

Pippa interrupted with a trembling voice, her eyes welled up with tears, "Oh, Dale, how could someone do such a cruel thing?" She reached out a paw to comfort him, her touch lending him the strength to continue.

With a slight nod of appreciation, Dale resumed, his voice breaking as he recounted waking up in a new, unfamiliar feline form, beside a trash can in a grimy alley. The vivid details of his transformation captured their attention, evoking a mixture of awe and terror as they hung onto his every word.

Ralph's practical mind broke in with a necessary, yet cautious question, "But how did you become a... a cat, Dale?" The question hovered in the air, with everyone sharing Ralph's puzzled expression, including Dale himself.

With a helpless shrug, Dale replied, his voice tinged with mystery, "I don't know, perhaps the next phase of my transformation, it's not with a sense of irony." He glanced down at his newfound feline body, a flicker of melancholy crossing his eyes.

He continued recounting his precarious escape from a marauding Great Dane, detailing his desperate climb up a fire escape. It was from this high vantage point that he had borne witness to the heart-wrenching capture of Spiffy by the infamous Dawg Dominion, a revelation that brought a collective gasp of horror and dismay from the group.

Sally chimed in with a tone of urgency, her eyes wide with fear, "You saw Spiffy? Is he... is he okay, Dale?" She asked, her voice breaking, the group leaning in, holding their breaths, craving reassurance, yet fearing the worst.

Dale nodded solemnly, the weight of the responsibility to convey the dire news evident in his grim expression, "He is alive, but in grave danger. He's been captured by the Dawg Dominion, a group notorious for their ruthlessness." The gravity of the situation hung heavily on them, each feeling a surge of rage and despair for their embattled friend.

"I followed them to the old cannery near the Hudson, that's where he will be," said Dale.

As Dale detailed Spiffy's perilous predicament, a silent vow of determination solidified among them. The group absorbed every detail with grave attentiveness, the information fuelling a rising tide of determination, ready to wage a battle against the adversaries to save their dear friend Spiffy. It was clear, through the veils of tears and with clenched jaws, that every one of them was prepared to stand united.

The spirit of unity enveloped them, drawing them closer than ever before as they braced themselves to face the adversities head-on. Spike voiced the group's collective sentiment with a heartfelt roar, "For Spiffy!" echoed unanimously, reverberating in the cold air as a vow of undying loyalty and camaraderie.

As they formed a huddle, with each one sharing their strengths and abilities for the mission ahead, the atmosphere buzzed with a fusion of fear, determination, and an unyielding spirit of friendship. They devised clever disguises, utilizing their knowledge of the streets and the knack for improvisation. The rescue mission would demand bravery, wit, and an immense spirit of teamwork.

With a final, solemn group nod, they dispersed, each carrying out their tasks with a fervent dedication, preparing to infiltrate the

Dawg Dominion's feared territory. The mood was tense yet hopeful, as a surge of adrenaline propelled them into action, ready to face any challenge, any adversary, with a fierce resolve to reunite their fractured circle.

In the mist of determination and urgency, Dale, even in his new form, couldn't help but bring in a touch of humor to lighten the grave mood. Waving his white napkin in the air once more, he declared with a mock solemnity, "I hereby pronounce this Operation: Save Spiffy!" evoking a round of nervous laughter that bore a hint of hope, a sliver of light in the looming darkness, as they set forth on their daring mission, with hearts brimming with bravery and the unwavering bond of friendship that transcended any form.

Underneath the shadow of dilapidated infrastructure in the far reaches of Manhattanville, the old fish cannery stood silent and abandoned, a stark testament to a bygone era. The structure bore the marks of time, with its rusty equipment, the smell of old fish still pervading the cold, damp air. The cannery was the perfect fortress for the Dawg Dominion, a place where their menacing operations were concealed behind weather-beaten walls and echoed through corroded steel hallways.

Capo led the procession, a commanding figure with piercing eyes that bore into Spiffy, who was bound and being pulled along in the little red wagon. The rest of the gang followed with militant precision, their fierce eyes focused and unyielding. Spiffy could feel his heart pounding violently in his chest, each beat echoing the impending doom that seemed to lurk in the looming dark corners of the cannery.

The Great Dane spoke up, his voice deep and ominous, setting the grim tone for the proceedings, "Boss, once we have the information we need, we can use that old canning line to seal him up like a tuna, a real masterpiece of cruelty, don't you think?" His sinister grin reflected a perverse enjoyment in the thought of such a horrific fate for Spiffy.

Capo nodded approvingly, his calculating mind already envisioning the execution of their ruthless plan, "Indeed, it would be a message to all, a demonstration of our power." The echo of his cold, hard words reverberated through the hall, heightening the chilling atmosphere that engulfed the place.

The gang reached the central area of the warehouse, a place dominated by ominous machinery that bore silent witness to the countless atrocities committed in the name of dominance and power. Spiffy was offloaded from the wagon with rough, uncaring hands, his small frame trembling violently under the scrutinizing gazes of his captors. The once busy production line now stood silent, a grotesque stage set for a terrifying act of cruelty, a perverse distortion of its original purpose.

Spiffy found himself surrounded by the cruel faces of the Dawg Dominion, his heart wrenching in his chest as the enormity of his predicament dawned upon him. Despite his terrifying surroundings and the malicious intent that emanated from the figures looming over him, Spiffy clung to a slender thread of hope, his mind frantically working to find a way out of this nightmare. Does he have one last escape left in him?

Facing the merciless gaze of Capo, who took a step forward with a menacing grace, Spiffy gathered every ounce of courage left in him. The room was heavy with the scent of dampness and decay, amplifying the sense of dread that curled in his stomach. Spiffy steeled himself, holding Capo's piercing gaze with a defiant one of his own, refusing to let the fear consume him completely.

"Now, little dog, you will tell us everything we want to know. Your friends, your secret meeting spots, everything," Capo demanded, his voice booming in the cavernous space, filled with echoes of malevolent promises and threats.

Spiffy swallowed hard, his throat tight with fear and determination as he spoke with a shaking voice, but surprisingly steady, "I won't tell you anything. We're just a group of friends who meet in the park. We're not part of any gang or involved in any crimes."

A silence descended upon the room, as Spiffy's words hung in the air, a bold declaration of resilience in the face of unspeakable fear. But as Capo's face contorted with anger, it was clear that Spiffy's act of bravery was just the beginning of a sinister game of power and resistance. The warehouse turned into a cauldron of malice, the machinery lying dormant, ready to spring into action at Capo's command, a foreboding presence in the horrifying tableau that was about to unfold.

The Great Dane, aka "Bruiser" grabbed a control button hanging on a cord near him. Spiffy, bound by chains attached to a device in the ceiling, stayed defiant.

"Alright little one, let's see how you like being a fish," said Bruiser as he pushed the button with his paw to raise Spiffy off the cold warehouse floor a few feet before he stopped the device.

"Going to talk now?" said Capo. "It is in your best interest to tell us what you know."

Another member of the DAWG, a gruff pit bull named Leon uttered, "He ain't gonna talk, let's just can him up and leave him in the center of the park, send a message to everyone, don't mess with the DAWG."

Amid the threatening atmosphere of the warehouse, a sudden tumultuous clatter echoed through the metallic canyons of the rusty complex. The clatter grew louder and more chaotic, slowly morphing into an indomitable rumble that shook the premises to its core. The Dawg Dominion members turned their heads in unison, their faces painted with confusion and fear as they tried to decipher the source of the uproar.

Out of the shadows emerged a band of audacious park dwellers led by Dale, the scruffy cat transformed from his squirrelly past life. Following him what they saw was a diverse assembly of animal friends, each carrying a determined yet comically serious expression. Their eyes locked onto their friend Spiffy, hanging helplessly from the ceiling, as they initiated their carefully conceived rescue plan.

Dale pointed his paw dramatically, orchestrating a series of maneuvers that seemed to be straight out of an action-comedy film. A group of squirrels, acquaintances from his previous form that he recruited vaulted through the air, their bushy tails swirling as they moved in to engage the enemy, their small but fierce forms a flurry of flying kicks and nimble jabs.

Leon and other gang members engaged in a messy fight, hilariously slipping on fish oil puddles created by Alex knocking over barrel after barrel tumbling into each other and causing a chaotic butterfly effect that activated the dormant machinery with an unintentional slap to a control panel. As the machines groaned to life, the Dawg Dominion members found themselves in an ironic reversal of their intended plan for Spiffy.

Mishap followed mishap in a series of comic but perilous events. A Doberman got enveloped in a sheet of plastic, stumbling around blindly before accidentally getting a labeling sticker stuck on his forehead that read "100% Fresh Fish." Meanwhile, another gang member, a hefty bulldog, found himself on a conveyor belt, rolling inexorably towards a canning device, his face a comedy of errors as he realized his predicament, his limbs flailing comedically before being canned neatly into a tin with only his tail sticking out.

Amid the chaos, Capo found himself being caught in the rapid shrink-wrap process, the machine wrapping him tighter and tighter in a clear plastic cocoon until only his head remained free, thanks to one of his gang members who managed to cut the wrapping around his neck. With glaring eyes and an immobile body, he could only utter furious but empty threats, vowing revenge as his body lay there, a ridiculous half-wrapped mummy on the warehouse floor.

Through a perfectly timed orchestrated chaos, Spiffy was lowered down by Alex. "I'm sure glad to see you all," said Spiffy. "I thought for sure I was a going to be canned."

The whole ensemble led by Sally, Ralph and Spike formed a protective circle around Spiffy, ready to guide him safely out of the perilous zone.

As the rescue team retreated, Dale couldn't help but shout back, "Remember Capo, it's always better to be a friend than a bully!" He then turned to Spiffy, offering him a comforting grin that translated into a promise of safety and camaraderie. "Where's Pippa with the backup plan?" he shouted.

"She should be here anytime," replied Sally.

Pippa's job was to run over to the animal shelter and get the attention of the animal control officers inside. She had traveled there, proceeded to taunt, and do a dance in the parking lot, only to have them hop in a truck and chase her into Manhattanville. There, she would lead them to the cannery warehouse.

Together, the group of friends made a hasty but triumphant exit from the warehouse, with Capo left behind, his furious shouts echoing emptily in the large cannery, vowing revenge but to no avail, as he was helplessly shrink-wrapped, unable to pursue them. The warehouse quickly turned into a scene of hilariously defeated Dawg Dominion members, some canned, others shrink-wrapped, a testament to the quick-witted and brave efforts of Spiffy's friends.

Once outside in the safety of the moonlit night, the group erupted into relieved laughter, just as Pippa arrived, out of breath.

"Ok, time to disperse, they are right behind me," she said.

Just as the group retreated across the alley into the next street, the animal control truck pulled up to the loading dock of the cannery only to hear a chorus of barks coming from inside.

"Hold on," said Alex. "Let's watch this."

The group watched as one by one the animal control officers emerged from the cannery with the members of the DAWG Dominion. Some taken out with slip leashes, some stuffed into crates and wheeled out, and some like Capo, being carried like a shrink-wrapped package of bacon. All of them were put into the truck for a trip to the shelter.

The night air echoed with their laughter, a melody of victory, ringing out as a testament to the strength of friendship, unity, and the comically perfect execution of a daring rescue. As the truck pulled away, the park dwellers had proven that with unity, courage, and a little bit of hilarity, even the most menacing of foes could be defeated.

"Let's get you home," said Sally, "before you are missed, it's getting late."

The gang headed back toward the park, keeping mind to avoid being noticed by any patrolling animal control trucks. After reaching the park, they went on their separate ways.

Alex returned home where Beatrice was just finishing up working in her studio in the basement. Alex, who had just laid down on his chaise lounge heard her say, "C'mon Pierre, let's make our dinner. Then I think we will go to the park for an evening stroll. What do you think about that?" she asked.

Alex turned a circle and wagged his tail, his way of showing his excitement. He was tired from the day's activities, but a walk with Beatrice would be calming.

# the wishing well

A cool morning rain doused the leaves of Central Park giving way to a sunny afternoon. With the Thanksgiving festivities a week away, the park was slowly losing its warm colors, and the magical glow dimming from the Bethesda Terrace & Fountain. The iconic Angel of the Waters statue stood majestically amidst the captivating panorama, an embodiment of hope and the keeper of countless whispered wishes.

Beatrice carried her easel and painting supplies, her keen eyes studying the landscape with a sense of purpose. She wanted to capture the last of fall upon the scene before winter grayed out the park. Her loyal companion, Alex, was at her side, eagerly absorbing the beautiful surroundings that were soon to become a part of Beatrice's artwork.

"Alex, this place... it has a soul, a heart pulsating with stories, wishes, and dreams of countless people. And this..." she pointed towards the Angel of the Waters, her eyes glinting with a profound connection, "...this is where magic converges with reality."

She paused, carefully setting her easel at a vantage point that encompassed the fountain in its full glory, against the backdrop of the flamboyant autumn foliage.

Beatrice continued to converse with Alex, her voice tinged with wonder as she poured her musings onto the canvas, and Alex listened with rapt attention. He seemed to understand every word, every nuanced emotion that flowed from Beatrice as she painted with a fervent intensity, aiming to capture the enchantment of the place that made it a beacon for dreamers and lovers alike.

The fountain before them shimmered with an iridescent play of sunlight, the famed "wishing well" of the city where countless individuals had thrown in coins accompanied by silent wishes, a tradition that spanned cultures and eras.

But amidst the magical aura, a concern hovered in Beatrice's mind, surfacing as a ponderous question that lingered in the crisp air, "I wonder, Alex... in a world swiftly adapting to digital currencies, plastic cards, and contactless payments, what becomes of a tradition so intimately tied to physical coins? Will the wishing well retain its magic when there are no more coins to carry people's dreams into its mystical depths?"

Alex tilted his head, seemingly pondering the depth of Beatrice's contemplation. He sensed the melancholy in her words, the fear of losing a cherished tradition in the whirlpool of change.

It was a concern that resounded on a deeper level with Alex. The group had seen transformations, experienced rebirths, and navigated changing terrains. The ritual of tossing coins and making a wish, he realized, was much more than a whimsical tradition; it was a tangible representation of hope, a physical act of entrusting one's dreams to the universe. It was an act as a human he never participated in, trusting his fate to his own ingenuity.

Beatrice's hands worked gracefully across the canvas, a dance of brush strokes that translated the enchanting vista before her onto the blank surface, giving it life and a hint of magic caught in the autumnal hues. Every line she drew, every shade she added was a silent vow to keep the magic alive, to encapsulate the spirit of the "wishing well" in her artwork.

As Beatrice worked, Alex stayed beside her, his eyes not just on the unfolding painting but frequently drifting to the Bethesda Terrace and Fountain, entranced by the complex mosaic of emotions it evoked in passersby. The hopeful eyes of a child throwing a penny, the whispered wishes of couples, the silent prayers of the elderly – all merged into the intricate dance of water and light.

After hours that seemed like fleeting moments, Beatrice finally stood back, her eyes scrutinizing every detail of the painting before she nodded, satisfied with her work. Alex watched as a beautiful recreation of the Bethesda fountain, with all its grace and hope, now resided on the canvas, ready to be a beacon of dreams in someone's living space. Beatrice packed her painting supplies with a sigh, her face glowing with the satisfaction of a job well done.

As they left the park, the sky turned a deep tone of crimson, blending into the shadows of the evening. Alex felt a connection, a deep-seated bond with the fountain, its spirit now captured in Beatrice's painting. He vowed silently to himself that he would return to this magical place, to understand more, to feel more, and perhaps, to share it with others who cherished it as much.

The next morning bore the fresh scent of damp earth and fallen leaves, a reminder of the transitory nature of time. Alex returned to the park; the image of the majestic angel etched in his mind. He was eager to share this newfound magic, this glimpse into human hope and tradition, with his group.

He convened with Dale, Spiffy, and others at their usual meeting spot. Alex relayed the magic of the previous day, his words forming a vivid picture in their minds, invoking a deep sense of curiosity and wonder.

Spiffy's eyes widened as he listened, his youthful spirit already coming up with adventurous plans. Dale, on the other hand, listened intently, his wise eyes reflecting deep contemplation as Alex described Beatrice's worry for the future of the "wishing well".

A deep hush fell over the group as they absorbed Alex's words, the vibrant image of the "wishing well" and the Angel of the Waters nestled in the heart of Central Park vivid in their minds. After a moment, the quiet was broken as they began to share their thoughts, memories, and legends that they had heard about the famous Bethesda Terrace & Fountain. The group was naturally drawn into a spiraling discussion, each speaking with genuine enthusiasm and interest, sharing and interchanging pieces of stories and personal experiences.

Dale started, his voice as steady as his personality, bringing a grounded perspective to the fascinating tale Alex had composed. "You know, the Angel of the Waters has been here for more than a century and a half. It is said to have witnessed the ebb and flow of life in Central Park through generations. Some believe it to be a silent guardian, a listener to all the prayers and wishes that people have whispered to it over the years," Dale shared, his face showing a smile as he spoke of the historical aura surrounding the statue.

Spiffy chimed in, his energetic demeanor echoing the lively spirit of the place described. "I've heard that couples who wish together at the fountain always end up having a strong bond. There's something about sharing a secret wish with someone you love right there, with the angel watching over you, that just seals the deal, you know?" His eyes twinkled with youthful wonder as he imagined the countless romantic moments that the fountain had hosted.

Sally, with her profound affinity for tales of magic and mystery, began sharing a more esoteric perspective. "There are rumors, legends I've overheard in the park, that on certain moonlit nights, the angel comes to life, reaching out to touch the waters, infusing them with a special kind of magic that grants the purest wishes made with a heartfelt desire." Sally's words cast a magical spell, adding a whimsical dimension to the discussion, and enveloping them in a web of magical intrigue.

"I got an idea," said Spiffy. "Why don't we throw a coin in the fountain and make a wish. We could wish for what we want to be in our next form or to finally reach the afterlife."

"I want to be a horse," said Ralph.

"A horse?" said Pippa.

"Yea, a big, majestic horse, and I want to pull the Budweiser wagon....... that would be the coolest ever," replied Ralph.

"I think we would all like to be something better someday. Perhaps wishes that come true should be unselfish ones, said Sally.

"Like wishing for someone else to be a horse?" said Dale.

"No, no, no," replied Sally. "I meant wishing for someone else to be happy, or get healthy or find love, etc."

"I say we all do like Spiffy said," exclaimed Alex. "We all toss a coin in the fountain, make a wish, and see if it comes true. So, make a wish that's not too hard and not too far in the future."

"I'm going to wish for a pizza to drop on the floor tonight at home," said Spike.

"I don't think you are getting the unselfishness wish idea Spike," said Pippa.

"Ok, Alex, then you can have the pizza and invite me over for dinner," replied Spike.

"You are too much Spike," said Sally.

"One problem," said Alex. "We are a pack of dogs and a cat. We don't have any coins. In fact, I have never seen any lying around in Beatrice's home. I didn't even use coins when I was a human."

The proclamation from Alex hung in the air, a hurdle in their freshly laid plans, almost tangible amongst the group, settling down like a little cloud of realization. Each one considered the conundrum in their own way, pondering the potential solutions in their imaginative minds.

After a brief moment of thoughtful silence, Dale lifted his head, his eyes showing a determined sparkle. "I think we can figure this out. You know, sometimes the humans leave coins in a little jar near the cash register at the corner store? Maybe we could find a way to get a few from there?"

Spiffy jumped in, his ever-active mind churning out ideas at a mile a minute, "Or maybe we could find some coins near the fountains in the park? You know, humans sometimes drop things when they are distracted. We have sharp eyes; we could find them!"

Sally looked at the others, her imaginative mind taking a flight of its own, weaving visions of a scavenger hunt filled with adventurous undertones, "What if we turn this into a kind of treasure hunt, a mission where each one of us uses our unique skills to find a coin, adding a layer of anticipation and excitement to our wish-making journey?" Her voice carried a ring of eagerness, igniting a corresponding glow in the eyes of the others.

The group nodded in agreement, drawn into Sally's picture of a prelude adventure leading up to the wish-making, the suggestion holding a charm that was hard to resist.

Pippa added, her voice thoughtful and deep, "Maybe we could also look around in the places humans frequent. The laundromat, the coffee shop...people lose things all the time. We just need to keep our eyes open and work together. It will be like a grand adventure, where everyone has a role to play."

The group exchanged excited, determined glances, the spirit of adventure taking hold firmly within each heart, setting a flame of resolve and eagerness.

With a sense of agreement settled amongst them, Alex took charge, his leader nature surfacing as he proposed, "Alright, then it's settled. We embark on a mission to find coins for our wishing at the Bethesda fountain. Let's meet back here in two days' time with our finds, and then we'll all go together to make our wishes." His tone was firm yet carried a delightful note of excitement, weaving them all into a pact of anticipation and wonder, laced with the spirit of teamwork and the joy of a shared goal.

Spiffy couldn't contain his excitement, his voice escalating in pitch, "Oh, this is going to be epic, a real mission! We are going to be like detectives, sniffing out clues, and finding treasure!"

Spike chimed in, his earlier wish momentarily forgotten in the thrill of the moment, "And who knows, maybe we might find enough coins to get that pizza too!"

"You and that danged pizza," laughed Sally.

A fresh wave of energy and anticipation filled the air as the group dispersed, their sights firmly set on the various locales and corners of New York that held the promise of undiscovered treasures. The world around them suddenly transformed into an expansive canvas, bearing hints and whispers of hidden riches, waiting to be discovered by keen eyes and eager spirits.

The next day, Dale headed towards the corner store, a place where the chimes of the door welcomed patrons with a warm embrace, filled with the rich aroma of coffee beans and freshly baked cookies. His eyes scoured the floor, every crevice and corner, with a hopeful glimmer. It wasn't long before he spotted a shiny object under a shelf laden with canned goods. He nudged it carefully with his nose, bringing it into the open. To his joy, it was a shiny nickel, gleaming with promise. He gingerly picked it up in his mouth, a smile of success blooming on his face as he trotted back home, his mission accomplished.

Meanwhile, Sally chose to venture into the labyrinthine paths of the park, her heart beating with the rhythms of nature, as she envisioned secret spots where humans would often sit and lose themselves in thoughts, sometimes leaving behind small tokens of the material world. As she wandered, her eyes fell upon a secluded bench, a place kissed by dappled sunlight. There, amidst the freshly mown grass lay a dime, its surface tarnished by years, telling stories of myriad hands it had passed. Sally carefully picked it up, her heart swelling with a sense of magic and connection to the countless dreams that coin had perhaps been a part of.

Spiffy, with his boundless energy, scampered through the streets with a nose for adventure, his young heart pulsating with exhilaration. He chose the bustling avenues where cafes and bistros lined the streets, a place of laughter and conversations. His eyes darted here and there, weaving through the maze of legs, each stride bringing a surge of anticipation. Finally, his perseverance paid off as he spotted a quarter lying forgotten near a vibrant street mural, a canvas of dreams and colors. It lay there, an unspoken wish waiting to be discovered. With a triumphant heart, Spiffy grabbed the coin, his spirit soaring with the taste of success.

Pippa had chosen the laundromat, a place of hums and rhythms, where the cycles of machines mirrored the ebb and flow of daily life. She moved with grace, her keen eyes scanning the corners and under machines, a silent ballet in the mechanical chorus. After what felt like an eternity, her gaze fell upon a glinting object nestled in a forgotten corner, a token of someone's day transformed into a beacon of hope. It was a penny, humble yet holding the warmth of countless hands, now poised to be a harbinger of dreams. With a silent nod of acknowledgment, she retrieved it, feeling a sense of fulfillment, a small piece in the mosaic of their shared dream.

Alex was the lucky one, he only had to venture out of the garden in his backyard where on the sidewalk he spotted the glint of light reflecting off the grass next to the sidewalk. He investigated to find a shiny quarter laying there like a git, a forgotten token a human had dropped.

Spike decided the easiest way was to look in his home. He often spent hours in the garage with his owner, Stan. Stan was a biker and spent a lot of time in bars drinking and playing darts. As he was lying on the garage floor while Stan was fixing the carburetor on his bike, he saw a penny underneath the workbench.

Without calling attention to himself, a walked over and laid down by the bench and in a stretching motion, he reached out and pulled the penny close enough for him to grasp with his mouth.

Meanwhile, Ralph scoured the lawn in his backyard and found a penny, old and covered with dirt, it would do the job. He was careful to repair the holes he dug while looking for the penny.

The day of their fountain gathering arrived sooner than they all had anticipated. Their adventurous spirits were alive with the enchantment of legends swirling in their minds as they reconvened, each carrying their found treasures carefully.

Dale was the first to arrive, carrying his piece of history gently in his mouth. He laid it down at the agreed meeting point, a secluded spot surrounded by lush greenery not far from the fountain. As each friend arrived, a neat little pile of varying coins started to form, a symbol of their collaborative spirit and their belief in the magic of the fountain.

Spiffy was practically vibrating with excitement, his tail wagging non-stop as he envisioned the magical transformation the angel would undergo under the moonlit night, awakening to grant their wishes. His eyes were filled with youthful wonder, a mirror reflecting the energy of dreams waiting to be fulfilled.

As they gathered, they couldn't help but admire the array of coins they had collected: a shiny quarter that reflected the sun's rays brilliantly, a well-weathered quarter with stories embedded in its curves, a forgotten dime rediscovered, a nickel and pennies that bore the marks of time and the earth's embrace.

There was a solemnity, a rare gravity that settled upon them as they stood before the heap of coins, each piece a token of their efforts and a vessel of their impending wishes. Alex, who naturally took the role of the group's philosopher and thinker, gathered them around as they prepared to impart their dreams and desires to the seemingly ordinary but suddenly extraordinary collection of coins.

"I think we've done an incredible job, everyone," Alex began, his voice carrying a hint of pride and wonderment. "Now, I guess it's time to make our wishes and toss our coin into the fountain. Remember, they don't have to be big. Just something pure, from the heart, and not too far in the future," he reminded them, his eyes scanning each face as he spoke.

"Oh, boy," said Spike, "Pizza, pizza, pizza."

"Would you stop it with the pizza," exclaimed Sally. "This is serious. We are here to test the legend of the fountain, I'm not sure pizza is how you want to spend your wish."

Spike said, "I know, I just love pizza."

The group moved closer and assembled near the fountain, the mystical "wishing well" watched over by the Angel of the Waters. The angel, a majestic statue of heavenly serenity, stood with grace as if welcoming them and their tiny yet profound wishes. The air was tinged with magic.

Alex went first, stepping forward with solemnity. The group watched in silence as he reached down and picked up the shiny quarter he had found. He weighed it in his paw for a moment, the metal cool and heavy, a physical manifestation of hope and dreams. He closed his eyes, taking a deep breath as he gathered his thoughts and desires, whispering his wish into his heart before letting the coin take a gracious arc into the water with a gentle splash. Alex opened his eyes, a new kind of light reflecting in them, filled with hope and a quiet joy that resonated with the still surface of the water, echoing with potentialities yet unseen.

Then it was Sally's turn. She moved with a grace that only she possessed, holding the quarter delicately. As she stood on the brink, she took a deep breath, her wish crystallizing in her mind, shaped from the pure desires of her heart. With a prayerful whisper that danced with the breeze, she released the coin, watching as it splashed in the water, creating ripples that seemed to spread the halos of energy of her wish into the very essence of the fountain.

Spiffy followed, As he let his coin fly, bouncing off the base of the angel and splashing int the water.

"Leave it to Spiffy to throw a bank shot," said Alex.

"He's lucky it made it to the water and didn't settle on the concrete," said Ralph.

One by one, they all took their turns, even Spike, who, after a jestful yet stern reminder from Sally, decided on a wish that was a tad more serious than pizza.

As Ralph took the last turn, the group held their collective breaths, it was the last of their wishes. Ralph had promised not to wish to be a horse. He released his coin, the water embracing it as a promise, a secret pact sealed between him and the mystical guardian angel overseeing the fountain.

After Ralph, they sat in a circle, the ambient sounds of the park in the background.

"Now remember, don't tell anyone your wish, or it won't come true. It's supposed to be bac luck," said Sally.

"If it comes true, can we tell?" asked Spike.

"Yes, Spike," she answered. "If it comes true, you have to tell, then we know that the coin works."

As they left the fountain, each of them filled with the hope that their dream would come true, they high fived and yelled, tails wagging and spirits high with anticipation of wishes granted and dreams awakened.

# reflections & revelry

The early morning sunlight seeped through the slits of the curtains, Alex, lying on his lounge, found himself ensnared in the branches of deep contemplation, a quiet turmoil bubbling under the surface of his usually call demeanor. It was a time of festivities, a time of gathering and cherishing the delightful ordinary moments of life. Yet for Alex, the looming festival induced an introspective mood, one where the questions of his spiritual path rose with a renewed vigor.

He wondered, with a tight knot of worry in his chest, about the journey that lay after this life. What did the cosmic forces that govern the realms beyond life expect of him? Of all his known trespasses, which did he need to atone for, and how? He pondered Max's words back in the recycling center, his selfishness and now the selfless joys shared with his close-knit group, were they a good and virtuous path toward salvation?

Alex's introspection expanded as he mulled over the concept of being "good." He found himself engulfed in the uncertainty of defining virtue. Being a kind and caring friend, a compassionate being in this world, he wondered if that would be sufficient to secure a tranquil afterlife, a serene existence post this vibrant yet transient life.

In the midst of his internal turmoil, Dale approached, pacing outside and then jumping onto the fence outside the downstairs window at Beatrice's home. Sensing the profound musings etched in Alex's reflective eyes through the curtains, he motioned for Alex to come outside.

Alex went out to the doggy door onto the terrace that overlooked the garden. Dale showed up a moment later and sat beside Alex, his presence a comforting warmth, a beacon of gentle wisdom as he began to share tales of life's intricacies. "You know, Alex," he started, with a voice deep and calm like the still waters of a pond, "life, in all its grandeur and complexity, often comes down to the simple act of living virtuously. Lord knows I have had my moments of being reckless, but transforming a couple of times recently I discovered that immersing oneself in the pure, innocent delights that life offers, one often finds the deepest spiritual fulfilment."

"That's deep thinking," said Alex. "I wouldn't have pegged you for that type of thought."

"As a squirrel, and now a stray cat, I have a lot of time on my paws to think about stuff. I only wish I could remember my human life like you," he said. "I wonder what I was and what I did and how the things I did in my human life landed me in this cycle of transformation."

Dale went on to share nuggets gained from his last two transformations. "Atonement does not always demand grand gestures, Alex," he advised softly. "Often, it lies in the simplicity, in the gentle hand of compassion extended to others, in the humble acceptance of our own imperfections and learning to forge a path of goodness amidst them. At least that's the conclusion I have come to. So, cheer up buddy, I think the worst is behind us. Besides, tomorrow is the festival and parade."

"You're right," said Alex. "I can't sit her and stew in my own gravy. I need to move forward."

"Speaking of gravy, the day of the festival last year, there was plenty of it left in the garbage cans," said Dale. "As a mosquito, I couldn't eat, but this year, nothing is going to stop me now."

"It's called Thanksgiving Dale," said Alex. It's a day when we, I mean the humans celebrate being thankful for the people and things in their life."

"Well, that sounds perfect," said Dale. "We can be thankful for the Alice Gang, that's what I am calling us now."

"Not a bad name, Dale," said Alex. "You've surprised me today. Thanks for cheering me up."

"Ok, gotta go," he shouted as he started walking atop the fence.

"Oh, Dale, if you see the rest of the gang, tell them there is usually a parade that starts right on the west side of the park by the lake next to Strawberry Fields.," yelled Alex. "Let's meet up after the parade next to the dog park there."

Dale acknowledged as he jumped down from the fence and gracefully navigated traffic as he disappeared down the street.

He visited the entire gang that morning, each of them in their own setting spreading the word about the parade and festival and how Alex explained it.

The next day, as the morning unfurled, the city seemed to pulsate with an effervescent energy, a concoction of joy, anticipation, and communal festivity. Slightly cloudy skies and a brisk 45 degrees, Alex found himself nestled snugly in the comforting crook of Beatrice's arm, a prime spot to observe the magnificent parade that had started to course through the heart of Central Park West.

Alex, with Beatrice by his side, stood at the vantage point that allowed him to witness the titanic balloons floating gracefully overhead. The sheer enormity of the balloons, caricatures of well-known figures and beloved characters from various realms of entertainment, filled him with a childlike wonder. Each balloon seemed like a gentle giant, a behemoth gracing the sky with vibrant colors and benign smiles, drifting in the sky as if in a dream. Alex's eyes twinkled with the reflections of the brilliant spectacle unfolding before him, his heart a whirlpool of emotions, ranging from sheer joy to a profound understanding of the collective spirit of thanksgiving that echoed in the cheerful shouts and merry laughter that enveloped him.

Spike's owner had picked up his girlfriend and brought her and Spike to a spot near the front lines. Each float that passed by was a burst of colors, a moving canvas depicting tales of joy, traditions, and the mix of cultures that displayed the dynamic narrative of humanity. The pulsating rhythms of the marching bands resonated with his heartbeat, encouraging a small wag of his tail in tune with the vibrant beats that filled the air. He marveled at the precision and harmony.

Ralph, stationed at a quieter corner with his young owners, found joy in the simpler elements. The colorful streamers strewn around, the laughter of children as they chased bubbles blowing in the air, and the warmth of the loving families gathered together were a mirror to his close-knit family of friends. Each face that passed by carried a story. His keen eyes observed not just the grandeur but the quiet moments of joy, the hand-holdings, the shared smiles, and in them, he saw a reflection of his journey, a path marked with friendships that enriched his soul.

As the parade progressed, **Sally** found herself entranced by the artistic prowess on display. The intricately designed floats, each depicting a theme, a story, a celebration of life's various facets, spoke to her sensitive nature. Each float was a moving artwork, inspiring in her a desire to create and making her wonder that perhaps she was an artist when she was a human.

Spiff's owners had chosen to watch the parade on television. Spiffy claimed a corner of the couch where he curled up, his head on a round sofa pillow, watching the parade as it scrolled down the screen.

In the midst of the jubilant crowd, Dale had positioned himself atop a branch in a nearby tree, a silent observer in the midst of the cacophony. His eyes danced with joy witnessing the sheer display of unity, of happiness that radiated from every individual, human or not, participating in this grand celebration of life.

Halfway through the procession of floats came the Alice in Wonderland float picturing the iconic items from the story. There were people dressed as playing card soldiers, the Queen of Hearts, the Mad Hatter and even the Chesire Cat.

Alex reveled at the float, significant as the likeness of Alice was the gang's meeting point. While looking at the details of the float he saw Pippa. She was sitting on the float next to her owner, Clara. It appeared that Clara was dressed to play the part of Alice on the float and Pippa was along for the right. How exciting he thought. This will make for a good story later.

As the parade ebbed to a close, Alex and Beatrice went for a walk in the park while the traffic cleared. Alex, as a human, never saw the parade live, much less tuned in for more than a few moments on television. His life was too busy, his priorities laid elsewhere.

The park was filled with activities that day. The ice-skating rink was open near 58th and 6th street, and nearby was the holiday market on 59th and Columbus circle. Alex wondered how he missed all of this. He never went ice skating or even knew about the activities that went on in the park. His last memory of Thanksgiving was having an argument with his father over something quite trivial. Thanksgiving was never a priority to him, it was more of a nuisance he thought, closing the stock market for a meal. Now, he might just understand. A wave of guilt washed over Alex as he and Beatrice continued their walk in the park. He looked up at her with soft eyes, thankful that she included him in this adventure.

After a short visit to the market where Beatrice bought a Christmas ornament in the shape of a black poodle, a colorful wool scarf, and some home-made dog cookies, they retreated back home where Beatrice was busy decorating the house for Christmas.

Alex slipped out the back door to head to the park and meet up with the gang. The streets were still alive with the residue of the day's festivities, whispers of laughter lingering in the air and remnants of joy scattered across the pavements. It was the perfect canvas for the group's next adventure, and Alex could feel a bubbling excitement as he neared their meeting spot.

Upon reaching the park, the gang convened, an eager bounce in their steps and twinkles of mischief in their eyes. The backdrop of the post-parade city was enticing, a playground of endless possibilities. The shared enthusiasm soon gave way to a boisterous exchange of stories from the parade, each dog offering hilarious anecdotes and observations, setting a jovial tone for the afternoon.

With their spirits high and bellies ready for some scavenger fun, they trotted towards Central Park West, a tightly knit pack on a mission to discover what goodies the parade-goers had left behind. What ensued was nothing short of a whirlwind of joyous chaos and uproarious discoveries.

The streets transformed into a playground of wonders. Sally spotted a group of kids with face paint and couldn't resist the urge to join in, sitting still while they dobbed on the paint, soon finding herself adorned with streaks of bright colors, a walking piece of parade art. Pippa found a discarded feathered boas and pranced around, casting colors in every direction, imitating a soap opera star, an enchanting figure in the dwindling daylight.

In the midst of their frolicking, Spike stumbled upon an abandoned coffee cup with a generous dollop of whipped cream still clinging to its sides. In his eagerness, he dove nose-first into the treat, emerging with a whip cream mustache and beard that brought bursts of laughter from the group. His new accessory, however, attracted more attention than anticipated as a passerby noticed his cream-adorned face and misinterpreted it, shouting, "Mad dog, mad dog!"

Panic ensued, the shout, getting the attention of a local patrol officer sent the group into a thrilling chase as they darted down the street, their hearts racing in excited tandem with their sprinting paws. As they raced away, the group found themselves in a veritable wonderland of forgotten parade goodies. The chase had led them to an alley where the parade's remnants were more concentrated, an unexplored territory of delights.

Ralph initiated a game of hide and seek amidst the enormous balloons that had been temporarily stored there, creating a labyrinth of giggles and playful yelps as they darted between the vibrant giants. Meanwhile, Pippa orchestrated a hilarious hat parade featuring discarded costume pieces, each dog taking a turn to strut down an improvised runway with exaggerated elegance, eliciting cheers, and laughter from their companions.

Further down the street, they encountered a cart of abandoned parade props, including giant foam fingers, which became the centerpiece of an impromptu puppet show led by Sally, with the dogs taking turns to manipulate the oversized props, creating a playful theatre of shadows on the walls of the nearby buildings, their exaggerated features setting the stage for a riot of laughter.

Their journey of discovery and joyous chaos continued, each turn bringing a new source of laughter, a fresh ground for hilarious interactions, and unexpected finds. From a playful tussle over a giant turkey leg prop to a group attempt at imitating the marching band they had seen earlier in the parade, their adventure turned into a scene of laughter, forged through shared hilarity and spontaneous fun.

As the sky turned gray and the wind began to pick up, the signs of an impending storm, they knew this was the end of their hilarious escapade. The gang reconvened, their faces glowing with the thrill of adventure, each bearing tokens of their joyous escapade — a feather here, a sparkle there, and Spike, still sporting his whipped cream adornment, now a badge of their exhilarating adventure.

With hearts light and spirits buoyant, they headed back to their meeting point. It was a walk back filled with animated chatter, a recounting of the day's silliest moments, and the shared warmth of friendship forged through laughter. With a bark in unison, and one faint "meow", they scurried home to avoid the inclement weather.

# night memories

The afternoon sun blanketed Central Park that holiday weekend after the Thanksgiving storm passed. Dale was fervently pursuing his mouse-hunting exploits. His ears twitched and nose worked overtime as he darted between bushes, his focus absolute. Suddenly, Dale halted, his body rigid, as an elderly dog appeared before him. The older dog bore an aura of enigmatic wisdom, his eyes deep pools of lived experiences that seemed to hold mysteries of a hundred lifetimes.

Dale cleared his throat nervously, breaking the stillness that enveloped them. "Uh, hello there, I haven't seen you around here before."

The elderly dog chuckled softly, the sound resembling the gentle rustle of leaves. "Well, young one, I've been around, just not always in plain sight. I've seen you and your vibrant group of friends having the time of your lives. My name is Alfred."

Caught between the sudden appearance of Alfred and his warm words, Dale felt a connection, a strange kind of familiarity that encouraged him to open up. "Oh, you mean the gang? Yeah, we are a close-knit family, but we are all trying to figure out our pasts, you know. Alex, the black poodle, is the only one who remembers something because of a glitch in the recycling machine."

Alfred's gaze turned thoughtful as he absorbed Dale's words, and then, with a hopeful gleam in his eyes, he spoke, "I may have something that could help you and your friends, young Dale. In my long years, I've learned ways to tap into the hidden recesses of the mind, to unlock memories that seem lost."

The sudden sparkle of hope in Dale's eyes was unmistakable. He ventured, "Really? You can help us remember who we were before? That sounds... incredible."

Alfred nodded, his expression tender yet gravely serious, "Yes, but it will not be easy. It demands courage and the willingness to embrace the truths that come with the memories. We will meet under the moon's guidance, surrounded by the whispers of the night. It is a journey of revelation, a voyage into the self. But remember, the night holds no deceit; it demands sincerity and openness to the experiences it unveils."

Dale swallowed hard, feeling the weight and gravity of Alfred's words settle in his young heart. Yet, within him, curiosity and yearning surged stronger, pushing him to agree, "Yes, yes, we are ready. I will gather the gang, and we will meet you. Where should we come?"

Alfred smiled, a rich, deep smile that bore the wisdom of ages. "Under the shadow of the grand oak in the heart of the park when the moon is at its zenith. There, surrounded by the guardians of the night, we will embark on a journey into the secret chambers of your past lives."

With that, the mysterious figure of Alfred receded, blending with the shadows, leaving Dale with a heart pounding with anticipation, holding a secret that bore the promise of discovery and perhaps, the unraveling of mysteries that tied them to their former human selves.

As Dale rushed back to find Alex and share this breathtaking news, the park seemed more alive, the leaves whispering secrets, and the air thick with magic and the promise of adventure. The stage was set for a night of revelations, where paths would cross, secrets would unveil, and lives would be transformed under the guidance of the enigmatic elder dog, Alfred.

The next day, the sun played hide and seek with the flitting clouds, casting a mesmerizing shadow across Central Park. Dale couldn't contain his eagerness any longer as he gathered the gang near their usual haunt. There was Spike, the mischievous and spirited one, and Alex, the black poodle with the soulful eyes that bore secrets of another life. They were soon joined by others.

Dale cleared his throat, his heart pounding with the weight of the secret he was about to share. Everyone turned towards him, their attentive eyes urging him on. "Guys, something incredible happened yesterday. I met someone who can help us... help us remember who we were in our past lives," Dale began, the words tumbling out in a rush.

Ralph leaned in, his ears perking up, a spark of hope ignited in his deep eyes. "Tell us everything, Dale," he urged, the collective breath of the group held tight, a tangible thread of anticipation weaving among them.

"Well, his name is Alfred," Dale continued, "He is an older dog, wise and carrying an air of mystery. He told me he could unlock our memories, help us remember who we were before we came to be... us."

A ripple of astonishment and wonderment flowed through the group. Spike couldn't contain himself, his tail wagging uncontrollably. "You mean, we could finally figure out why we have these strange dreams, these flashes of another life?" he blurted out, his voice tinged with excitement and hope.

Dale nodded vigorously, "Yes, exactly! But it is going to be a deep journey, a spiritual one. Alfred mentioned it would require courage and a readiness to face whatever we might find."

"Hold on," said Alex. "Are you sure he's not pulling your leg or trying to lure us into someplace dangerous?"

"I don't think so," replied Dale. "His story is too good, and the details are stunning. At least hear him out, and then we can decide amongst ourselves if we want to follow him on this adventure."

The group exchanged thoughtful glances, a mixture of hope and apprehension swirling in the air. Muffled agreements of readiness to face their past, to unearth the buried truths, echoed among them.

The idea of a journey to find out who they were carried a charm that was irresistible.

As the discussion flourished, plans began to take shape. "We have to meet him at the grand oak near The Loch, close to The Paws of Honor, the pet cemetery for heroic police dogs. It's a place filled with stories, tales of bravery and honor," Dale added, the location bringing a gravity to their endeavor, linking them to a place of respect and homage.

Excited whispers traversed the group, ideas and questions bubbling up, filling the space with electric energy. "What if I was a famous musician, bringing joy to people with my music?" pondered Pippa, while Spiffy wondered, "Could I have been a guardian, a protector of a family?"

The midday sun warmed the wind as they planned their meetup. "Let's meet here tonight, after your humans go to bed," said Dale. "We need to be at the Loch, before the moon is straight above us."

"Agreed," said the group in unison.

"Tonight, it is then," uttered Sally as the group slowly separated, heading back to their homes.

Later that evening, as the moon cast long shadows and the city sounds mellowed, a palpable anticipation hung in the air, stirring the leaves, and whispering secrets to the quiet world. One by one, the group convened at their chosen rendezvous point, the whimsical and iconic Alice statue, which seemed to nod encouragingly at them as they assembled.

Each member wore an expression of eagerness mingled with apprehension, as if standing on the threshold of a dream, ready to step into the hallowed annals of their history. Under the silver beams of the moon, they moved as one, with Dale leading them with a sense of purpose and reverence for the path they were embarking upon.

The group navigated their way around the reservoir, their reflections ghostly figures in the still waters, transient and fleeting as memories themselves. The moon beamed down upon them, lending a magical shimmer to their path as they trotted through North Meadow, where night critters paused and acknowledged them with knowing glances, a silent tribute to their brave venture into the unknown.

As they approached The Loch, the sound of the North Loch Waterfall greeted them, a gentle roar that mirrored the beating of their collective hearts. And there, atop an embankment that overlooked a quietly babbling stream and The Ravine, stood the grand oak tree, a silent guardian keeping watch beside the solemn grounds of the Paws of Honor cemetery.

It was here they found Alfred. His large, towering frame silhouetted against the moonlit night, his fur a sea of grey that seemed to merge with the twilight hours. The group could not help but feel a deep reverence for the elderly Irish Wolfhound who seemed like a living embodiment of wisdom, his profound eyes reflecting ages of untold stories and experiences.

Alfred greeted them with a gentle nod, a warm smile breaking across his noble face as he regarded each one of them, acknowledging their courage to undertake this journey of self-discovery. As the group introduced themselves one after another, a ripple of respect and wonder flowed between them, establishing a connection that transcended their immediate existence.

Once the introductions were completed, Alfred cleared his throat, commanding attention effortlessly with his serene yet potent presence. "My brave young friends," he began, his voice deep and resonating with the whisper of the wind through the trees, "I am here to guide you on a path of rediscovery, a voyage into the chambers of your hidden memories, a journey through time."

He paused, letting the gravity of his words sink in before continuing. "Before we begin, we must visit a very special place, a magical wildflower garden that holds the secrets to unlocking your pasts. It is not far from here, a place where the wildflowers dance with the spirits of the ancient heroes resting nearby, a garden steeped in magic and mystery."

With a sense of heightened reverence, they followed Alfred, who led them with a graceful yet purposeful stride. They walked in a solemn procession, the night embracing them with open arms, ready to reveal the secrets hidden in the garden of memories. As they reached the wildflower garden, a sense of peace enveloped them. It was as if the wildflowers themselves were waiting for them, ready to share their ancient secrets and to guide them on a path of enlightenment, a path that promised revelations, tears, joy, and a deeper understanding of who they were and who they could become.

Their adventure had officially begun, under the watchful eyes of Alfred, the mystical moon above, and surrounded by the beauty of the magical wildflower garden that whispered of secrets, of memories locked away, ready to awaken to the call of brave souls venturing into the chambers of their past.

As they traveled along familiar paths, the haunting beauty of the night enveloped them, and the older dog regaled them with tales from his rich life, weaving a narrative that was at once captivating and laden with wisdom. He spoke of his experiences as a human, as a soldier whose bad decision cost the lives of his platoon. His self-imposed penitence for his shame was to remain as a navigator on earth, which led him to choose the path of a dog for over a decade and a half.

As Alfred spoke, a profound stillness settled among them, each absorbed in the wisdom imparted, resonating with the depth of his experiences. He encouraged them to dive deep into their reservoir of memories, to explore and revisit fragments of their past with newfound perspective and understanding.

With the moon at its zenith, they arrived at the magical wildflower meadow, a place where time seemed to hold its breath, and nature bestowed its deepest secrets. Alfred gestured to the wildflowers bathing in the moonlight, their silver petals glowing with an ethereal luminescence, granting them a hypnotic aura. It was these silver wildflowers, Alfred explained, that held the key to unlocking their hidden memories, a magical conduit to the depths of their subconscious.

"Only pick the ones reflecting the moonlight as silver," he said. "Each of you need to have three flowers for the journey through your memories."

They worked together to carefully select the silver glowing wildflowers, each one a beacon of hope, a fragment of the bridge to their former selves. They placed them delicately into a basket, their hearts aflutter with anticipation and a deep reverence for the mystical journey they were embarking upon.

As they gathered the last of the wildflowers, Alfred gathered them close, his towering frame a comforting presence in the moonlit night. "Now," he said, "we must travel to the sacred cave of memories, nestled deep within The Ravine. It's a stone's throw from the Loch."

He explained it was a place steeped in legends, a sanctuary where the veil between worlds was thin, allowing them to traverse the boundaries of time and self. With the basket secured, the group followed Alfred with a renewed sense of purpose, their hearts beating as one in harmony with the rhythmic symphony of the night. They traversed through the meandering paths with an undercurrent of excitement tinged with solemnity, aware that they were venturing into a hallowed space of remembrance and discovery.

The journey seemed to go on forever, yet no time passed at all. The world around them shifted and morphed, the whispers of the trees guiding them, the song of the stream narrating the chapters of countless stories that echoed in the heart of the Ravine.

At last, the silhouette of the cave entrance came into view, a gateway to the hidden corridors of their souls, beckoning them with the promise of revelations untold. The group paused at the threshold, exchanging nervous yet hopeful glances, united in their courage to face the hidden realms of their pasts.

Alfred turned to them, his deep eyes glimmering with wisdom and compassion. "Gather your courage," he said. "Where we go, is the place of memories lost and found, This is your last chance to back out. Sometime, there are questions we should not ask, as that answers may disappoint you."

"We are ready," said Sally.

The group nodded in agreement. Alex turned to the group and said, "You know my story, and the struggle I have had because I retained my memories. Please, if you don't want to know, it's ok, nobody here with think the less of you for it."

Alfred chimed in, "Alex is right, there is not shame in backing out, but if your all-in agreement, less press forward into the cave."

Alfred led them into the heart of the cave, behind the gushing waterfall at the Loch. Moonlight peered into the cave from cracks in the rocks above lighting their path. The group felt a reverential hush settle over them as they entered the hidden chamber, a place untouched by time, where the ancient stones bore witness to countless secrets. The sounds and dull roar of the waterfall were heard above them.

In the center of the chamber stood a massive stone bowl, worn and weathered by centuries. Alfred solemnly instructed each of them to place their share of silver wildflowers into the bowl and use a rounded rock to crush them into a fragrant, shimmering pollen then take a big deep inhale of the silver dust of the pollen. He told them their memories would play out like an ethereal movie on the cavern wall for all to see.

Ralph stepped forward first, his heart pounding in his chest. As he inhaled the mystic pollen, the chamber transformed. Ralph found himself immersed in his past life as a talented chef, painting the world with flavors unknown. His tale was one of passion and joy, bringing people together with his culinary creations until a peaceful end in his sleep. Laughter echoed in the chamber as Ralph recounted moments of kitchen disasters turned into delicious surprises. His reason for recycling was that he was too busy to fall in love, and not tolerant of those who worked with him who did, and the pain they felt to live up to his expectations.

Ralph stood back, "It all makes sense now," said. "What a heal I was." He sat back relieved but saddened and enlightened by the truth.

Sally came next, shyly stepping forward with a glance at her friends. She grinned as the visions unfurled; she had been a mischievous yet beloved comedian, lightening the burdens of those around her with her wit. Sally recalled a life filled with laughter, a beacon of joy in the lives of many, and her tales brought warm smiles and chuckles from her friends. She died from breast cancer, found in time to save her life, but the shine of the spotlight was too great, and she robbed herself and her love and her two young daughters of her presence, her selfishness was her greatest sin.

After coming out of the hypnosis, Sally started crying, now remembering the names of her daughters, Anne, and Lacy. As she walked back to the group, Alex placed his paw on her shoulder and said, "Now that we know our sins, our reason for being in this place, we can move forward. I know it hurts to think that you had a loving family."

Sally sniffled and hugged Alex while Pippa was stepping up to the stone bowl.

Pippa followed, her delicate frame shaking slightly. What would she find out she thought. The group watched as her face transformed through a range of emotions. She had been a brilliant ballet dancer, expressing stories through graceful movements, her life a beautiful, yet tragically short dance, ended abruptly in an accident.

The room filled with solemn nods of understanding and soft tears of empathy as they envisioned her dancing gracefully in moonlit stages. As the scene played out, images of Pippa addicted to painkillers and other drugs and an accidental overdose. Her sin was depriving the world of her graceful beauty in the ballet. She returned to the group, saddened by her fate but understanding her penance.

Spike's turn came with an energetic hop to the center. The group was soon laughing hysterically as he recounted a life as a bumbling detective who somehow always managed to solve the case despite his often-absurd antics. His life had been a riot of unpredicted actions, filled with heroic bravado in surprisingly successful operations.

He was laughing very loudly when the event of his demise showed up. The group reacted in surprise to fine out he died alone in his apartment. It seems he skipped training to attend a football game, training that would have helped him avoid the accidental shooting of a young child. A wave of remorse came across his face as he returned to the group. "Sorry gang, I wasn't a real good guy," he said.

"Sure you were," said Alex. "You just made one mistake, in a storied life as a decorated police detective. If it were unforgivable, you certainly would not be here."

Alfred chimed in, "It's not over Spike, come back and see the ending."

Spike returned to the bowl, and he saw a woman, the child's mother, come to his door many years later after the event and forgave him for his mistake. While grateful, it was too late to change his fate.

"See," said Alfred. "That forgiveness saved you from eternal damnation and gave you a chance to ascend."

"Yea," said Alex. "Just like the little girl who blessed me when she received my eyes as a donor recipient. Something made me sign that card when I was so young. It was after that where I went wrong. You were on the right side from the start."

Spike felt a smile come across his face as he once again returned to the group.

Next was Spiffy. He stepped forward with a solemn expression. As he watched his story, the group watched intently, learning of his past as a devoted therapist, helping others navigate the stormy seas of their minds. His life was a rich tale of deep connections and healing, touching countless lives before succumbing to old age surrounded by the people whose lives he had transformed.

"That's it!" Spiffy shouted.

"Oh my," said Alfred. "Looks like the adjudication center made a mistake with you right from the start. I've never heard of someone without a significant sin being recycled.

"Well, I hope they discover their error soon," said Spiffy. "I mean, I like being here with you all, but I would rather be in the afterlife."

"Perhaps they will discover their mistake, but you can't be hung up on where you want to be, and not enjoy were you are," said Alfred.

Lastly, it was Dale's turn. A deep breath brought forth visions of a life as a children's book author, weaving tales of magic and adventure for young minds. His past was filled with creativity and the joy of seeing young eyes light up with wonder. He had brought magic into the lives of countless children before a peaceful departure in his beloved garden. His sin was that although children enjoyed his tales, he never wrote any original material. Along life's way he had cheated his way to success, much like he cheated death as a mosquito and squirrel.

As each one's pollen's magic wore off, they found themselves back in the stone chamber, their faces reflecting the deep journey upon which they had just embarked.

Through tears, laughter, and deep reflections, they nurtured a newfound depth of understanding for one another. The chamber resonated with the complex melody of shared vulnerability and strength drawn from their vivid revelations. They huddled closer, their bonds strengthened, souls intertwined with threads of golden memories, their past human lives revealed, fostering deeper connections, and carving a rich narrative into the annals of their timeless friendship. They had ventured into the secret chambers of their past lives, and had returned united, ready to forge a future filled with understanding, enriched with the kaleidoscope of experiences carried from their human lives into their present. The group, now more a family than ever, embraced each other with renewed affection, ready to face whatever adventures lay ahead, together.

After they huddled and gave out hugs, they turned around to thank Alfred, but he was gone. Vanished into thin air or so it seemed. He would have had to walk right through the group to leave the chamber and cave. Perhaps there is some mystical magic here after all.

# second chances

December air, crisp and infused with a spirit of anticipation, guided Alex and Beatrice on their Sunday midday walk. Beatrice was headed to the holiday market at the south end of Central Park. Unlike the market in November, additional vendors would show up to sell their holiday decorations, cookies, and other items. Along their path, Central Park West was more alive than ever, embracing the vibrant holiday market that glittered with hope and the promise of new beginnings. Fresh pine scent permeated the air, a fragrance both cleansing and rejuvenating, while the magical luminescence of twinkling lights adorned every corner, weaving tales of magic in the daylight.

A fresh layer of snow from the night before lay upon the park and the air filled with the hint of snowflakes to come. As they moved, a heartwarming sight slowly unfolded before them. The Holy Trinity Lutheran Church stood as a pillar of faith and community, now playing host to a jubilant event adorned with deep connections and heartfelt vows. A large gathering had converged at its steps, a harmonious amalgamation of laughter, joy, and the blissful echoes of union.

The church steps were transformed into a canvas depicting joyous celebration. Two lines of well-wishers formed a path of honor, down which walked Lisa and Justin. Alex, trotting along at pace with Beatrice looked over and did a double take. He was surprised, there dressed in wedding attire, were Lisa and Justin. The happiness emanating from them seemed almost tangible, their smiles lighting up the chilly morning, perhaps brighter than the sparklers held by the attendees to celebrate this beautiful milestone.

Alex and Beatrice watched silently; unseen yet deeply moved by the commitment being honored here today. Lisa and Justin were taking a precious step, initiated from love and a shared dream of a future filled with mutual understanding, respect, and endless adventures. The sparkling white limousine awaiting them bore witness to this pledge of shared dreams and a harmonized journey into tomorrow.

As Alex observed this significant milestone in Lisa and Justin's journey, a profound realization dawned upon him. A curious meld of joy for the couple and a reflective contemplation on the path his spirit had traveled so far, both as a human and in his present form. The wedding, a beautiful depiction of second chances and renewed beginnings, kindled a flame of hope in Alex. Could there be a second chance awaiting him? Could his diligent assistance and heartfelt efforts to help Lisa be his ticket to ascension, his pathway to the heavens that awaited with open arms?

As the day matured, Beatrice had moved along, her spirit lifted, and heart warmed by the witnessing of the beautiful ceremony. The holiday market at the southern end of Central Park was vibrant, alive with the spirit of the season. Amidst stalls adorned with twinkling fairy lights and the captivating aroma of fresh pine wreaths and baked goods, Beatrice found herself absorbed in the festive spirit, purchasing intricate ornaments, a jar of homemade cranberry sauce, and a set of hand-knitted mittens, gifts that bore the personal touch of those who crafted them with love and care. With a heart full of joy and a bag filled with delightful finds, she returned home, the snow crunching under her feet echoing the rhythmic heartbeat of a day that celebrated love and unity in the most enchanting manner. As she settled into her rocking chair to read Alex slipped out into the garden.

Alex, now with a few hours at his disposal, chose to head towards the park, a place that had witnessed countless reflections and shared stories of the Alice Gang. The fresh layer of snow seemed to have added a layer of quietude, a tranquility that draped the surroundings as he made his way to their usual rendezvous point.

Upon his arrival, he noticed the rest of the Alice Gang already assembled, their fur slightly dusted with snow, giving them a somewhat mystical appearance. Spiffy was wearing a green winter doggy jacket.

"Hey Spiffy," said Spike. "You look like one of Santa's elves."

"Go on," he said. "Make fun of the little dog. At least I am not cold."

"You don't have a heavy coat of fur like Sally and I," said Pippa. "Even Alex has a thick layer. It's just you and Spike with the flat coat."

"Hey," said Alex pausing, "I have some great news to share."

"Go on," said Sally. "Don't keep us in suspense."

"Guess who I saw at the church over by the holiday market getting married today?" said Alex.

"Oh, me, me, me," said Spike.

"It's not a contest Spike," said Alex. "I saw Lisa and Justin getting married."

"Really?" exclaimed Sally. "My word, that was fast!"

"I agree," said Alex. "Guess it was true love."

Pippa slapped Alex on the back with her paw and said, "See, I think you just earned your wings."

"I'm not sure," said Alex. "But it sure feels good to do a good deed."

Alex embarked upon the narrative, recounting the morning's events with a reverence that the event warranted. Each detail was lovingly portrayed – the joyous atmosphere that pervaded the area around the Holy Trinity Lutheran Church, the luminous smiles of Lisa and Justin, and the twinkling sparklers that seemed to be streaks of starlight brought down to earth to grace the human festivities. As he ended the story that highlighted the event of the morning, he sighed in relief. This was something he wanted for her when he was human, it took being a dog to finally contribute to her happiness.

In the hushed sanctuary of the park, under the soft, wintery sky, the Alice Gang realized this unspoken agreement bore a weight unlike any they had had before. The sighting of the blissful couple, amidst an ambiance of renewed beginnings and fresh hopes, had left a resounding chord in each of them.

Alex broke the solemnity of the past several minutes first, his voice wavering slightly as he said, "Seeing Lisa and Justin today...it got me thinking about our journeys — the ones we've had and the ones that might still be ahead of us."

Each face turned, one after the other, expressions of silent agreement passing amongst them. They were not just a group of animals sharing space and time; they were beings with rich histories, with tales stretching back into years of human experiences, now brought together in their current forms with a shared longing — the eternal desire for redemption, a chance to make things right, to find a pathway to ascension.

Spike, the ever optimistic and vibrant soul, was the next to speak. "We've all had our share of mistakes, but we've also had our moments of goodness, of love. We were given this second chance for a reason, don't you think? Maybe we can find our way back to the heavens by helping others, just like Alex did with Lisa."

Sally nodded; her wisdom gleaned from years of living emanating from her. "Indeed. This world is full of opportunities, filled with individuals seeking guidance, love, or even a simple act of kindness. We have been given a precious gift – the ability to observe, understand, and influence the course of events, albeit in small ways."

Pippa chimed in, her voice holding a tinge of eagerness, "Perhaps we could be guardians, silent watchers who steer individuals towards happiness, towards the right paths. That's an idea."

Spiffy, albeit the smallest amongst them, held a heart grand with dreams. Donning his green jacket like a knight would his armor, he stated with conviction, "I want to find someone lonely, someone lost, and be their beacon of hope, their tiny little warrior fighting off despair."

"Though he be but little, he is fierce," said Alex.

"What's that, Alex?" asked Pippa.

"It's a quote from a famous poem by Shakespeare, A Midsummer Night's Dream, although I changed, she to he," said Alex.

"Oh, I love, uh, who's Shakespeare?" asked Ralph.

"Never mind," said Alex. "It's a memory from my past."

As they spoke, the park around them seemed to resonate with their noble intents, a silent witness to their shared vision. They spoke of deeds big and small, from guiding lost children home to helping reconnect old friends, from protecting other animals to simply being there, a comforting presence for someone in need.

Each member brought forth ideas rooted deeply in their understanding of human emotions and complexities, leveraging lessons from the visions of their past lives to envision deeds that could potentially offer them a road to redemption. The circle was a riot of hopes, a symposium of dreams forged from their individual yet now shared desires for redemption. It was a rich mosaic of perspectives, each contributing to a broader vision, a plan that harbored potential paths of kindness, of light.

Alex, his spirit engulfed in the fervent exchanges, found himself silently committing to this path of hope and righteousness. He felt a surging kinship, a bond strengthened by the purity of their intent. This group of unique individuals had become a family, tied not by blood but by shared experiences and a united front in their quest for redemption. It was a plan born not just of personal desires for redemption but of a collective dream to bring goodness, to bring light into the world.

As the gang dispersed, with a pact sealed in heartfelt determination and a shared vision of better tomorrows, the snowy park bore witness to the inception of a noble journey. A journey of second chances, a journey of redemption forged in goodwill and a promise to be forces of kindness in a world that still held beauty, still cradled hope in its snowy embrace.

Each member returned to their respective homes or in Dale's case, his cardboard box in the alley near Beatrice's and Alex's home. They stood ready to embark upon individual quests tethered to a unified, noble objective – to earn their ascension.

# the artist in the park

The Alice Gang reconvened under the perpetual witness of the Alice statue in Central Park, their energetic and vibrant collective pulsating with stories ripe for sharing. Each individual brought with them a rich mosaic of experiences gathered over the week, tales sprinkled with goodwill, adventure, and the vibrant colors of humor. Alex, Spiffy, Spike, Sally, Dale, Ralph, and Pippa each carried a sparkling twinkle in their eyes, a mirror reflecting their exciting and sometimes hilarious ventures in the spirited pursuit of ascension.

As they huddled closely under the statuesque guidance of Alice, Alex initiated the round of story-sharing with a jovial nudge towards Spiffy. Spiffy, with a spring in his step, jumped to the fore, eager to share his latest adventure. The gathering braced themselves for an account teeming with Spiffy's customary enthusiasm and, perhaps, an overabundance of protective zeal.

"So, get this," Spiffy started, painting a vivid picture with wildly gesticulated paws, "I was guarding this squirrel, right? Picture this tiny creature, furiously munching away, completely unaware of the vast dangers of the park!"

The group chuckled as Spiffy detailed the squirrel's nonchalant demeanor, disregarding an exaggerated list of dangers Spiffy had conjured, including potential bird attacks and squirrel nappings. Spike interrupted with a teasing question, "Oh Spiffy, was it a secret agent squirrel on a top-secret mission?"

The group erupted in laughter as Spiffy played along, adding layers of espionage and dramatic flair to his tale. The park around them came alive in their imagination, transforming into a ground for secret squirrel missions with Spiffy as their designated guardian.

As laughter subsided, Pippa gracefully took her turn, sharing a heartwarming tale sprinkled with a touch of humor. "I helped this tiny human, barely knee-high, find her way back to her mom. But you won't believe how she thanked me!"

A ripple of intrigue spread as Pippa narrated how the grateful toddler offered her a very soggy, half-eaten cookie as a token of gratitude, a gesture so innocent and pure yet undeniably funny. Ralph couldn't resist asking, "Did you take a bite, Pippa?"

With a mock serious expression, Pippa retorted, "Well, one does not simply reject a gift offered with such heartfelt gratitude, does one?" before breaking into a heartwarming smile that echoed the pure and innocent spirit of the young child she had assisted.

As they wandered through the park, each sharing their experiences in turn, the area seemed to embody their joyous friendship, each tree and shrub playing audience to their tales filled with laughter and light. Spike shared an amusing anecdote about a playful encounter with a jogger, involving a shoe that seemingly 'accidentally' ended up in his mouth. The group visualized the startled jogger hopping on one foot, Spike's expression of feigned innocence, and the subsequent chase that ensued, followed by laughter from the group.

Sally, with a motherly glow, narrated her tale of assisting a young fledgling struggling with its first flight, adding a delightful spin as she mimicked the bird's clumsy yet determined flaps with her paws. The reenactment had the gang in splits, as they envisaged the earnest yet comically struggling fledgling under Sally's encouraging 'wings'.

"The little guy just wouldn't listen," said Sally. "It wasn't long before his mother showed up and pecked me on the rear end."

"Tora, Tora, Tora," cried Ralph. "A dive-bombing bird with a direct hit."

The group busted out in laughter as Dale stepped up to tell his story. With a theatrical flair, recounted a whimsical tale of ushering a chaotic ensemble of ducks across a busy pathway, a mission that transformed into a comical parade as he navigated the indecisive ducks amidst human spectators amused at the charming yet chaotic sight. They laughed at the visual of Dale acting like a spirited marching band leader for a group of whimsically marching ducks.

Ralph took the stage ceremoniously next, sharing a tale filled with an overzealous sense of duty as he stood guard over his owner's new baby, assuming the role of a vigilant guardian against a perceived yet entirely absent threat posed by a nearby butterfly. The mental image of stern and protective Ralph being distracted by a butterfly brought forth a burst of laughter from the group, a picture of endearing vulnerability coupled with a heightened sense of duty.

"It landed on my nose," said Ralph. "It tickled, and I started turning around but it would not leave. My owners were in stitches trying to grab their phones and snap a photo."

"Headline, dog attacked by butterfly, story at five," said Sally as the group busted out in laughter.

"Better watch out, might be on the front of that paper they sell on the street," said Spike.

Alex moved to the center and shared how he comforted Beatrice at home.

"Yea, I was laying in the studio while she was painting. She received a phone call, and what I could make out was that an old dear friend passed away," he said.

"Awe, how terrible," said Sally.

"Yea," Alex replied, "She went upstairs to the sofa and began to cry. I followed her up and sat next to her on the sofa and put my head in her lap."

She said, "Oh, Pierre, thank you for sympathy. My dear old friend passed away. I have known her for over 50 years."

"It was heart breaking," said Alex., "but she seemed to appreciate my gesture and later that evening she toasted her friend with a glass of wine on the patio."

As they shared and laughed, inquiring, and adding delightful embellishments to each other's tales, a rich assortment of their experiences unfurled amidst the vibrant backdrop of Central Park. Eventually, they returned full circle to the Alice statue, their laughter echoing through the park, shared adventures in pursuit of life's light-hearted moments.

At the conclusion of their joyful story exchange and return to the Alice statue they noticed a figure busily engaged in a vibrant act of creation. It was a woman of a senior age, with an easel delicately positioned under the mighty oak tree that graced their meeting area. Beside her stood a small rolling suitcase, an intelligent solution harboring all her painting necessities for easy mobility.

The artist was deeply absorbed in her work, her brush dancing gracefully on the canvas, painting bright and loving strokes that captured the serene beauty of the Alice statue. The sun played artistically on her canvas, lending life to her creation with its rays produced by her skillful hands. Her presence brought an added depth of artistry and warmth to the park, mirroring the fantastic tales the gang had told just moments before.

Alex's heart leaped with recognition and joy as he realized that the artist was none other than Margaret, a cherished friend of Beatrice's, who had graced their home with her presence on numerous occasions. Memories flooded in, each visit of Margaret marked with a gesture of love — a new toy or a delightful treat, creating a gallery of joyful recollections in Alex's mind.

Turning to the gang, his eyes sparkling with fondness, Alex shared, "That's Margaret, a dear friend of Beatrice's. She visits us often, and you know, she always brings along a delightful surprise, either a treat or a toy. She has a heart as warm as her art is vibrant."

"Oh, I hope she doesn't notice that it is me," Alex said. "I will be in big trouble."

"Just act like a stray," said Pippa. "She probably never suspects that her friend would let you just wander around."

As if on cue, Margaret looked up from her canvas, her eyes landing on the animated gathering that was the Alice Gang. A smile spread across her face, a reflection of kind-hearted recognition and tender affection as she acknowledged the group with a gentle nod.

Margaret's artist's eye couldn't help but be captivated by the gathering before her. The rich variety and color of their fur, the animated expressions, and the evident friendship they shared — all of it painted a live scene more enchanting than any canvas could hold. She found herself intrigued, even amused, by the apparent rich discussion, although incomprehensible, happening among the spirited group, a scene so full of life and zest that it breathed life into her artistic soul.

The atmosphere became infused with a creative and affectionate energy as she continued to observe them. As Margaret surveyed her canvas, a burst of inspiration danced in her eyes, lighting them up with a playful spark. She realized that the group before her would breathe life, charm, and mystic into her portrayal of the Alice statue. However, to capture their true essence, she needed them to strike poses that were natural and joyful, embodying their playful and spirited nature.

A brilliant idea bloomed in Margaret's mind as she delved into her suitcase, pulling out a white paper-wrapped sandwich. A knowing smile adorned her face, hinting at the delightful plan brewing in her creative mind. The Alice Gang watched with curious eyes and twitching noses, their attention honed in on the mysterious parcel as Margaret unwrapped it to reveal a tempting turkey sandwich. The park's atmosphere became alive with eager anticipation, a delicious aroma wafting through the air, drawing them closer with an almost magnetic force.

The group exchanged enthusiastic glances as Margaret lovingly broke the sandwich into generous pieces, placing a share before each member of the gang. The alluring scent of turkey coupled with the kind and inviting gesture turned the space around the Alice statue into a banquet of joy and laughter, encapsulating the very essence of friendship and spontaneous joy Margaret wished to capture on her canvas.

As they settled down to enjoy the treat, a chorus of animated commentary erupted, tinged with quirky remarks and hilarious observations. Alex, with an expression of sheer bliss, mused aloud, "Oh, this might just be the finest banquet under the Alice statue yet!" while Ralph, ever the protector, kept a vigilant eye on the surroundings even as he nibbled, ensuring the safety of their little feast.

Spiffy was all praises for Margaret, stating emphatically, "She's not just an artist with paints, but with sandwiches too!" He was on a roll, offering generous, exaggerated compliments that had everyone chuckling.

Dale brought in a touch of theatrical commentary, likening the sandwich to a royal feast, and each bite a narrative of culinary artistry, while Sally gently reminded everyone to eat properly, motherly concern reflecting in her kind eyes, even as she herself could not stop the joyous trembles that each bite invoked.

Spiked amused everyone with his playful antics, pretending to find a "secret message" in his portion, drawing out the fun with a series of "aha!" and "oh, what's this?" that had everyone grinning from ear to ear.

Pippa was the picture of grace, enjoying her share with poised delight, and adding with a wink, "Well, this is indeed a delightful twist to our adventures today, isn't it?"

As the gang engaged in their animated, joy-filled banter, they were unaware of the careful, loving strokes Margaret was making on her canvas. She seized the moment of delightful chaos to sketch the Alice Gang's vibrant personalities into her painting using her pencil, their joyous laughter, the sparkling friendship, and the playful banter finding a forever home on her canvas. There was not enough time to fully paint the group.

Through the dance of her pencil, their playful, individual personalities came alive beneath the Alice statue. When she was finished, and just in time as Dale darted off to chase a mouse, she started packing up her paints and supplies, folding her easel and preparing to leave. The group took that as the signal they could scamper off, before she really noticed that Alex was the black poodle in the frame.

They watched Margaret leave from the other side of the bushes behind the statue.

"Wow, that was a close one," said Alex. "I better get home before Beatrice realizes I am gone."

Alex and the gang ran off in the direction of their homes, hopeful that the acts of kindness they attempted would be noticed by the Recycling Center and pave the way to their redemption.

Alex, tired and panting sneaked into the house and headed straight to his favorite place to lay, under the coffee table. It wasn't more than a few minutes when Beatrice, with hands nurturing and tender, ascended from her art sanctuary into the familiar embrace of her living room, where she headed to the kitchen to make a cup of fresh tea. She halted mid-step as her eyes caught the tranquil sight of Alex nestled under the coffee table, basking in a warm sunbeam that found its way through the living room window. A tender smile adorned her face, reflecting the warmth illuminating Alex as she whispered, "Awe, sleeping in a sunbeam." The serenity enveloped the room, a testament to the deep bond shared between the two.

Transitioning to a gentle ritual, she brewed herself a comforting cup of tea, a symphony of steam spiraling upwards, intertwining with the sunlight filtering through the kitchen window. Easing onto the sofa, Beatrice settled into her afternoon rhythm, embracing the simplistic joy that the company of her favored soap operas brought her.

The following morning was ushered in with a symphony of wind, blustering through the naked trees, announcing a wintry spectacle of expected snowfall that aimed to blanket the city in a clean, pristine six-inch layer of white. As Beatrice navigated through her early routines, a knock resounded at the door.

As the door swung open, a beaming Margaret greeted her, cradling a large, framed painting shrouded in paper, its essence further shielded by a luxurious velvet cover that hinted at the treasures within. Excitement and curiosity danced in her eyes as she recounted the meeting with the Alice Gang amidst the backdrop of Central Park, her suspicion growing stronger that Alex had been the enigmatic black poodle that had graced the gathering with his presence.

"Hi Margaret," said Beatrice. "How have you been?"

"Wonderful," said Margaret. "Let me tell you. I was in the park yesterday painting, and I could swear that the black poodle in my painting was Pierre. He looked just like him."

However, Beatrice shook her head, her voice infused with loving conviction as she assured Margaret, "It couldn't have been him; he was asleep all morning under the coffee table, bathing in his favorite sunbeam." Margaret's insistence met with Beatrice's firm, yet affectionate denial, painting a picture of Pierre's serene morning spent in the comfort of their home.

With anticipatory hands, Margaret slowly unveiled her labor of love, pulling back layers to reveal a canvas full with life, a meeting of joyful souls captured in an aura of warm sunlight giving way to a dreamy twilight canvas. The painting showcased the Alice Gang in their vivacious element, each member delineated with meticulous detail that brought a lifelike essence to their playful poses.

Underneath the wise watch of the Alice statue, the painting depicted their spirit, each member encapsulated in a day to night transition, a gradient of golden rays descending into tones of gray, gradually succumbing to a rich canvas of night, sprinkled generously with twinkling stars. Margaret explained her artistic choice with a voice tinged with reverence, "I added the nighttime sky because there was something truly heavenly about them, almost as if they were divine souls enjoying a day under the sun."

"I want you to have it," said Margaret. "One, I don't have room for it, besides, since there is a black poodle in it, perhaps you can assume it's Alex with his friends. It will make a good conversation piece."

"Oh, thank you Margaret," said Beatrice. "It's a beautiful painting. I never thought about painting the Alice Statue before. What a wonderful choice you made."

Beatrice, with eyes shimmering with emotion, could not deny the evocative beauty before her, a work painted with threads of joy, friendship, and a touch of heavenly allure, it spoke to the viewer on a profound level. Despite her previous convictions, a part of her, a tiny, whimsical part, dared to entertain the enchanting possibility that Alex had indeed embarked on a magical adventure, dancing under the day sun and twinkling night stars with the spirited Alice Gang. The painting stood as a testimony to a moment of pure, unbridled joy, a celestial dance of souls bathed in both sun and starlight, a blend of day's warmth and night's serene mystery, a canvas bearing the imprints of heavenly souls enjoying a terrestrial frolic, a snapshot of joy unfurling under the affectionate gaze of the Alice statue, caught between realms, yet absolutely real in their joy and companionship.

A couple of days later, Alex lit out to find the gang and tell them about the painting. He wanted them to see it. A fresh canvas of snow greeted the world, a pristine layer that crunched softly underfoot as it bore witness to the flurry of tiny paw prints marking a path of camaraderie and eager anticipation. Leading the charge was Alex, his adventurous spirit undeterred by the snowy carpet that blanketed the surroundings. The Alice Gang congregated with an undercurrent of exhilaration, intrigued by the urgent summons from Alex who beckoned them with tales of a magical portrait, a snapshot of a moment frozen in time that now adorned Beatrice's living room wall.

With little hearts pulsating in harmony with the rhythmic dance of falling snowflakes, they forged a path through the white wonderland, eventually reaching the welcoming abode that bore the embodiment of their joyous essence on canvas. In a stealthy procession, they snuck into the warm interior of Beatrice's home, drawn magnetically towards the painting that hung with grace and elegance on the living room wall above the sofa.

There it was, a rich depiction of life and laughter, a masterstroke that exhibited the imprints of their shared adventures. They circled around, transfixed by the vivid shades that danced across the canvas, their own animated forms brought to life through Margaret's skilled hands. Their mesmerized silence gave way to a ripple of laughter as they began noticing the intricate details, the playful nuances that captured their energetic personalities so perfectly.

Ralph couldn't resist a good-natured jab at Pippa, teasing her for the exaggerated elegance of her portrayed stance, while Sally, in turn, faced mock scolding for seeming to steal a larger portion of the sandwich although there wasn't a sandwich in the painting. The room buzzed with laughter, playful nudges, and jovial jests as each of them found humor in the caricatured exaggerations.

Yet, amidst the laughter, a shared wonder blossomed as they lifted their gazes to the starry canopy that adorned the upper reaches of the canvas. A ripple of reflective silence engulfed them as they pondered the possibility of Margaret having glimpsed deeper, recognizing the celestial journey woven in their earthly sojourns, their spirits in pursuit of redemption under the benevolent gaze of the stars.

This poignant moment of contemplation was abruptly interrupted by the familiar creaking of steps, a precursor to Beatrice's approach, as she ventured to refill her coffee cup. Panic ensued, a synchronized chaos as the group dispersed in a frantic search for hiding spots within the warm and welcoming confines of Beatrice's home. Spiffy found refuge behind a tall vase, while others ducked under furniture and behind curtains, transforming the space into a hide-and-seek playground pulsating with suppressed giggles and muffled whispers.

Beatrice entered, blissfully unaware of the lively hide-and-seek championship unfolding in her living room, her focus consumed by the embrace of her coffee cup. A dance of shadows played across the room, a delightful secret shared between the Alice Gang and the sun passing behind the clouds as they watched Beatrice from their clever hiding spots.

Eventually, Beatrice retreated, her footsteps fading away as she descended back into the comforting embrace of her art studio, leaving behind a lingering fragrance of fresh coffee. This signaled the end of their indoor adventure, and one by one, the group emerged from their hiding spots, sharing whispered giggles and playful nudges as they recounted their close shave with discovery.

With hearts full and spirits rejuvenated, the Alice Gang navigated towards the exit, venturing back into the winter wonderland that awaited them. A world cloaked in a blanket of fresh snow. They dispersed with a jubilant spirit, leaving behind a delicate imprint of their presence, a playful dance of paw prints embellishing the pristine snow, a transient testimony to their joyous rendezvous and a promise of many more adventures to unfold under the benevolent gaze of the starry heavens above.

# dreams and echoes

Christmas came and went followed by the New Years and the terror each member felt upon hearing the fireworks celebrating the new year. January held new depths of cold as several nor'easters plowed through the city that month. Each member of the Alice Gang found themselves snuggled into their chosen spots in their homes. Alex in his chaise lounge, Spiffy, aka "Taco" in a small bed in the shape of a taco, the others in comfortable places on couches, beds, and rugs, and of course, Dale curled up in his cardboard box in the alley.

A peculiar sensation began to envelop them; a deep tranquility that was both alien and familiar enveloped them, coaxing them into a deeper state of sleep than usual. Each of them could feel an invisible thread, tender and warm, joining them together in the intricate setting of dreams, bridging distances and blurring the lines between reality and the ephemeral dream world.

And as their eyes closed and their breathing became synchronized with the gentle hum of the wind outside, a magical dreamscape began to unfold, a realm where the subconscious minds could roam free, unburdened by the physical confines of their daytime world.

The stood together in their meeting spot. The Alice statue, which had stood silent witness to their daily exploits, transformed into a living entity in this dreamscape, an enigmatic guide leading them through a landscape that bore a strange resemblance to Central Park, yet stretched and contorted in surreal ways. Pathways spiraled into the sky, trees whispered secrets into their ears, and familiar landmarks took on mystical, shifting forms, offering doors to deeper layers of the dream world.

Their dream-selves congregated near the breathing, pulsating version of the Alice statue, now a beacon of light and a nexus of their collective consciousness. With heightened senses, they could feel each other's emotions, desires, fears, and hopes echoing in the space that connected them.

In the ethereal haven of their dream world, the members of the Alice Gang found themselves at ease, enveloped by an environment that encouraged openness and fostered deep connections. The landscape around them was ever shifting, reflecting the innermost recesses of their souls, and presenting an external canvas where their deepest desires and fears were welcomed with understanding and empathy.

As they settled in a circle under the caring gaze of the sentient Alice statue, a blue orb of light surrounded them, fostering a safe and secure space for the confessions to begin. The atmosphere was charged with a tender energy, an unspoken agreement of trust binding them in this vulnerable moment.

Ralph was the first to speak, his voice trembling yet determined as he opened up about his deepest wish.

"I...I always wanted to fly," Ralph confessed, his voice breaking as he articulated a dream he had never voiced aloud. His eyes carried a distant longing, a dream so powerful yet unattainable. "Every time I see birds soaring in the sky, I feel this... this pull, a desire to join them, to feel the wind beneath me and to see the world from above, unbounded and free."

The group listened, their eyes soft with an understanding, their spirits sending waves of empathy and encouragement. It was a simple wish, yet it echoed with a deep yearning for freedom, a primal desire that resonated with everyone present.

Sally, moved by Ralph's vulnerability, took a deep breath before sharing her own secret, one she had kept locked away, buried deep within her soul. The blue orb around them seemed to pulse, as if encouraging her to share her burden with her trusted friends.

"I have always been terrified of water," she said softly, her voice carrying a tremble that echoed the deep fear living within her. "In my past life, I... I faced a water tragedy. I remember when I was a child, the overwhelming sense of dread, the cold water swallowing me, stealing my breath away..." Sally paused, her breath hitching as she fought back tears.

The group rallied around her, their energies converging to create a warm, comforting embrace, a gentle buffer against the cold memories that haunted her. The dream realm responded to her distress, the blue orb growing brighter, more comforting, cradling Sally in a nurturing embrace.

"How is it we remember more of our human life," asked Ralph. "Is this a lingering effect from our magic wildflower experience?"

Just as he finished his question, the entity of the Alice Statue spoke. "Don't be afraid, here in the dreamscape you remember everything."

The group began asking questions to the entity, but received no answer, only its ominous gaze, both comforting and frightening.

The group turned their attention back to each other. There was a beautiful solidarity in their shared vulnerability, a deeper bond forming as they each took turns sharing their deepest desires and fears, no matter how profound or frivolous they seemed. The space felt safe, almost sacred, as they allowed themselves to be seen in their full complexity, their dreams and fears validated by the empathetic ears of their friends.

Alex then shared a frightful dream when he was a child of his parent's divorce and being raised by his father, an unforgiving and hard man, and his desire to reconnect with his mother, whom he never saw again.

And thus, they continued, unraveling the threads of their truths, desires, and fears, deepening their connections, and finding in each other a safe harbor for their souls to rest, to heal, and to dream together, baring their souls to each other in the purest form of friendship, fortified and enriched by the magical haven of their collective dreams.

With each nightly meeting in the dream realm, the Alice Gang grew closer, learning to navigate this shared space with a growing sense of wonder and openness. As they ventured deeper into their dreams, guided by the now sentient Alice statue, they stumbled upon realms of breathtaking beauty, fields of luminescent flowers that hummed with life, rivers that flowed with melodies so sweet it could heal the deepest of wounds.

Yet the dreamscape also held sections of haunting shadows, spaces where their deepest fears and insecurities took form, forcing them to confront the echoes of their past lives, the regrets, and the unfulfilled desires. It was a place of healing and understanding, a sacred space where they could work through the pains that still clung to them, scars from past lives that needed to be acknowledged and released.

And as morning approached, pulling them gently from the embrace of the dreamscape, they awoke with a profound sense of connection, a new layer of understanding enriching their bond. The park would hold a new magic, a deeper resonance, as if the dream had imbued their waking world with a touch of the mystical, the surreal.

As they opened their eyes to greet the new day, they each realized that it had been a dream, they were still snuggled up in their beds, confused but enlightened by the dream they experienced.

In the vivid daylight, the Alice Gang congregated again under the familiar shade of the oak tree, with the Alice statue casting a gentle gaze upon them. They all seemed to wear expressions of bewilderment mixed with wonder, a residue of the transcendental experience that unfolded in the dream realm.

Spiffy was the first to break the silence, his eyes wide and voice tinged with awe. "You guys won't believe the dream I had last night.

It felt so... real, almost as if it wasn't a dream at all., you were all there and the Alice Statue was alive." He paused, trying to gather words to describe the surreal experience.

Alex chimed in, his face lighting up with realization, "Wait a minute, I think I had the same dream. We were all there, and we were sharing our deepest fears and desires." He looked around, his eyes meeting similar nods of agreement and dawning understanding from the others.

Sally's eyes widened, "Yes, yes, exactly! I've never experienced anything like that before. It felt like we were all connected on a different level, understanding and feeling each other's emotions." She recounted with her eyes gleaming with wonder.

A murmur of agreement rippled through the group, as they began to share and compare notes on the dream, their expressions oscillating between wonder and apprehension. The dream had revealed sides of them that were both beautiful and painfully raw, yet here they were, back in the waking world, still united, still together. It was clear that their bonds had deepened, the dream serving as a mysterious yet beautiful conduit that connected their souls more intimately than ever before.

As they were engrossed in the passionate discussion, a sudden rustling noise interrupted them. They turned to see a rather comic sight unfolding before them. Spike and Dale emerged from the bushes, with a tremendously long chain of sausages dangling between them. The duo was involved in a hilarious episode, each holding one end of the sausage string in their mouths, each trying to guide the chain of sausages without tripping over it as they approached the group.

The sight was so absurd, so delightful, that it immediately brought a round of laughter and joyous shouts from the group. Even the serious and deep conversation couldn't withstand the infectious hilarity of the sausage-chained duo, who had managed to steal the sausages from Billy's Hot Dog cart, bringing a piece of delightful chaos to their gathering.

"Sausage!" cried Ralph. "My favorite."

Spike and Dale laid the chain of sausages in the center of the group and Dale said, "Eat up, we need to dispose of the evidence."

The gang jumped in and grabbed a sausage to eat.

With Spike and Dale joining in, the conversation took a lighter turn, slightly muffled due to mouths full of sausage. The group inquired to Spike and Dale if they had the same dream last night which they both validated. They started sharing bits and pieces of the dream, Spike expressing his secret desire to be a hero, saving others in dramatic, daring rescues, while Dale shared a whimsical desire to create a sculpture so large it could be seen from space.

The atmosphere became a delightful mix of deep revelations and light-hearted banter, accompanied by the munching of sausages. The group embraced both the profound connections formed in the dream and the simple, unadulterated joy of the moment. The contrast between the deep, mystical shared dream experience and the delightful chaos of the sausage heist perfectly encapsulated the essence of their friendship.

As another day past and evening commenced, the Alice Gang found themselves once more slipping into the grasp of the shared dream. The dream landscape mirrored their familiar surroundings but carried a deeper intensity, shadows stretching long and eerie under the spectral moonlight. The air was thick with anticipation as the dream unfolded to reveal the iconic Alice statue, surrounded by the mysterious blue orb that pulsated gently with a beckoning light.

The stood outside of the orb, each member of the gang felt a strange pull towards the orb, a calling that vibrated deep within their souls. The statue communicated, "One by one you will step into the light, you will confront your greatest fears, the ghosts of your past and the very events that bound your spirits in chains."

An expression of fear appeared on each face of the gang. A collective sigh could be heard echoing in the group.

One by one, with hesitant steps, they entered the orb. Inside, the world transformed, bending to reflect their previous human incarnations in ethereal forms, flickering with a fragile, luminous glow. The dreamscape shifted for each individual, revealing haunting scenes from their past lives, moments of despair, failure, and loss that had scarred their souls deeply.

Ralph stepped in first. His image of a tall man in a chef's coat found himself in the midst of a furious storm, his ethereal wings flapping wildly as he struggled against the fierce winds that threatened to pull him apart. The figure of a man, his father, yelling at him, and he at his co-workers who were cowering around. It was a fierce representation of his inner turmoil, his fear of losing control, yet in a boat below him, a young woman, the love that was never reciprocated, calling his name. The group encouraged him to fly down with the wind and rescue her. Just as he turned around with the wind, he found himself back as a dog.

He lowered his head in shame and said, "Now, I understand. When I went one way, I should have gone the other way."

Sally was next. Upon stepping into the orb, she found herself in her human form, long flowing brown hair, and a beautiful dress on stage in a comedy club. Television cameras around her capturing the show, broadcasting it to millions. In the back, a handsome man in slack and golf shirt holding hands with two beautiful grade schoolgirls, both will long flowing black hair wearing identical flowered dressing. She could barely see them from the stage due to the spotlight that shone in her face, a symbol of her blindness, her lack of vision to her family.

The scene cuts away to a hospital where a doctor informs her that she has stage 1 breast cancer. The next night, she books a four-month tour of North America with a noted headliner. The group urging her to go for treatment, She turns around to go back into the doctor's office to get treatment, but the door leads to the stage of the comedy club. The scene cuts to after the tour, the doctor informs her she now has stage 4 breast cancer, asking her why, when they diagnosed her condition months before, did she not seek treatment. She was informed that she only had three months left to live. Then the image of her girls standing next to her hospital bed, barely tall enough to see their mother, moments before she passed away.

The scene was far more vivid than in the cave with the wildflower pollen. It wasn't like watching a movie, she was actually reliving the experience. Sally broke down and cried again.

"It's ok, Sally," said Alex. "This time you made the right decision."

"I really miss my husband and girls," she said, "I hope they have forgiven me; I don't know how I can say this now, only remembering recently, but it's so painful."

Each faced a scenario equally terrifying, yet with the encouraging presence of the others at the periphery of their consciousness, they found the courage to confront their fears head-on. With every victory over fear, the ethereal forms of the members shone brighter, their luminous glow intensifying as they forged deeper connections, their bonds strengthening with the knowledge of each other's vulnerabilities and the shared experience of overcoming them.

Pippa faced a drug addition with images of hypodermic needles chasing her while pain pills blocked her way. Spike was shown the day he skipped training, instead this time, attempted to leave before it started to attend the training he miss that cost the life of a young boy. Dale in turn, found himself eager to write his own material, knowing that he had enough life experience to make it on his own without depriving other people of the spotlight.

When Alex stepped into the orb, he found himself again at the art exhibition, having a cocktail and mingling with colleagues. When time came for donations, this time he tried to write a check, putting down his drink and saying he didn't need any more alcohol.

Last was Spiffy. He stepped into the orb, and nothing happened. The blue orb started to pulse rapidly and then not at all. He stepped out of the orb and said, "Strange, I didn't see anything."

Alex said," That's the second. time to find out they might have made a mistake with you."

Just as the were about to discuss what had happened that night, they awoke the next morning in their beds, confused by the abrupt end to their dream and eager to rejoin the group to assess what had happened.

That morning after their owners went to work, the Alice Gang assembled once again in their cherished meeting spot, each bearing the weight of vivid, evocative memories freshly etched in their minds from the shared dreamscape that had become a setting for their deepest fears and desires.

They gathered close, their faces mirroring a somber understanding, a shared vulnerability that spoke of experienced truths and unearthed secrets. Each carried a glimpse into the others' soul, having ventured into the landscape of their deepest fears and most fervent desires; a sacred space where spirits bare all.

With careful, respectful tones, they initiated a discussion, a collective therapy of sorts as they navigated the remnants of the dream that clung to their memories. Alex, with a reflective demeanor, broached the subject of the ethereal transformations they had undergone, the visions of their former human selves that had played out in the vivid theatre of the dream world.

A profound understanding shimmered in their eyes as they gathered, now knowing that their journey towards redemption was entwined, a path forged with collective strength and empathy.

Ralph initiated the sharing, his voice wavering as he recounted his ethereal voyage through a tempestuous storm. A vivid tableau of fear and misplaced priorities relived with the backdrop of a furious storm, haunted by past decisions. The tumultuous sky echoed the turmoil within him as he navigated a space torn between his demanding father and the unreciprocated love calling for him from a boat below. Ralph recounted how the dream vision of his friends encouraged him to soar downwards, to choose the path of love over conflict. He returned as a dog with an understanding, a realization of the directions not taken, haunted by the lost opportunity to choose love over anger. His eyes moist, he acknowledged his error, a quiet commitment to choose differently in his spiritual journey henceforth.

Sally took her turn with tears already welling up in her eyes. Her story unveiled a setting of vibrant stage lights and dark hospital rooms, of fame sought at the expense of health, and a family waiting in the wings. She relived the moments of standing before the glaring spotlight, blinded to the precious moments slipping away with her family. Even as the dream offered her a chance to make a different choice, to choose health and family over career, it led her back to the stage in a painful cycle of lost opportunities. Sally wept openly, her heart aching for the family left behind, her spirit yearning for redemption and forgiveness for the choices made in her past life.

The circle of sharing continued with raw, earnest narratives of fear and redemption. Pippa recounting her desperate flight from the symbolic representation of her drug addiction, a scene thick with looming needles and obstructing pills. Spike confronted the day he had shirked responsibility, a decision that had devastating consequences, but this time, encouraged by his friends, he chose to attend the crucial training. Dale found his voice within his dream, embracing self-belief and choosing not to overshadow others but to build from his life's experiences.

Alex brought them back to an art exhibition, a place of culture and sophistication, where once he had immersed himself in the intoxications of alcohol, neglecting his philanthropic duty. This time, encouraged by the dream narrative, he chose sobriety and charity over self-indulgence, a step towards atonement in his spiritual path.

Finally, it was Spiffy's turn, yet as he recounted stepping into the enigmatic blue orb, he encountered an enigma — an absence of visions, a pulsing rhythm that abruptly ceased, leaving a void of experience. The group listened with bated breath as Spiffy recounted his non-experience, a stark contrast to the distinct journeys each had undergone.

As Spiffy stepped back, puzzled and a touch disappointed, the group enveloped him, reassuring him that perhaps his journey was different, perhaps the lack of visions indicated a different path to redemption, one not tied to past fears or regrets but forward-looking, a path of possibilities yet unseen.

With each narrative, the Alice Gang found themselves drawing closer, their ethereal forms glowing with a renewed luminosity forged from shared vulnerabilities and victories over inner demons. They sat together, united in a sacred circle of understanding and empathy, their bonds strengthened through the shared journey through the labyrinthine pathways of fear and redemption in the dreamscape.

"I wonder if I'll sleep tonight," said Pippa. "I can't imagine going through that again."

"We will know by tomorrow," said Sally.

"Right, so meet up tomorrow, same time and place, and hope we have a good night's sleep," said Alex.

# the mirror of truth

As the gang reconvened under the dappled sunlight filtering through the branches overhead, there was a collective exhale of relief; the nightly dreamscape that had been their constant companion for the past two nights had remained absent in their slumbers the previous night. They gathered in quiet solace, sharing their experiences of a peaceful, uneventful night's rest, and all agreed - with a mix of relief and a faint trace of nostalgia - that that part of their journey had reached its end.

But as if the universe conspired to keep their adventure alive, Spiffy arrived late, a noticeable urgency in his pace. The others noticed the folded piece of paper he carried carefully in his mouth, and a fresh wave of curiosity surged as he narrated his morning escapade. He spoke of a menacing German Shepherd that broke free from its leash, of a chase that led him to stumble and fall into a concealed hole near the historical Greywacke Arch, which stood sentinel by the familiar softball fields.

The gang gathered around as Spiffy laid the paper down, unveiling a slightly worn and folded mystery that he had found at the bottom of his accidental haven. The group's heartbeat seemed to sync in anticipation, their recent vow to normality already fading as they eyed the piece of paper that beckoned with a siren's call to the depths of the unknown.

With reverent hands, Alex unfolded the parchment, revealing lines written in an elegant, swirling script, yet tinged with the weight of age. It was a riddle that sung of secrets hidden under the cold grasp of January, of an ancient pathway cradled by silent trees, and a beacon of lunar light that promised guidance through shadowy realms to an age-old sentinel holding truths untold.

Alex read the letter to the group,

"Under January's freeze, a secret rests,

There a path that time forgot,
Seek the time when the full Wolf moon peers,
And lights the night with lunar spears.
In shadow's grace, where silence basks,
Find the ancient obelisk, a sentinel from time,
With cryptic tales in stone it asks,
To unveil truth beneath its mask.
Two thousand paces southwest tread,
Through whispers of the time long dead,
A pilgrimage through silent wood,
Where nature's heartbeat still holds good.
Find the looking glass held dear,
In hidden realms now drawing near,
A portal to the depth unswirled,
A gate to an inner, secret world.
Gaze deep within its silver pool,
A mirror in the quiet cool,
And there amidst reflections swell,
Discover true self, break the spell.
There in clarity's embrace,
Meet yourself in silent grace,
Journey's end with truth unfurled,
A revelation in the world.
Know that in this mystic place,
With open heart and tender face,
The riddle's end does truth foretell,
Within thy self, all answers dwell.
Now the path that lies ahead,
An open book where life will tread,
In inner worlds with riches rife,
Find the meaning, find your life."

A hushed stillness fell over the group as Alex's voice resonated with the last word of the riddle, the poetic lines hanging in the air like a rich fabric sewn with threads of mystery and promise. The riddle spoke of paths untrodden, and secrets buried deep within the woods, guided by a blue moon's light, and guarded by an ancient sentinel forged from stone and time itself.

Their spirits, previously hushed and at peace with the notion of the end of their mystical journey, stirred to life once more, pulsating with the lifeblood of adventure that flowed once more through their collective veins. Every member of the group felt it — a resonating chord of connection and a mounting anticipation, their hearts dancing to the beat of the mystical drum heralding the deep secrets that awaited to be unraveled.

Gathering in a tight circle, a spirited discussion ignited amongst them. With the shared objective clear, they embarked on a deliberative process, pooling together their perspectives and skills to interpret the words from a bygone era, which lay before them, eager to yield its secrets to the worthy seekers.

The mention of the 'Wolf moon' quickly took center stage in their dialogue, as Sally overheard her owners talking about it as something they could see from their balcony.

"That's tonight," Sally cried. "I heard my owners talking about it at breakfast before they went to work. They were going to go to the top of the office building to see it."

"Well, we better decipher the rest of this riddle, or we will have to wait a long time," said Alex.

As they dwelt deeper, various members of the gang brought forth interpretations of the landmarks mentioned in the riddle, using their collective experience in exploring the park as a reference.

"Ancient obelisk?" inquired Ralph. "Not sure I know of one of those. I don't even know what an obelisk is."

"Maybe it's a dragon," said Spike.

"No, you nut case," said Sally. "It's not a dragon."

"Oh," said Alex. "I know what it is. It's that tall skinny triangle thing the moved here from a land called Egypt. It's called "Cleopatra's Needle", and it's over 3,000 years old."

"Great," said Pippa. "Then we have the distance in paces, well, human paces, we will have to make up our own version of dog paces. We also have the direction; the rest of the poem is there to throw us off or just tell us what we will find."

"It says we will find our true self, truth and the meaning of life," said Alex.

And yet, in the midst of their concerted effort to unravel the mystery, there was a sacred respect for the personal journey the riddle alluded to. A journey inward, a courageous confrontation with the self that lay deep beneath the surface, untamed and pure. A mirror that held the promise of revelation and transcendence, urging them to delve into the mysterious realms within their beings. where fear danced with desire, and truth whispered in the shadows of doubt.

"All right," said Sally. "Then we go tonight."

"Don't be late," said Alex. "That means you Spike and Spiffy. Leave the hotdog and sausages at the stand. You won't need a snack."

The group scattered with plans to meet after the moon appeared in the night sky, a moon like no other moon, the brightest of all the moons that calls the howl of the wolf. It signifies new beginnings, the victory of light over darkness.

As dusk approached, the earth whispered secrets to the trees, and the wind carried tales of ancient times, of moonlit paths and hidden realms. The world around them seemed to prepare for the event, a sacred convergence of celestial forces that would guide their journey to discovery. All around, nature whispered in anticipation, the sky painting itself with the deep colors of twilight, preparing to host the rare celestial visitor.

Under the watchful eyes of starry hosts, the gang gathered again, a motley ensemble of curious hearts and spirited souls ready to undertake the night's adventure. Faces reflected the pale light emanating from the heavens, illuminating the expectation and quiet determination carved in their features.

Sally arrived first, her eyes wide with the spirit of adventure, followed by the others, who came laden with an assortment of tools they deemed necessary for their expedition. There was a palpable sense of unity as they stood together under the emerging moon, their shadows long and wavering, bearing testimony to the magic that began to unfold in the silvery tones.

Spike and Spiffy appeared just in time, having heeded Alex's admonition, and abstaining from their usual detour to the hotdog stand. The gravity of their mission had imposed a rare discipline on the duo, their faces displaying a mix of excitement and solemnity as they joined the circle, completing the congregation of eager souls ready to embark on a mystical sojourn guided by the moon's radiant light.

The first glimpse of the wolf moon rising heralded the beginning of their adventure. With hearts pounding in harmony with the rhythm of the night, they set forth, following the whispered guidelines of the riddle, their pawsteps a silent pledge to the silent grace that awaited them in the depths of the mirror of truth.

The night was alive with mystery as they moved, the moon leading them like a luminescent shepherd through The Ramble, past Greywacke Arch, and the hole that Spiffy fell into earlier in the day. Each step they took was one towards discovery, into the mystical heart of the night.

As the path unfolded in front of them, they reached the historic obelisk centered in a grove of dead trees, partially covered with snow, the water in the fountain the obelisk overlooked, frozen solid. The group oriented themselves with the park, knowing exactly what direction was South and West.

"Ok, I think we are here," Alex said.

"Well if we point southwest, we point directly to the fire department building. I can see the tower on the building reflecting in the moonlight," said Ralph.

"How do we know what a pace is," asked Spiffy.

"We walk like this," said Spike, as he took giant steps on his back legs walking upright until he tripped and fell down.

"No, Spike," said Alex. "When I walk with Beatrice on the weekend mornings, she keeps me at pace next to her. I noticed that two of my walking steps equals one of hers, so we just multiply the steps by 2 and I can walk the paces."

"Great idea," said Pippa. "You take the lead; we will watch behind you to make sure you stay on course."

Dale said, "I'm glad our doing the walking, it would take like thirty of my steps to be pace, not sure I can count that high."

And there, in the quietude of the moonlit night, where darkness met light in a silent ballet, Alex walked off four thousand dog steps in a southwest direction toward the fire station, the entire remainder of the group in tow.

As the adventure continued, the group found themselves in sync with the night's magic, their individual energies humming in quiet harmony with the pulsating glow of the moon that led them forward with a reassuring grace. The soft crunch of the snow beneath their feet whispered secrets as they meandered through the hushed woods, with each step drawing them closer to the unveiling truth.

A tacit understanding seemed to envelop the group as Alex slowed, his paces more deliberate, each step a conscious movement as the thousandth milestone approached. The silent woods bore witness as he marked the 4000th step, the soft crunch of snow underfoot resonating in the cool air, echoing a silent testament to their journey. Right there, nestled in a quiet embrace of the woods, lay the small circular outcropping of Turtle Pond, a familiar site transformed into a mystical landscape under the silvery glow.

Despite the frozen veneer that masked its surface, a pulsating glow beckoned from beneath, a faint luminescent heartbeat that rhythmically throbbed, pulsating with a dull yet irresistible call. It was as if the pond harbored a secret, concealed under the protective embrace of snow and ice, yet vibrant and alive, ready to emerge from its icy cocoon to reveal its truth.

Spiffy, bearing the spirit of courage and a heart untamed, responded to the beckoning call. With nimble steps, he ventured onto the icy canvas, a living paintbrush that brought forth the latent image hidden under the snowy layer. His playful energy, coupled with a sense of purpose, facilitated the magical unveiling as he removed the last of the snowy veil, revealing a portal that resembled a luminous mirror, encased within the frozen water.

A hushed gasp escaped the group as they watched the transformation unfold, the icy surface gaining a crystalline clarity that harbored an ethereal reflection of luminosity and grace. Even Spiffy paused, momentarily caught in the hypnotic reflection that seemed to radiate from the very depth of his being as he viewed his reflection.

As Spiffy retreated, Sally approached, a tide of anticipation passing through her. As she gazed upon the icy surface, she didn't see a physical form but a magnificent phoenix, a palette of reds dancing in harmony, representing her ever-renewing spirit and untamed vitality. The firebird also displayed her dynamic spirit, and the transformations she had yet to undergo. She met the gaze of the phoenix, recognizing the depths of her own resilience and the unyielding fire within her.

Spike took his turn, stepping forward with a heart swelling with curiosity and a gentle, unassuming grace. As he peered into the mystical mirror, he encountered a gentle yet sturdy oak tree, its branches wide and welcoming, offering shade and protection to all who sought it. The tree stood tall, roots deep into the earth, representing a deep connection to the world around him and an unspoken wisdom gathered from witnessing the cycles of life and time. Its leaves whispered secrets of harmony, understanding, and the gentle power of kindness, reflecting his role as a peacemaker, a transformation from his former gruffer personality when he ruled the dog park.

Spiffy returned, a playful light dancing in his eyes. As he gazed into the mirror, it was not a canine form that gazed back but a luminous sprite, a playful spirit of the forest, embodying curiosity, and adventurousness. The sprite darted and played, a swirl of sparkles trailing behind it, representing Spiffy's light-hearted nature and the joyous, playful spirit that animated his adventures. Yet the sprite also had depth, revealing layers of courage and resourcefulness as it navigated through the mystical realms depicted in the mirror, underscoring Spiffy's bravery and readiness to face the unknown with a heart full of wonder and joy.

Ralph and Pippa took their turns. Ralph, revealed as a creative soul, full of resilience and calm, evident by his extended stay in the animal shelter. His ethereal form, that of a mountain, time tested, sturdy, and supportive. Pippa's, that of a winged lion, courageous and graceful in flight like the ballerina she once was.

Lastly, Alex moved forward, the unofficial leader, the one who often guided the group with a steady hand. As he peered into the luminous circle, he saw not a human form but a majestic dragon, a creature of legend and lore, imbued with a spirit of nobility and wisdom. The dragon soared high, its wings enveloping the sky, a guardian of dreams and a seeker of truth, reflecting Alex's deep-seated desires to protect and guide his friends towards enlightenment and self-discovery. As the dragon glided gracefully in the reflected sky, it also portrayed a deep inner wisdom, a calm, steady force guiding him towards a destiny filled with depth and understanding. It was a powerful image, resonating deeply within Alex, igniting a silent vow to honor the majestic, wise spirit revealed to him on this magical day and not return or dwell on the being he once was that dishonored and marginalized people.

The group stood in a circle, their eyes still entranced by the magical reflections, a sacred stillness enveloping them as they silently acknowledged the profound journey within that they had just embarked upon, guided by the mirror of truth that revealed the spiritual essence residing deep within each one of them. As they stood there in this moment of reflection and reverence, the lighted circle disappeared below the ice, melting away, as if it were removing the fears that prevented them from travelling down the path of self-discovery.

"It's getting late," said Alex. "We best be off before our owners notice we are missing."

"Yea, I almost got busted last time we were out at night," said Ralph. "I had snow all over my feet, but the backyard didn't have any, They got up to check the baby and were like, "Now were did you find snow...", and before I could play puppy eyes game, they baby started crying and saved me."

They bid each other goodnight and spread out across the park, the wolf moon now disappearing behind the New York skyline, and the journey of self-enlightenment complete.

# a mistake corrected

A few days later as agreed on their schedule, the group gathered at the familiar meeting point by the iconic Alice statue. Although warmer than previous days and void of snow, a pall of uneasy silence hung heavy over them, replacing their usual lively banter. Alex was the first to break the silence, his voice echoing the concern that was etched on everyone's face.

"Spiffy's not here yet, isn't he?" he asked, his brows furrowing deeper with each passing second, his glance darting from one familiar face to another, seeking confirmation of the unspoken worry that bound them all.

Sally shook her head, her lips pressed tightly in a thin line, "No, and it's not like him to be late without any reason. Especially not after... everything we've been through."

The air felt heavier with her words, a swirling maelstrom of fear and anticipation settling in each heart as they pondered over the ominous twist their adventure seemed to be taking. Yet, amid the growing concern, Dale felt a flicker of hope ignite within him, propelled by a deep-seated belief in their bond, stronger than any adversary they might face.

"Maybe he is at home..." Dale suggested hesitantly, the slight quiver in his voice betraying the rising tide of worry gnawing at him.

The group exchanged uncertain glances, and it was Spike who finally spoke, his voice carrying a determination that steadied them all, "Then we should split up and look for him. If he's somewhere in the park, we'll find him."

Dale nodded, feeling a surge of resolve as he met Spike's steadfast gaze. "I'll check his house," Dale decided aloud, a sense of purpose guiding his steps as he set off towards Spiffy's known residence.

As they dispersed, branching out in different directions, their hearts carried a unified beat of worry and hope, intertwining in a solemn dance of amity and faith in each other. It was a promise, silent but potent, carried in each determined step as they sought to bring their friend, safe and sound.

Dale approached Spiffy's home with cautious optimism, a flicker of hope lighting up his heart with every step closer. However, as he neared, an unfamiliar yet robust barking erupted, jarring the still morning air. Dale's steps faltered as he caught sight of a black Labrador Retriever guarding the premises vehemently. Each attempt Dale made to approach was met with louder barks and fierce thuds against the window.

A heavy sense of unease settled in Dale as he retraced his steps, his mind swirling with confusion and worry. A part of him hesitated, yet the urgency pulsating from the group's anxious faces when he rejoined them propelled him to share his discovery.

"There's a new dog at Spiffy's place, a big black Labrador," Dale informed the group, his voice betraying the unsettling encounter he just had. "Every time I tried to get closer, he just... he started barking like mad, hitting the window. I didn't want to be his lunch."

A collective moment of apprehension grasped the gang, a new layer of complexity added to their unfolding drama. Alex rubbed his chin thoughtfully, a deep furrow marking his brow as he contemplated their next course of action.

"We need to find a way to talk to Spiffy without alarming that Labrador," Sally said, her sharp mind already weaving through potential strategies, her eyes flickering with a resilient spark of determination.

They gathered in a close-knit circle, voices rose and fell, intertwining in a collaborative brainstorming session, with each one offering ideas, voicing concerns, and providing reassurances. The air buzzed with the vibrant energy of unity as they focused on a singular mission, formulating a plan to reunite with their beloved friend.

After much discussion, it was decided; a stakeout was in order. The team relocated to a vantage point across the street from Spiffy's home, hearts pounding in harmonic rhythm as they kept a watchful eye on the house, awaiting the opportune moment to implement their meticulously crafted plan. Their gazes sharpened, and bodies tensed, prepared to spring into action at the right signal.

As luck would have it, the tense and silent vigil bore fruit much sooner than anyone had anticipated. Just as the afternoon started to peak through the clouds, one of Spiffy's owners appeared, fastening a leash around the Labrador's neck, and leading it out for a walk. The group exchanged quick, significant glances; their bodies charged with a sudden surge of adrenaline.

"This is it, folks. Time to make a move," Alex whispered, rallying the troops with a determined nod. With a collective breath held in suspense, they carefully approached the house, their every move calculated and silent, hearts pounding in their chests as they neared the now unguarded fortress.

The soft whispers turned into a flurry of frantic, hushed gestures, a silent dance of desperation and hope as they motioned towards the window trying to grab Spiffy's attention. It was Spike who managed to get through to him, pointing towards the backyard, his expression a vivid picture of urgency and beckoning friendship.

With hesitant steps and a clear look of confusion marking his features, Spiffy emerged from the home, drawn to the familiar yet somehow foreign faces before him. He approached the fence, his head slightly tilted in a bewildered expression as he surveyed the group that greeted him with a mix of relief and tense anticipation.

"Do I know you?" said Spiffy.

"Spiffy," Sally said. "It's us, the Alice Gang. What's up with you? Why didn't you come to the park?"

"I... I think you have the wrong dog. My name is Taco, not Spiffy," he stated with a hint of uncertainty clouding his words, his eyes darting between each face, a clear sign of inner turmoil starting to brew.

The group exchanged heavy, burdened glances before Alex took a step forward, his voice shaky yet determined as he embarked on the challenging task of finding out what was wrong with Spiffy. He looked the brown Chihuahua up and down, stared into his face and said, "I don't know what's going on, but this is not Spiffy. He looks like him, but I don't see Spiffy in him."

Alex gathered his thoughts, his voice brimming with emotion as he began to speak, "Spiffy... he had this undying curiosity, a spirit that was ever vibrant, always eager to explore the unknown. He was the brave one among us, with a heart as big as the sky itself. Spiffy carried with him a joy that was contagious, a kind of joyful rebellion that broke through the mundane. He had a way of seeing the beauty in everything, a perspective that brought light into every situation. Even in the face of danger, he carried a youthful exuberance, a zest for life that encouraged us all to live a little more fully, to seek out the adventures that lay hidden in the everyday."

The description flowed, a vivid painting of Spiffy's quirks, his joyful spirit, and his adventurous heart; a heartfelt recollection of a friend loved and missed.

Taco's eyes, growing brighter and more intense as the image of Spiffy built up in front of him. There was a moment of silence, a pause in which the world seemed to hold its breath before Taco finally spoke, his voice breaking with the weight of realization.

"I... I remember now. Bits and pieces... flashes of another life, another... well, me." Tears welled up in his eyes, a clear struggle of identity crashing within him.

It became apparent to the group that Spiffy's soul must have ascended and Taco, whomever he was in a previous life took Spiffy's canine form.

"I hate to say it," said Sally, tears welling up in her eyes. "But our friend has finally found peace in heaven. Obviously, they corrected the mistake."

"We knew that this might happen, ever since the cave with Alfred and then again at the mirror," said Pippa.

"I just wished I would have had a chance to say goodbye," said Alex.

Ralph chimed in, "I think we have to face the fact that if and when it happens to the rest of us, there will be no warning, no fanfare, no goodbyes, just poof, and you're gone."

The group remained silent, the air heavy with empathy and understanding as they allowed Taco the space to find his words. The sky seemed to mirror their mood, a gentle breeze rustling the leaves sympathetically.

Finally, Taco began, his voice tinged with an uncertain tremor, "It was... strange, you know. There was this mix-up, a kind of chaos and before I knew it, I was... here." He paused, collecting his fragmented memories before continuing, "I was supposed to continue on my journey, move towards the light that promised peace and eternity. But somehow I ended up back here, in this world, within this... new form."

His gaze seemed distant as if he were looking at something far beyond their physical realm, narrating a surreal series of events that defied the very norms of life and death. The group listened intently, their faces a canvas of complex emotions, weaving between surprise, sadness, and understanding.

The wind carried his words, filling the space with a soul-stirring narrative shown to him in the Recycling Center that spoke of the mistakes he made in life that initiated his cycle of reincarnation. As Taco narrated his return to the earthly realm, there was an undercurrent of grace, a silent acknowledgment of the strangeness of life, and the unforeseen paths it often took.

As he finished his tale, a solemn stillness enveloped them, a respectful acknowledgment of the depth of his experience. Sally broke the silence, her voice tender and reassuring, "Well, it seems life has given us a second chance to be friends, to build new memories while cherishing the old ones."

The others nodded, a resolve strengthening within them as Alex added, "And we will stand by you, Taco, helping you navigate this complex weave of old and new, of Spiffy and Taco." The sentiment echoed in their firm, supportive nods, a united front of friendship ready to face the unique journey ahead.

A beautiful balance began to form, a harmony between acceptance and the deep-seated nostalgia that resided in each of their hearts. Pippa chimed in with a hopeful smile, "Together, we will find a way to honor Spiffy's memory and accept you into our group. What do you say?"

Taco replied, "It would be nice to have friends, it gets kind of boring listening to Zues complain all day. Zues is the black Labrador, which reminds me, they will be back shortly, so you better get moving."

"Sure," said Alex. "We meet at the Alice statue in Central Park every three days unless we plan an adventure. You will need to sneak out when your owners go to work and use the board we came in through as your escape route."

And with these words, a fresh chapter in their friendship unfolded, one of rediscovery and growth, as they embraced Taco with open hearts, ready to forge a path filled with shared memories, a path that respected Spiffy's vibrant spirit and Taco's eager curiosity to embrace life anew.

A conscious choice to welcome change while honoring the past marked a new beginning, a poignant yet hopeful juncture in their journey, as they stood together under the comforting shade of the olive tree in Taco's back garden, whispers carrying promises of understanding, of adventures to come, and of a friendship reborn, as rich, and deep as the intertwining roots below.

# dance of the spirits

The surreal glow of the moon danced across Central Park, lending a silver brilliance to the dormant trees. The world felt softer, tinged with the enchantment of a moonlit night that seemed to invite whispers of magic and mystery. It was as if the moon had cast a spell over the park, summoning the Alice Gang to its luminescent stage.

They had decided to do a night meeting, slipping out as their owners went to bed, to capture more of the magic the park had previously shown them. As they assembled near their iconic meeting point, the Alice statue, a sense of wonder and anticipation united them. Dale voiced what was dancing in all of their hearts, "Do you all feel it? The park... it's like it's alive, more than ever." His eyes twinkled, reflecting the heavenly body that graced them from above.

A laugh escaped Sally as she twirled, her arms open wide, "I feel like a child again, expecting fairies to come out any moment now!" The group exchanged smiles, the magical setting encouraging them to abandon the weight of their usual worries and fears, even if just for a fleeting moment.

Newcomer, Taco said, "So, this is a night adventure."

As they ventured deeper into the park, they decided to head towards the Cherry Hill fountain and down the path to the Aaliyah Weeping Willow Tree. The very fabric of reality seemed to weave new patterns before their eyes. The shadows cast by the trees started to sway gently, even though the air was still. It wasn't long before they noticed ethereal figures timidly emerging from various elements around them.

The playful fire spirits danced gracefully amidst the flickering flames of a nearby fire pit, their forms conjuring images of fiery ballet dancers lost in a passionate performance. Pippa couldn't help but giggle at a particularly chubby fire spirit attempting to keep up with the more graceful entities. "He looks like he's having the time of his life," she remarked, her laughter infectious as the group found joy in the fire spirit's enthusiastic attempts.

Meanwhile, from the park's lake, water nymphs began to rise, their forms flowing and graceful, resonating with the calm fluidity of the water they represented. They moved harmoniously, forming intricate patterns in the air as they danced.

At the willow tree, they were greeted by gentle beings of air, swirling in harmonious dance, intertwining with the others in a delightful aerial ballet. Last but not least, spirits crafted from the very essence of the earth joined the fray, their forms sturdy and comforting, a testament to the nature of the element they represented.

The grand assembly of spirits danced in perfect harmony; an ethereal ballet orchestrated by the natural forces that cradled them. Their forms merged and separated, creating a dance that spoke of ancient rhythms and primordial connections.

Sally voiced the collective awe they were experiencing, "It's like watching the very heartbeat of the earth, the raw energy of life itself."

With eyes wide and hearts open, the Alice Gang witnessed the spirit dance, a vibrant display of the deep connections binding all elements. It was an event that transcended the mundane, offering a glimpse into the interplay of nature's most fundamental forces, wrapped in the embrace of the moonlit night. It was a dance of unity, of joy, and the cyclical dance of life and death, weaving the tale of an interconnected universe through an ancient and timeless dance.

The stage was set as elements danced in unison together, gracefully embodying the forces that governed the natural world. Each spirit carried a story, an elemental truth of existence, and as they danced, they bore their essences naked before the Alice Gang, revealing the harmony underlying the visible and invisible worlds.

The spirits of the earth moved with a grounded rhythm, each step a homage to the vast mountains and expansive lands. Their moves were powerful, confident, embodying the strength and steadiness of the earth. Their presence was comforting, a firm embrace from Mother Earth herself, offering shelter and nurturing every life within her bosom.

In contrast, the water spirits flowed with grace, their bodies undulating with a rhythmic fluidity, portraying the gentle caress of streams and the deep waves of the ocean. Their dance testified to life's currents, to change and adaptation, and the ability to carve paths through the hardest of stones with gentle persistence.

Meanwhile, the fire spirits embodied a fervent zest for life, their movements dynamic, full of passion and raw energy. They danced a wild, unrestrained ballet, a testament to the flames that harbored both creation and destruction in a loving embrace, showcasing a desire that burns bright, instilling warmth and bringing light into darkness.

Last, were the spirits of air, twirling lightly with the grace of butterflies, their motions whispering secrets of the vast sky and the gentle breeze. They floated with a celestial charm, representing freedom, potential, and the boundless potential that the heavens bestowed upon the world.

The park was transformed into a canvas where the grandest painting of all time was being created. As the spirits engaged in a harmonious ballet, a vibrant picture of synergy and grace unfolded before the Alice Gang, an expression of a universe in perfect harmony.

The gang watched in awe, their hearts in tune with the spectacular insights being unveiled through the dance. Dale murmured, almost in a trance, "It's like...seeing the song of the world, every element in a harmonious melody."

Sally whispered, tears glistening in her eyes, "It's beautiful... it's like a gentle reminder that in the grand scheme of things, we are all connected, in life and in death."

The dance slowed, each element bidding farewell in a graceful exit, leaving the group in a solemn hush, hearts expanded, and spirits elevated with the divine performance that illustrated the grandeur and symbiotic grace of the universe.

After the spectacular performance by the spirits, the Alice Gang lay down under the majestic willow tree, their hearts full yet longing for the guidance and connection that the dance of the spirits had invoked within them. The moonlit night seemed even quieter now, as if the world itself was absorbing the scene that had graced the park.

Suddenly, a soft, warm voice caressed their ears, it was tender yet full of the wisdom of ages. It felt familiar yet heavenly, an essence that reverberated with the universal truths of heartache, courage, and hope. It was the weeping willow tree singing. Its presence was all-encompassing, soothing, and nurturing as she sang, weaving words of fear, courage, and the undying hope of finding one's home into a melody that echoed through the silent night.

Heart don't fail me now
Courage, don't desert me
Don't turn back now that we're here
People always say life is full of choices
No one ever mentions fear
Or how a road can seem so long
How the world can seem so vast
Courage, see me through
Heart, I'm trusting you
On this journey to the past
Somewhere down this road
I know someone's waiting
Years of dreams just can't be wrong, no
Arms will open wide
I'll be safe and wanted
Finally, home where I belong

Well starting here my life begins
Starting now I'm learning fast
Courage, see me through
Heart, I'm trusting you
On this journey to the past
Heart don't fail me now, no
Courage, don't desert me
Home, love, family
There was once a time I must've had them too
Home, love, family
I will never be complete until I find you, hey
One step at a time
One hope, then another
Who knows where this road may go?
Oh, back to who I was (I was)
Onto find my future
Things my heart still needs to know
Yes, let this be a sign
Let this road be mine
Let it lead me to my past
Courage, see me through
Heart, I'm trusting you
To bring me home

As she vocalized the deepest yearnings of a heart in pursuit of home, love, and family, the group felt each word resonating with their own individual journeys and struggles. The lyrics bore witness to the fears that oftentimes shackled them, yet invoked a bravery that urged them to forge forward, to trust in the journey towards rediscovering their lost selves, and reclaiming the sense of belonging that eluded them.

Each word sung was a gentle balm, a lullaby that spoke of hope, the courage to face the vast and unknown world, and a trust in the heart's guidance. The song carried them through a landscape of dreams deferred yet fiercely held onto, of arms waiting to embrace them, a place of safety and acceptance that awaited at the end of the lonely road.

"I've never heard such a beautiful song," said Sally. "The words really resonate with what I am feeling. Our time here together, our journey and our past, all connected somehow. I often think about Spiffy. Is he happy?"

"I hope so," replied Alex. "Or all of this wouldn't make any sense. It kind of puts things in perspective, a view of the world I never had as a human and missed out on so much."

As the song approached its end, the group felt a connection to a pain deeper, a longing more poignant; a calling to rediscover the places, the loves, and the family that once were. The song became a pledge, a vow to forge forward one step at a time, one hope followed by another, guided by courage and an unyielding trust in their heart's compass.

When the last note drifted into the night, a profound silence embraced them, a silence that carried the weight of truth and the tender embrace of understanding. The soft voice urged them to embody courage, kindness, and reverence in all their dealings, reminding them that these virtues would be their guiding lights on the road home.

As they lay there, under the willow's protective branches, the majestic tree began to fade, dissolving into the moonlit night until nothing remained but the cool grass beneath them. The song, the voice, and the tree had gifted them a precious memory, a beacon of light in their journey of rediscovery.

They would later find out that a hurricane had claimed the willow tree, a tribute to a young, vibrant R&B artist whose life was a kaleidoscope of dreams, courage, and tragically cut short. The tree had been a shrine to her.

The group exchanged solemn, understanding glances, their hearts heavy yet filled with a deeper resolve. The tree's ending was not in vain; it had bestowed upon them a legacy of courage, a melody of hope, and a path illuminated by the virtues of bravery, kindness, and reverence. They carried that forward with them as they headed to their homes.

# return of the dawg

The animal shelter was an arena of wild barks and frantic footsteps. It was their great escape, the day the DAWG Dominion had been plotting for weeks.

"Quick, follow my lead!" Capo, the shrewd Rottweiler leading the gang, shouted over the ruckus. The group darted with fervent urgency, each one fueled by the smell of freedom that teased their senses.

Bruiser, the Great Dane with not-so-great awareness of the surroundings, took a moment to pause amidst the chaos, a befuddled expression on his face. "Wait, are we escaping or playing tag? I love tag!" His voice boomed, echoing through the halls as other DAWG members groaned at the untimely confusion.

"Bruiser, just move your giant paws, will ya!" retorted Leon, the quick-witted Pit Bull as he nudged the Dane into motion, albeit with considerable effort. The DAWG Dominion had been strengthened with recruits like Sly, the fox with stealthy moves, and Spark, a small yet fiery Shiba Inu, both running with determined expressions.

A flashback to days before painted a picture of careful planning under Capo's leadership. In the secluded corners of the yard, strategies were forged with new and old members alike. Doberman Chopper had been a vital addition member of their group in the past, his sharp intellect proving to be a resource during planning sessions.

But even Chopper had his moments, stopping abruptly as they approached the exit point, his voice breaking the tense atmosphere. "Hey, did anyone remember to bring the snacks? I heard the outside world has a serious lack of kibbles." The others stared at him, wide-eyed, before Leon broke into a hearty laugh, shaking his head in amusement.

The yard was their stage now as they put their plan into motion. Capo's sharp voice cut through the noise, directing his team with precision. Spark and Sly were the experts of diversion, drawing the attention of the staff in a frenzied dance of feints and distractions. Spark belted out an exaggerated rendition of an opera, her voice scaling high howl notes that left everyone, including the shelter staff, stunned and slightly amused.

"Now, Bruiser!" Capo ordered, signaling the great Dane to tackle the fence that stood as the barrier to their freedom.

With a baffled expression, Bruiser trotted over to the fence, mumbling loud enough for everyone to hear, "You know, I've always wondered why humans don't just dig holes like us, much easier, right?" Yet, with a Herculean effort, Bruiser tore through the fence, creating a pathway to freedom, his question left hanging in the air as others sprinted through, laughter and barks filling the air as they embraced the vibrant life of New York awaiting them.

As they dispersed into the streets outside the shelter, hearts were light, spirits high, and a few of them even chuckling at the hilarious commentary provided by Bruiser and Chopper throughout the escape. The DAWG Dominion was not just back; they were back with a roar of laughter, a spirit of unity, and perhaps, just a tad more humor in their grand tale of freedom.

"C'mon," said Capo. "We need to find a new base of operations and start planning our revenge on the Alice Gang."

With the thrill of the escape still fresh in their paws, Capo led the DAWG Dominion northward through Central Park, their eyes scanning for the perfect new lair. "Stay alert," he growled softly, "we're not just finding a home; we're finding a fortress."

Bruiser, slightly behind and obviously enamored by a butterfly flitting nearby, piped up, "A fortress, you say? Does that come with a moat? I've always wanted to swim in a moat!"

Rolling his eyes, Leon nudged Bruiser back into focus. "You'll be lucky if you get a puddle, big guy."

Soon enough, the gang arrived at Nutter's Battery, the historical remnants of a fortification lost in time. Sly, living up to his name, sniffed around a cluster of bushes and uncovered a hidden opening. "Hey, Capo, you might want to see this."

Eagerly, the group squeezed through the hidden passageway and descended into a world they never knew existed. Damp, dark chambers connected by tunnels stretched out before them. The narrow beams of sunlight that filtered through cracks in the rocky outcroppings above provided just enough light to navigate. It was as if the earth itself had conspired to offer them sanctuary.

Chopper, taking in the dank surroundings, chuckled nervously. "This place could use some interior decorating. Anybody up for some 'Paws & Gardens' magazine inspiration?"

Spark, her eyes gleaming in the dim light, turned to Capo, "Well, boss, what do you think?"

A grin spread across Capo's snout. "Ladies and Gentlemen of the DAWG Dominion," he announced dramatically, "welcome to our new headquarters!"

Leon pawed around a side tunnel that seemed to connect toward Fort Fish and Fort Clinton, looking back at the gang with approval. "It's like we have our own subway system but without the annoying passengers and train delays!"

"And no ticket inspectors!" added Bruiser, clearly pleased with his own wit, causing another collective eyeroll from the team.

Capo surveyed the labyrinthine hideout, already envisioning the endless possibilities. "From here, we can traverse the park unnoticed. And these chambers are perfect for hatching plans. It's time to start planning our revenge on the Alice Gang."

As if on cue, each member of the DAWG Dominion howled in agreement, their voices echoing through the tunnels, drowning out even the distant hum of New York City above them.

A sense of purpose, tinged with the triumph of newfound freedom and a home, filled the air. The DAWG Dominion was back, and this time, they were not just a gang but a force to be reckoned with. And perhaps, Bruiser thought to himself, they could still get that moat.

The memory of their prior encounters with the Alice Gang still stung, serving as a painful reminder of what they had lost and what they were fighting to regain. The humiliation at the cannery, some members canned, requiring the shelter staff to use oddly enough, a can opener to rescue them. The smell of fish they swore still permeated their fur with a pungent lasting odor.

Once, the DAWG Dominion and the Alice Gang had run in separate circles, each ruling their own respective territories without much overlap. But that confrontation at the cannery had altered the equilibrium, putting both gangs on a collision course. The skirmish had escalated, magnifying the Dominion's hunger for redemption. They had been outsmarted, outmaneuvered, and it had cost them not just their territory, but also their pride. For the DAWG Dominion, revenge was no longer a mere choice—it had become a necessity.

As days passed in their newly discovered underground lair, Capo's focus was unwavering. "We're going to reclaim what's ours," he declared during one of their secret meetings, "but we'll need more paws on the ground."

Capo's words were met with solemn nods. It was clear that the Dominion needed not just paws, but skills—each member had to bring something invaluable to the table.

It was Leon who first found the brothers, Tank and Bullet, two Boxers who had escaped from an underground dog-fighting ring.

They were muscular and intimidating, but also smart—ideal recruits for their cause. Capo welcomed them into the fold with a stern reminder of the sacrifices they'd all made to be there. "Welcome to the DAWG Dominion. Just remember, it's not just about brawn here; it's about brains, loyalty, and the drive to take back what was unjustly taken from us."

They also enlisted the help of Rosie, a resourceful Australian Shepherd who had a knack for gathering crucial information. She was adept at blending in with different groups and had become their eyes and ears in Alice Gang territory.

"Resources," Bruiser announced during one strategic meeting, holding up a shopping list that included disguises, and oddly enough, bones for gnawing. "We need to stock up if we're planning an epic battle."

Even Chopper couldn't resist the gravity of the situation as he shifted from his usual quips to a laser-focused mindset. "This isn't a game anymore, it's a full-scale operation."

Their meetings were clandestine, their strategies meticulously crafted. Crude maps of the Alice Gang's territory were spread across the ground as they plotted key points for ambush and escape. "We're not just fighting to regain our territory," Capo would often growl, eyes meeting each member of his team, "we're fighting to regain our dignity."

"What's that?" said Leon.

"It's the hot dog stand by the dog park," said Chopper. "I figured we would need to eat too."

"Get your head in the game," said Bruiser as he batted him on the head with his giant paw. "And get that mess off the map."

A palpable sense of urgency hung in the air during these meetings. Each member understood that the impending showdown would either resurrect the DAWG Dominion to its former glory or crush it into oblivion.

"Desperation can often be the best motivator," Capo said, as they concluded one such intense strategy session. "And right now, we're desperate to win, desperate to prove that the DAWG Dominion is not to be trifled with. I think we will need to take another hostage, but this time be prepared for any response, got it?"

"Take a hotdog you say boss?" said Chopper.

"Get your mind off the hot dogs Chopper," said Capo. "It's hostage, as in we need to find one of the members alone and dognap them to our new lair. Then we can use them to lure the others into a trap. Remember, they know the park better than us, but, they probably have never run into this part of the park and within this fortress."

As they dispersed into the labyrinthine darkness of their lair, each member felt a mix of anticipation and resolve. Their once tarnished pride was gradually being replaced by something stronger, more enduring determination.

There was a collective, unspoken understanding among them: The DAWG Dominion was no longer playing defense. With each new recruit, each acquired resource, and each hatched plan, they were taking control of their destiny, meticulously plotting their course toward an unavoidable, decisive clash with the Alice Gang.

And this time, they vowed, the outcome would be different.

The Alice Gang gathered under the old oak tree near the Alice statue in the park a few days later, after some rest and relation from their night adventure and the paranormal cinematic show the ethereal sprits gave them. Alex, Sally, Pippa, and Ralph took their usual spots around the base of the monument, each one looking as though they had a story to tell. Spike and the new addition, Taco, were playing in the water.

"Good to see everyone," Alex started, his voice tinged with the comfort of familiarity. "I hope the week's been good to all of you. Sally, you look like you've had some adventure."

Sally chuckled. "Oh, you have no idea. My owners decided it was 'family bonding time' and took us on a hiking trip. The outdoors are great and all, but I could do without the bugs."

Ralph grinned. "That's nothing. I got to go to a ball game. It was dog day in the park. The atmosphere is amazing; you guys should really try it."

As they exchanged stories, Pippa, the usually jovial Husky, seemed particularly quiet. Noticing this, Sally nudged her gently. "Hey, everything alright?"

Pippa was about to reply when Dale jumped down from the oak tree onto the ground. His eyes were wide, his fur a tad ruffled. The sight was enough to shift the mood drastically.

"Sorry I am late," said Dale cautiously. "I overheard something I think you need to hear." Dale began, his voice tinged with seriousness. "I was down by the donut shop where those alley cats usually hang out. They mentioned that the DAWG Dominion managed a daring escape from the shelter recently."

Everyone's attention was suddenly razor-focused on Dale. Memories of past confrontations with the DAWG Dominion flooded back into their minds.

"And there's more," Dale continued. "They're looking to settle a score. The cats didn't know who the Dominion was after, but given the events at the cannery, it might be us and it might be wise to stay vigilant."

Sally's eyes met Alex's, both sets of eyes reflecting a blend of concern and determination.

"Thanks for the heads-up, Dale," said Alex, finally breaking the silence. "We'll need to talk strategy, perhaps even bolster our numbers. If it's a fight the DAWG Dominion wants, then we should be prepared for any eventuality."

The Alice Gang members nodded; their faces set in stoic determination. Whatever the DAWG Dominion was planning, the

Alice Gang would be ready. They had friendships to protect, innocents in the park to defend, and now, potentially, a conflict to face.

As they disbanded for the night, the weight of Dale's news lay heavy on their minds, turning their thoughts away from family trips and ball games and towards the darker corners of the animal world they inhabited. Would this be the onset of a new rivalry, or the closure of old wounds? Only time would tell.

As the members of the Alice Gang dispersed into the shadows of Central Park, a figure in the foliage watched intently. Sly, the fox with eyes that missed nothing, sat in the overgrowth near the Alice statue with Spark, they were tasked with surveillance. The events of the meeting had unfolded before him, and although he couldn't catch every word, the change in mood had been palpable. Dale's arrival and subsequent hushed conversation had sent a shiver through the group. A shiver that mirrored the one Sly felt at the prospects that lay ahead.

Under the veil of the shadows of their cover, Sly told Spark, "Head back and tell Capo that the feline friend in the Alice gang had gotten got wind of their escape. They are on high alert. Proceeding to next stage."

Spark quickly darted off in the direction of the fort.

Sly was tasked with finding out who the weakest link is in the Alice gang and tail them.

Sly watched as Sally, who had always struck him as slightly more cautious and reserved than the others, broke away from the group. Her eyes flitted nervously as she made her way through the park. She was the one.

He padded softly, making sure to use the natural camouflage of the park to his advantage. Sally seemed to sense something and glanced back a few times, but she saw nothing. Sly was too good, too stealthy.

He followed her through winding paths, over wooden bridges, and past empty benches until the cityscape changed from the wooded canopy of Central Park to more urban surroundings. She turned into a house that looked modest but comfortable.

Sly took a mental note of the address. This information could be valuable for Capo and the DAWG Dominion's plans. Time to return to their new underground lair and strategize.

Back at the labyrinthine tunnels of Nutter's Battery, Capo awaited Sly's return. When he finally arrived, the rest of the gang — Bruiser, Leon, Chopper, and the energetic Spark — gathered around, eager for news.

"Well?" Capo asked, eyes piercing into Sly's.

"She's the one—Sally, a member of the Alice Gang," Sly reported. "She's cautious, and her body language revealed that she's a bit on edge. I think she's our best bet for... applying pressure."

Bruiser, the Great Dane, looked puzzled. "Pressure? Like, should we ask her politely to go away? I don't get it."

Sly grinned, finding Bruiser's naivety amusing. "Not exactly, big guy. By 'applying pressure,' I mean we're going to make them an offer they can't refuse."

Chopper chimed in, "I still can't believe they have donut shops, and we don't. You'd think someone would've thought of a kibble store by now."

Leon laughed, "Chopper, you have the most impeccable timing for off-topic remarks."

"Enough," Capo growled. "We've got the information we need. It's time to plan our next move."

As the DAWG Dominion settled into their newfound lair, maps spread out and eyes locked in a mutual understanding, a single thought united them: the Alice Gang wouldn't know what hit them. And for the first time since their escape, Capo felt a sense of impending triumph. A chessboard lay before him, pieces moving, risks calculated. It was time to make a move that would tilt the game in their favor, once and for all.

He looked at each member of his gang, from Sly's cunning gaze to Bruiser's blissful ignorance. "We were born from adversity, molded by it. We've fought for every inch of our freedom, and now it's time to reclaim our place, to write our own destiny."

Deep in the winding tunnels of Nutter's Battery, the atmosphere was thick with tension and anticipation. Capo stood over a makeshift table, a worn-out map of Central Park and the surrounding neighborhood spread out before him. Sly, Bruiser, Leon, Chopper, and Spark gathered around, their eyes fixed on the marker that represented Sally's house.

"Sly," Capo began, his voice steady and low, "you've been watching the place. What have you got?"

Sly looked up, his eyes meeting each member's gaze before focusing on the map. "Two days of surveillance," he said, detailing his findings. "Sally goes out to the yard like clockwork—9 PM for her evening break. She's back inside in minutes and doesn't emerge until 6 AM, before her owners head to work."

Bruiser scratched his head. "That's a tight window. How do we get in and out without getting caught?"

"We'll need to be precise," Sly continued. "We've got maybe five minutes to get in, secure Sally, and retreat back to base."

Chopper chimed in, half-distracted by his own thoughts of a kibble store: "What about the stuff we need for the mission?"

"Ah, yes," said Leon, holding up a roll of duct tape. "Courtesy of our scouting near the fire station. This should keep Sally from alerting anyone."

Capo nodded, his eyes narrowing as he envisioned the plan coming to fruition. "This is it, everyone. Our first significant move against the Alice Gang, and our chance to turn the tides. We go in at 9 PM, three nights from now."

On the appointed evening, the DAWG Dominion, led by Capo and Sly, gathered at the edge of Central Park, shrouded by darkness. The members went over their roles one last time. Sly and Leon were to sneak into Sally's yard and secure her, while Bruiser and Spark would serve as lookouts, ready to signal any unexpected activity. Chopper was in charge of the supplies.

The clock struck nine.

"Move," Capo whispered.

With a synchronized grace born of countless drills and a shared sense of purpose, Sly and Leon moved effortlessly through the darkness. They reached the fence surrounding Sally's yard and waited for the signal from Bruiser and Spark.

A soft chirp from Bruiser's whistle told them it was time.

Within seconds, Sly and Leon had cleared the fence. They found Sally in the middle of her yard, eyes squinted, nose sniffing the air.

Before she could make a sound, Sly moved in, quickly but carefully placing the duct tape over her muzzle. Leon, acting as backup, stood ready for any surprises.

Sally's eyes widened; a muted whimper escaped her taped mouth as she realized her predicament. Sly gestured towards the exit, and together with Leon, they led the muzzled Sally out of the yard, into the veil of night.

Back in their lair, the DAWG Dominion celebrated their flawless operation. But Capo knew the real work had only just begun. He looked down at the captured Sally, her eyes filled with a blend of fear and defiance.

"Welcome, Sally," Capo said, his voice tinged with a satisfaction he hadn't felt in years. "We meet again, I think it's high time we had a talk, don't you?"

And with that, the room fell silent. Every member of the DAWG Dominion knew that this moment marked the beginning of a new chapter in their ongoing struggle. A chapter that, for the first time, bore the ink of potential victory.

# Grey wolF rising

Inside the damp, dimly lit chambers of Nutter's Battery, the atmosphere was fraught with both tension and triumph. Capo stood on a makeshift stand made of old crates and pallets. Sally was held in a small pen to one side of the room, her eyes still burning with that unsettling blend of fear and defiance. The members of the DAWG Dominion—Sly, Bruiser, Leon, Chopper, and Spark—sat in a semi-circle, their gazes shifting between their leader and their captive.

"Phase one is complete," began Capo, his voice tinged with both gravity and a trace of satisfaction. "But Sally here isn't talking, and we need information. For that, we need leverage."

His eyes scanned his loyal gang, stopping at Sly and Bruiser. "You two are up for the next task. There's a cat that frequently visits the donut shop just north of our hideout—the same one that's been seen with the Alice Gang. We're going to bring him in."

Sly nodded, his foxy eyes gleaming with anticipation. "Broad daylight, Capo?"

Capo smirked. "Bold moves for bold times. Besides, it'll send a message. We're not hiding anymore."

The next morning, the sun shone brightly as it started its ascent over the cityscape. A new day had dawned, but for the DAWG Dominion, it was another day of subterfuge and planning. Sly and Bruiser positioned themselves in an alley that gave them a clear line of sight to the entrance of the donut shop.

Within an hour, they spotted their target: an orange tabby sauntering towards the shop, its eyes scanning for any treats or scraps that might have been left outside.

"Ready?" Bruiser asked, his bulky frame tensed like a coiled spring.

Sly's eyes narrowed, focused on the target. "Ready."

With the precision of a sniper and the agility of a sprinter, Sly shot out of the alleyway, Bruiser right on his tail. Before the cat knew what was happening, Sly had lunged, pinning it down with a swift, decisive move. Bruiser quickly produced a small net, expertly tossing it over the stunned tabby.

"We've got you now," Sly whispered, his eyes meeting those of the captured cat. "No sudden moves, and no one gets hurt."

The return to Nutter's Battery was swift and uneventful, a testament to the Dominion's increasing competence and confidence. As they pushed through the hidden opening behind the bushes, the cat wrapped securely in Bruiser's net, each member sensed that the balance of power was slowly but surely shifting in their favor.

Capo greeted them with a nod as they entered, his eyes lingering for a moment on their new captive.

"Excellent work," he said. "Now, let's see what our new guest has to say for himself."

Sly and Bruiser placed the cat, still wrapped in the net, next to Sally. The tension in the room spiked as eyes met eyes, predator met prey, and captor met captive.

"You might not want to talk, Sally, but perhaps your feline friend will be more forthcoming," Capo sneered, relishing the moment. "You see, we're done playing games."

"What's your name cat?" said Capo.

"It's Dale, and I won't talk either," replied Dale.

"Fine," said Capo. "We have ways of making you talk. One of you will spill the beans sooner or later."

A heavy silence filled the chamber, thick with the weight of choices yet to be made and destinies yet to be sealed. Whatever happened next, one thing was certain—the war between the Alice Gang and the DAWG Dominion had escalated, and there was no turning back.

"Spark," said Capo. "Bring the barrel."

"Yes Sir!" Spark replied.

Spark left momentarily and returned rolling an old empty oil drum, probably used to house gun powder during the war. He turned it up on its end, so the opening was on top.

"Leon," said Capo. "Start the water flow."

Leon reached over to a wooden trough and lever. He pulled the lever and the trough swiveled toward the barrel positioning its end above the opening of the barrel. Suddenly water began flowing down from the ceiling, obviously coming from Harlem Meer, the lake overhead of the caverns below.

When the water reached the top of the barrel, Leon reversed the lever and the flow of water stopped. Sally and Dale gulped in fear. What were they going to do with the water in the barrel?

Capo circled the room, a sinister laugh emerging from his mouth. "All right Bruiser, string him up."

Bruiser tossed a rope over the beam above the barrel then tied it to the net enclosing Dale. Then hoisted Dale up in the air over the barrel and tied it to a hook on the wall.

In the suffocating darkness of Nutter's Battery, each member of the DAWG Dominion felt the weight of the moment. But for Sally and Dale, held captive and facing the immediate threat of physical harm, the psychological torment was unparalleled.

Sally's thoughts swirled in a vortex of guilt and regret. Could she have prevented all of this? Her mind was a battleground between her sense of loyalty to the Alice Gang and the immediate peril facing her and Dale. Each second that ticked by was a second closer to making an impossible choice.

Dale, the usually independent and daring tabby, felt his usually unshakable spirit waver. He looked at Sally, their eyes meeting for a brief moment. Dale had always admired her courage, but now, he could see the visible strain on her face. He wondered, now for the first time, how the Alice Gang would manage to get out of this crisis.

"Bruiser, lower him," Capo's voice echoed, pulling everyone's attention back to the present.

As Bruiser moved toward the rope, his burly paw shaking just slightly, Leon glanced at him and then at Sly. "Are we really doing this? Dunking a cat?"

Chopper, who had been quiet all along, added, "This is getting out of hand. We've never gone this far before."

Capo cut in, visibly annoyed, "You think the Alice Gang would hesitate if the roles were reversed? We have to do whatever it takes to protect our territory and establish our dominion. They brought this on themselves."

Sly, always the tactician, chimed in: "Capo's right. It's a dog-eat-dog world. No pun intended."

Satisfied with the show of support, Capo turned to Sally. "This is your last chance. Give us what we need to know. The details of your meetups, the timing, the homes of the Alice Gang members. Or else."

Sally looked at Dale, who was now hovering just inches above the water-filled barrel. She felt the walls closing in on her. "No," she finally said, her voice almost a whisper but steady.

"Bruiser, dunk him," Capo ordered.

With a reluctant pull on the rope, Bruiser lowered Dale into the barrel. The water swallowed him up, muffling his instinctive yowl. Seconds felt like hours. When Bruiser finally lifted him out, Dale was a sopping mess, his fur clinging to his body, his eyes wide with shock and fear.

Silence weighed down on the room like a stone. Then Sally, her voice breaking, shouted, "Okay, okay, I'll tell. Stop."

The room exhaled as if it had been holding its collective breath. Whatever the future held for the Alice Gang and the DAWG Dominion, the line had been crossed, and there was no going back.

Dale was slowly lowered, his paws touching the ground, his drenched fur making him appear even more pitiable. The water dripped from his whiskers, each droplet a testament to the dark and perilous road that lay ahead for all involved. The line between right and wrong had blurred into a gray haze, and each member of this twisted drama had to ask themselves: at what cost comes victory?

As Dale was set down next to her, still dripping and visibly shaken, Sally felt her resolve crumble. She looked at Capo, his eyes cold and calculating, and realized there was no way out but to cooperate.

"I'll tell you what you want to know," she said, her voice tinged with a mix of relief and resignation. "We meet twice a week, or every three days, usually around mid-morning. Our gathering spot is the Alice statue. There are about seven regular members, although we occasionally make new friends."

Sly scribbled the details down on a scrap of paper, his eyes never leaving Sally's face.

Capo grinned. "See? Was that so hard? You just made things a lot easier for yourself, Sally. And for us."

Just as Capo was basking in his triumph, a new series of events were set in motion elsewhere.

The morning activity was lively as Ralph paced around the dog park. His owners often brought him so he could get some exercise. The home they lived in had a small backyard, only room enough to stretch your legs.

Suddenly a sprightly white Maltese walked up to him and said, "Are you part of that group that meets at the Alice statue?"

"Yes," replied Ralph.

"Great," she said. "My name is Nanas and everyone that comes to the park has heard the DAWG is back. I was wondering why your friend Sally was with them the other day?"

Ralph's heart sank. If Sally was with the DAWG Dominion and they were in the park, it was undoubtedly bad news.

"She wasn't going with them willingly, I could see tape on her muzzle," said Nanas.

"Thanks, Nanas. I need to find Alex, fast," said Ralph, darting off towards the streets on the west side of the park where Alex lived.

Back in the DAWG Dominion's subterranean stronghold, Sally felt the eyes of her captors on her. "You'll never break the Alice Gang," she said, finally breaking the silence. "Someone will come looking for us."

"Let them come," said Capo, his voice dripping with menace. "We're ready for them."

Sly rolled up the scrap of paper with Sally's revelations and tucked it securely into an old jar for safekeeping. As he did so, he couldn't help but wonder what the cost of this newfound information would be.

Capo turned his attention to Dale, who had managed to shake off some of the water but still looked like a soggy dishrag. "Your feline friend here better hope that you've told us everything, Sally. Because if you haven't, he'll be the first to pay the price."

The weight of her decision hung heavily on Sally, as did the ominous cloud that had settled over the entire underground chamber. As Capo's words echoed in her ears, she prayed that her friends from the Alice Gang would sense her plight and come to their rescue soon.

Unbeknownst to her, Ralph was already on a desperate search for Alex, and the clock was ticking for both the DAWG Dominion and the Alice Gang. With each moment that passed, the stakes grew higher, complicating the web of loyalty, betrayal, and survival that ensnared them all.

Ralph made it to Beatrice's home, she had just left the room, her footsteps fading down the hall. Ralph seized the opportunity and softly pawed at Alex's garden window. When their eyes met, Ralph's gaze was frantic.

"What's going on?" Alex pushed the window open with his nose and hopped onto the garden ledge.

"It's Sally," Ralph panted, urgently lacing his words. "I spoke with this little white Maltese named Nanas at the dog park. She saw members of the DAWG Dominion with Sally, heading towards Harlem Meer. I think she's in trouble, Alex. Serious trouble."

Alex's eyes widened; his heart sank like a stone thrown into a pond. "Oh no, Sally... We've got to do something."

"I thought as much," Ralph said.

"Gather everyone," said Alex. "Meet me at the Alice statue as soon as possible. We don't have time to lose."

Ralph nodded, his gaze steely. "I'm on it. I'll get everyone I can."

As Ralph darted off, his paws barely touching the ground, Alex paused for a moment, his heart heavy in his chest. His connection with Sally had been unlike any he had ever felt, even back when he was human. It was genuine, unguarded, free from the complexities that often taint human relationships. And now she was in danger, held by a gang he knew all too well.

He shook off his apprehension, leapt back through the dog door, and bounded through the house, biding his time until Beatrice was distracted enough for him to slip out unnoticed.

Once he was sure she was occupied in another room, Alex went through the dog door and sprinted through the yards, leaping over fences, and darting through alleys. His thoughts were a whirlwind of emotions and plans, but a single name echoed repeatedly in his mind: Sally.

Within the hour, members of the Alice Gang began to congregate around their iconic meeting point—the Alice statue. Pippa, Spike, Taco along with Ralph and Alex, had arrived, their faces etched with concern.

"We're all here," Pippa declared, looking around at the assembled group. "Ralph told us what has happened. We are so concerned."

Spike spoke up, "We have another problem."

"What's that?" said Alex.

With a tremor in his voice Spike said, "On my way hear I got hungry and thought I could swing by and get a donut, you know, swipe one off a table out front. I got one while this man went inside to get more coffee and as I went into the alley, I ran into a cat named Puddles."

The group attentively listened to Spike. "She said the DAWG catnapped Dale in broad daylight using a net and hauled him off into the park."

"Dang," said Alex. "The are just smart enough to use him and Sally against each other to get information."

Murmurs of disbelief and apprehension rippled through the group but overriding it all was a sense of resolve. They knew what they had to do.

"All right, listen up," Alex began, taking on the mantle of leadership. "This is not going to be easy. The DAWG Dominion is ruthless, and now they're desperate. But we've got something they don't have—unity. We look out for each other. Sally and Dale are one of us, and we're not leaving them behind."

As the members of the Alice Gang nodded, a collective understanding filling the air, Alex's gaze drifted away for a moment. He couldn't shake the gnawing feeling at the pit of his stomach. The stakes were incredibly high, and the road ahead full of peril. But he knew they had no other choice. For the first time in his life, human or canine, something—someone—truly mattered to him, and he would go to any length to protect that. With a resolute nod, he turned his attention back to the group.

"Ok, let's meet up after dark, when you hear the church on the corner of the park ring their bells nine times. We will rescue Sally and Dale."

"Do we know where they are?" asked Pippa.

"Knowing the gang and because I've retained my human memories," replied Alex. "I suspect they set up their lair in the northern part of the park. They could not have carried Dale far in a net in broad daylight without being seen by everyone. There are old fortifications and alcoves in the area. We will start our search there."

"Nine bells it is," said Ralph as he and the other group scampered off. Alex head back to his home. He needed to sit and think about the history of the park. Could his human memories and experiences be the key to rescuing his friends?

Alex sat quietly in a cozy corner of Beatrice's home, his eyes unfocused as he stared into the distance. Thoughts whirred through his mind like a swirl of leaves caught in a gust of wind. Harlem Meer, the northern part of the park—each word triggered a flicker of memory. A series of images unspooled in his mind, hazy yet insistent, each picture clearer than the last.

He remembered his school days, sitting in a classroom filled with the smell of chalk and the sound of his teacher's voice explaining the history of the park. Yes, that was it! The northern area of the park had historical fortifications, remnants of times long gone, and Alex's heart leapt as the thought struck him, they were all interconnected with a maze of hidden tunnels and chambers. A tactical advantage perhaps, or a hidden sanctuary; either way, it was information that could change the game.

Just then, the distant tolling of the church bells reverberated through the air, each chime echoing the urgency he felt. Nine times it rang, and as if on cue, Alex bolted through the dog door and sprinted towards their rendezvous point.

The members of the Alice Gang were already there, their faces etched with concern and a collective sense of purpose.

"I've got something," Alex declared as he arrived, panting but resolute. "I remember my history lessons from when I was a human. The north end of the park, by Harlem Meer, has historical forts and monuments. More importantly, those forts are interconnected with hidden tunnels and chambers."

"Hidden tunnels?" Pippa's ears perked up with interest. "That could be useful."

"Very useful," Ralph agreed, his eyes narrowing. "It gives us an element of surprise."

"Or at least a better chance at finding them," Taco added.

Spike wagged his tail, "Let's give those DAWG Dominion ruffians a lesson they won't forget!"

Taking these affirmations as a sign, Alex led the group in the direction of Harlem Meer. As they maneuvered through the maze of park trails, lit only by the moon and the distant city lights, the weight of their mission pressed down on them. Each of them carried a blend of hope, fear, and steely resolve in their hearts. Alex, in particular, felt a sense of gravity he had never felt before, even in his human life.

Moving through the conservatory garden, they reached the Fort Clinton, the eastern most of the structures, Near McGowan's pass was a massive structure that seemed to loom even larger in the dim light. A flag stood upon the outcropping. Below the structure amongst the boulders near a small waterway was an opening, just large enough for the largest of them to squeeze through.

"Remember," Alex began, his gaze sweeping over each face, "we stick together, no matter what. Keep your eyes peeled for any members of the DAWQ. The tunnels could be our best shot at finding Sally and Dale. When we hear them, we will launch or plan."

Earlier before leaving the Alice statue, the gang had formulated a plan to use a common trigger for dogs: food. Spike, on his way to the statue, scavenged behind the various food carts that were closing that populate the streets around the park for scraps of delicious food.

The group carried with them an array of delightful treats, a half-eaten hot dog, three falafels, a bag of potato chips, and a slightly dirty hamburger patty.

As the group nodded in agreement, each of them took a fortifying breath, ready to plunge into the labyrinthine unknown. The forts and tunnels might have been remnants of a bygone era, but tonight, they would serve as the stage for a modern-day battle, waged not with guns and cannons, but with courage, unity, and an unyielding will to protect their own.

"Let's move," Alex ordered, and with a collective nod, the Alice Gang stepped into the shadows of history, each second ticking by like a countdown, each step echoing with the names that reverberated in their hearts: Sally and Dale.

It wasn't a very long journey in the tunnels until the gang heard the faint sound of talking. It was Capos' unmistakable voice reverberating through the chamber and tunnels.

"Ok," said Alex. "This is where we have to be quiet. Walk softly and don't make any noise."

They walked further into the tunnel in the direction of Capo's voice. Closer, and closer they got until suddenly, Capo's voice went silent. The air seemed stale and damp. Alex looked at Ralph and shrugged his front shoulders. Needless to say, they kept moving forward.

As they peaked around the corner into the next chamber, they found their mission objective. In the center of the chamber was a dog crate, Sally was inside, sleeping. Next to the crate was Dale, lying on an old burlap sack, legs and feet bound so he could not escape.

"Psst," Alex whispered. "Psst."

Dale craned his head around in an effort to see what was making the noise and saw Alex. He tried to talk, but with the tape on his mouth, you could only hear the inaudible meows of desperation.

Sally woke up, hearing Dale move and turned around to see the gang just in the opening of the chamber. Unmuzzled, she said, "It's a trap. They have been watching you. Run, it's a trap!"

Just as Alex and the gang were trying to process what Sally was saying, the DAWQ Domination surrounded them, each holding a large stick, ready to engage the Alice Gang.

"Thanks for bringing us some food!" said Capo. "We were getting kind of hungry."

"Let them go," said Alex.

"Or what?" said Capo. "You are outnumbered and outsized. We have you this time. No machinery and other things to trip us up, no animal control to come to your rescue. Just us and you. We have the edge."

"What is it you want," said Alex. "Why take Sally and Dale?"

"They were pawns in our little game of chess," said Capo. "Luring you into our new base of operations to exact our revenge."

"And what revenge is that?" Pippa asked.

"To see the last of you, and declare this entire park, the Kingdom of the DAWQ!" pronounced Capo.

In the suffocating darkness of the chamber, as both the Alice Gang and the DAWG Dominion stood frozen in their respective stances, a low rumble broke the silence. It wasn't an earthly sound, nor was it one any of them recognized. The echo reverberated along the walls, accompanied by the soft, rhythmic thud of footsteps.

Both gangs looked at each other, a flicker of unease dancing across their eyes. Whatever or whoever was coming seemed to be getting closer, the footsteps growing more distinct, almost deliberate in their pace.

Then, a shadow—colossal and indistinct—cast itself on the chamber wall. As the contours became more defined, it was clear this was no ordinary dog. A silhouette far too large and towering for that.

He stepped into the chamber. Alfred, the grey Irish Wolfhound, was an imposing figure. He stood at 5 feet tall and weighed 150 pounds, his coat a haunting shade of dark grey that seemed almost spectral in the dim light. His eyes had a glint that left no room for questioning his authority.

"I trust I am interrupting," he boomed, his voice dripping with a gravitas that seemed to fill the chamber and silence both gangs instantly. "But as it seems you've all forgotten, I am the King of this Park. I reign supreme over all animals and spirits that call it home."

The Alice gang felt a sigh of relief, for Alfred was their friend, was he there to rescue them? The room was so quiet you could hear a leaf rustle above ground. Both gangs, previously so filled with bravado and strategy, could only look on, astounded, and dwarfed by Alfred's presence.

"Release them," Alfred commanded, gesturing toward Sally and Dale. "Leave this park, and never return. Failure to comply will give you a firsthand lesson in what it feels like to become a spirit."

Capo, usually so full of arrogance, could only stammer. "Y-y-yes, Your Majesty."

Alfred's eyes narrowed as he surveyed the DAWG Dominion, ensuring his command was heeded. One by one, they unlocked the crate and untied Dale, keeping their heads lowered in deference.

"You're making the right choice," Alfred declared. "Remember it, should you ever think of transgressing again."

As Sally and Dale scurried over to the Alice Gang, Alfred turned to Alex. "You've shown great bravery and loyalty. But remember, this park is a sanctuary for all creatures. Disruption of its peace will always be quelled."

Alex bowed his head, an understanding passing between them. "We owe you our gratitude, King Alfred. Your wisdom guides us."

Alfred simply nodded, then looked at both gangs once more. "Remember this night, for the rules of this park are not to be bent or broken. I trust there will be no need for a second reminder."

And with that, the towering Irish Wolfhound turned and ambled back down the tunnel from whence he came, his exit as majestic as his entrance.

The Alice Gang looked at one another—still processing the extraordinary event that had just unfolded—then at Sally and Dale, who had just escaped the jaws of danger. Though many questions remained, one thing was crystal clear: the unity and resolve they'd shown had been rewarded, and they had just witnessed the intervention of a living legend.

As they made their way back to their familiar grounds near the Alice statue, each carried within them a new sense of the larger community they were part of—a kingdom, ruled by a King who was as mysterious as he was just, in a park that was more magical and complex than they had ever realized. They also knew that they had been part of something much bigger than themselves, a chapter in the ongoing history of a park where the spirits of past, present, and future held court, presided over by a king named Alfred.

The DAWG as they retreated and ran up the alleys to the north of the park were arguing amongst themselves.

"Whose stupid idea was this?" said Chopper.

"Don't call me stupid," said Capo. "We'll just have to find another place to rule.

"Well, it better be near something to eat," said Bruiser. "After all that excitement, I'm hungry."

Tails between their legs, they disappeared into the night,

And so, the Alice gang walked on, their hearts lighter, but also more solemn, for they had seen firsthand the rewards of unity and the costs of disruption. They would not forget the lessons of that night. They were the Alice Gang, and they were part of a greater story—a tale of courage, community, and the mysterious powers that govern the delicate balance of life and harmony in a park that was, in itself, a world.

# the sacrifice

It had been more than a month since the incident with the DAWG, the last few weeks had been filled with regular meetups, adventures in the park, and stolen hot dogs from the cart. Taco had become close to the group through his repeated participation in their outings. Alex and Sally's fondness for each other grew. All was perfectly beautiful in the park, or so it seemed.

It was an afternoon in March, the sun arced through the azure sky, occasionally hiding behind a cloud over Central Park. Birds chirped their timeless songs, children laughed as they played by the Alice statue, and couples walked hand in paw. It was the kind of day that lulled one into a sense of timeless tranquility, almost as if the park itself were a sanctuary away from the struggles and complexities of the outside world.

Alex lounged atop a small mound, eyes half-closed, soaking up the serenity of a world he had fought to protect. Nearby, Ralph playfully chased butterflies, embodying a joy so simple and pure that it felt almost rebellious. Spike, engrossed in a new digging project, sent little sprays of dirt into the air with each scoop of his paw. Pippa looked on approvingly, occasionally giving direction.

In these moments, the world seemed right. Sally and Dale lay side by side in a patch of sun-dappled grass, their recent ordeal now a receding nightmare, thanks in part to the ever-vigilant Alice Gang and the legendary King Alfred. The gang's unity was their strength, a bond forged through shared trials and triumphs.

Yet, even in this idyll, there were subtle disruptions in the fabric of their peaceful existence, ripples in the water, whispers in the wind. Alex noticed a murder of crows gathering in the trees, their cawing a discordant note in the otherwise harmonious symphony of the park.

"Is it just me," Pippa asked, looking upward, "or do those crows seem a bit more... restless today?"

"I've noticed it too," Alex replied, slowly standing up. "Something doesn't feel right."

Ralph, ceasing his playful antics, bounded back to the group. "Yeah, I don't like it. Feels like a storm's brewing, but the sky's clear with the exception of just a few clouds."

These forebodings did not go unnoticed. Spike stopped digging and sniffed the air, as if testing it for an invisible threat. "Guys," he said hesitantly, "I smell something different. Can't put my paw on it, but it's not normal."

"Maybe you farted," said Ralph who broke out laughing.

"Could be nothing," Sally suggested, always the optimist, "maybe they're just migrating or something."

"Or it could be a sign," Dale mumbled, his eyes narrowed, "a warning. Birds always know first, then squirrels. When I was a squirrel, I could smell rain hours before it started."

"Let's stay vigilant," Alex finally said, his voice betraying a note of gravity that was rare for such a beautiful day. "Something tells me we're not out of the woods yet. Literally and figuratively."

The others nodded, a somber understanding passing between them. They knew not what tomorrow would bring, but the winds of change were stirring, and the uneasy feeling settling in their hearts was but the calm before an impending storm.

In that moment, they all shared an unspoken realization: their lives were intertwined in a series of unpredictable events, those created by unseen hands. The world around them was far more complex and volatile than it seemed, a place of light and shadow, peace and peril, life and, though they shuddered to admit it, potentially death.

As the sun moved lower in the horizon, the Alice Gang looked at one another with a newfound sense of urgency. Each one felt it, the weight of the unknown, the burden of what was yet to come. And so, they prepared themselves for whatever lay ahead, each silently vowing to protect the unity they had worked so hard to forge, even if it meant making the ultimate sacrifice.

This day may have been calm, but a storm was indeed brewing, one that would test the bonds of friendship and loyalty, pushing each member of the Alice Gang to their limits. It was a storm that none of them could see, yet all of them could feel, a storm that promised to change the course of their lives forever.

And so, with the afternoon getting late, they headed back to their homes and owners, cautiously but optimistic about the future.

The next morning, Beatrice, sensing an uncommon lethargy in Alex, bent down to scratch behind his ears. "Pierre, you've been moping under this coffee table longer than usual," she observed. "Is something bothering you?"

Alex looked up with a half-hearted wag of his tail. Beatrice saw through him, as she often did. He could sense the weight of concern in her eyes and felt a warm rush of appreciation for his human caretaker.

"Tell you what," Beatrice began, her voice tinged with excitement. "I was going to head down to my studio today, but instead, how about we treat ourselves? There's a new place I heard about near Times Square called The Dog Mom. It's a spa for both of us. What do you think? Would you like to be pampered today?"

The idea appealed to Alex, an unexpected but welcome distraction from the unsettling undercurrents he had felt in the park. A spa day could be precisely the thing to rejuvenate both body and spirit.

"Great, let's get you ready!" Beatrice exclaimed, interpreting his enthusiastic bark as a definitive yes and placing his harness on him.

Beatrice arranged for a cab to take them near Times Square, where The Dog Mom was located. As they navigated through the streets of Manhattan, Alex couldn't help but be struck by the city's magnificent chaos, something he had often ignored in his human days. The cab finally came to a halt, and as they stepped out, the panorama of Times Square unfolded before them.

Bright neon lights, giant billboards, and the ceaseless ebb and flow of people. Times Square was a spectacle that never slept. Alex was stunned. How had he missed the magic of this place before? The towering digital displays, the loudness of city sounds, the variety of scents wafting from nearby food stalls, it was sensory overload, but in the best possible way.

"Why didn't I appreciate this when I was human?" he mused internally, shaking his head in wonder and regret. Perhaps it was the dog's heightened senses, or perhaps he was seeing the world through less jaded eyes now. Whatever it was, the vibrancy of life around him was nothing short of miraculous.

The Dog Mom was an oasis amidst the sensory carnival. It had a calming ambiance, with soft music playing in the background and an aroma of lavender in the air. Beatrice and Alex were led into a room with two adjacent grooming stations. While Beatrice got into a comfortable robe and sank her feet into a warm, bubbling foot bath, Alex was guided to a small tub designed just for dogs.

As Beatrice had her hair shampooed, Alex felt the warm water enveloping him, followed by the gentle massage of hands lathering soap into his fur. A sense of peace washed over him. For a moment, the foreboding that had been shadowing him since yesterday seemed to dissolve, carried away by the soothing suds and the loving touch of the groomer.

Once both were rinsed and towel-dried, Alex had his feet shaved and nails cut, and his tail shaved up to within a few inches of the end with a pom-pom on the end. Perfectly groomed, a spectacle of pure Poodle.

They met back in the lobby, looking and feeling like the best versions of themselves. Beatrice looked down at Alex, her eyes meeting his, and for a moment, there was a mutual understanding—an unspoken agreement that, come what may, they were in this together.

"Feeling better, Pierre?" Beatrice asked, even though she knew she wouldn't get a verbal answer.

Alex barked happily, his tail wagging with renewed vigor. Beatrice smiled. "I'll take that as a yes."

As they stepped back into the cab to return home, Alex couldn't shake off the feeling that they had just fortified themselves for challenges that lay ahead. The uncertainties of the future still loomed large, but for now, the strength they drew from each other—and from these small moments of reprieve, was enough to sustain them.

Times Square receded into the background, its brilliant lights a colorful blur through the back window of the cab. Alex lay his head on Beatrice's lap, comforted by her presence, as they headed back towards Central Park. The unknown awaited, but they were fortified, emotionally and spiritually, for whatever came next.

As they neared their home, Alex glanced back toward the park. It seemed peaceful from a distance, but he knew better. Though the spa day had been a wonderful escape, he sensed that the real trials were yet to come. And when they did, he would be ready.

A few days later, Alex couldn't contain his enthusiasm as he recounted his day with Beatrice to the Alice Gang. The gang was all there—Ralph, Spike, Pippa, Taco, Dale, Sally, and him. They had congregated around their usual rendezvous point, the bronze Alice statue that had seen so much of their collective experience.

"You should've seen it, guys! Times Square is like another world. The lights, the sounds, it's unbelievable!" Alex started, his eyes shining as he remembered the dazzling spectacle. "Beatrice took me to a spa called The Dog Mom. We both got groomed, and the experience was, well, it was something else."

Spike, always the food enthusiast, interjected, "Did you smell any good food? I've heard humans talk about Times Square like it's some sort of food heaven!"

Alex chuckled, "Oh, you have no idea, Spike! The aroma was a medley of everything you could imagine. Hot dogs, pretzels, and get this, a whole stall dedicated to international candies!"

Spike's eyes widened, "International candies? That's...that's like a treasure trove!"

Pippa, whose sensitivity to auditory stimuli was second to none, asked, "What about music, Alex? Was there any music playing?"

Alex smiled at Pippa's question. "Music was everywhere, Pippa! From street performers to giant speakers blaring the latest hits, it was a feast for the ears. I even heard some jazz from a saxophonist on a corner."

"Jazz, you say. That's classy stuff," Pippa mused, imagining herself lost in the intricate notes of a saxophone.

Ralph, who had been quietly listening, finally spoke. "Sounds like a dream, Alex. But you're talking about it like it's a fairy tale. Is something bothering you?"

The question caught Alex off guard, but he should have expected it from Ralph, who had an uncanny ability to sense emotional undercurrents.

Alex sighed, "It was a great day, Ralph. It was. But something feels...off. I can't quite put my paw on it, but I feel like we're on the brink of something big. Something... ominous."

The Alice Gang shared a moment of silence. They each knew what Alex was talking about. Despite their best efforts to maintain a semblance of normality, there was no denying the electric tension that tingled in the air, like static before a thunderstorm.

Ralph broke the silence. "Well, whatever it is, we'll face it. We've got each other, and that's more than any looming danger can reckon with."

"So," Alex began, reclaiming his initial enthusiasm, "when do you all want to go see Times Square?"

"We should see it soon," said Sally. "Sounds like a neat place."

"It's a long way away," said Alex. "It will take all day to get there and back."

"How about tomorrow?" said Spike.

"Yea," said Pippa. "I don't see a reason to wait."

"Fine," said Alex. "Meet here tomorrow morning after your owners go to work. We will venture to Times Square and have some fun."

The calm before the storm was a precious thing, a time to gather strength and savor the small joys. They didn't know when the storm would come, but when it did, the Alice Gang would be ready, but they weren't going to let it deter them from their adventures. And so, as each member departed, they carried with them the unspoken but palpable reassurance that no matter what transpired, their bonds would be their greatest asset and most trusted ally in the uncertain times that lay ahead.

The next morning was inauspicious. Dark clouds scuttled across the sky as if even the heavens were warning of impending danger. Howling winds carried a foreboding message, a sharp contrast to the general peace and tranquility that Central Park usually offered. Yet, despite nature's dark omens, the Alice Gang met as usual by their namesake statue.

Alex looked at the sky and then at his friends, "It doesn't look like the weather is on our side today. Should we proceed?"

Spike sniffed the air, his nose twitching as if trying to smell the day's fate. "I've been through worse," he finally grunted.

Pippa looked hesitant, her ears drooping a little. "If you all think it's okay, then let's go. But we should be careful."

"Alright," Alex confirmed, his eyes meeting each of theirs, imparting a sense of gravity to the decision. "We go, but with caution."

They had not ventured far into the paths of The Ramble when the sky broke open, unleashing a torrential downpour that caught every animal and human off guard. Squirrels dashed for their burrows, birds fluttered frantically toward any available shelter, and humans scurried, umbrellas inverting in the wind, as they ran for cover.

"Quick, under that tree!" Alex shouted, leading the gang toward an old oak tree, its limbs gnarled like ancient arms. As they huddled underneath, they found that the thick canopy offered scant protection against the rain coming in sideways, driven by the relentless wind.

"This won't do. We need better shelter!" Pippa yelped, as she tried to dodge the wind-driven droplets.

"Bethesda Terrace. Now!" Alex commanded, no longer willing to negotiate with the fates.

With hearts pounding, they bolted out from their meager refuge, their paws splashing through mud and puddles as they ran. They crossed the Bow Bridge, its beautiful ironwork blurring in their peripheral vision as they focused solely on their destination. Finally, they skidded into the sanctuary of Bethesda Terrace, its grand arches providing immediate respite from the rain that still battered the park outside.

Panting, each took a moment to shake off the water from their fur, but Alex noticed something, or rather, someone, was missing.

"Sally! Where's Sally?" he asked, his voice tinged with panic.

Each member of the Alice Gang looked at the others, their eyes widening as the realization sunk in.

"We lost her," Spike muttered, his ears flattened against his head.

As they huddled beneath the arches of Bethesda Terrace, a faint sound wafted through the howling wind, a desperate, unmistakable bark.

"Sally!" Ralph exclaimed, his ears perked up.

"Where is it coming from?" Pippa asked, her eyes widening.

Ralph's keen eyes scanned the chaotic landscape. "There! In the lake by the Bow Bridge!"

The torrential rain and gusty winds turned the usually placid lake into a roiling mass of water, whipping up waves that clashed against the banks with unyielding force. Amidst this turmoil, a desperate head bobbed in and out of the water, Sally.

"Forget the rain! Move!" Alex roared, leading the charge back into the storm.

By the time they reached the edge of the lake, Sally's struggle had grown critical. Her panicked barks were now intermingled with desperate gasps for air.

Without a second's hesitation, Alex plunged into the swirling waters, muscles tensing against the cold shock. Biting onto Sally's collar with a grip borne of sheer willpower, he began to battle the fierce current and towering waves. As he neared the bank, Sally found her footing on the soft lakebed, scrambling out with the help of Ralph and Spike's strong paws.

Alex was close behind, but just as he was about to clamber onto solid ground, a rogue wave reared up and slammed him back into the water with crushing force. He went under, his body disappearing beneath the turbulent surface.

It was in that harrowing moment that Alfred, the grey Irish Wolfhound, appeared like a guardian spirit. With a powerful leap, he plunged into the water, grasping Alex's limp body, and hauling it back to safety.

The rain eased as if the sky itself was holding its breath. Alex lay motionless, waterlogged, and lifeless on the ground.

"He's not breathing!" Pippa cried out.

Quickly, she placed her paws on his chest and began compressing, pushing rhythmically with an urgency that defied the drumming rain. Water spewed out of Alex's mouth and, after what felt like an eternity, he drew a ragged, shuddering breath.

The black Poodle woke to a circle of anxious faces, and for a moment, disoriented and struggling to reconcile the events that had unfolded he asked, "What happened?"

"Alex, you gave us quite the scare," Ralph said, his voice tinged with palpable relief.

"Who is Alex?" said the black Poodle. "What happened?"

"What do you mean?" said Spike.

Alex, now no longer Alex, looked around, his eyes meeting each of theirs but showing no recognition.

"What do you mean, 'Who is Alex'?" Spike asked, bewilderment painting his face.

Before any further confusion could spiral, Alfred, the grey Irish Wolfhound, spoke with an air of gravity. "Cease your questioning for a moment, all of you. I believe there's something else at play."

The circle went silent, all eyes on the towering figure of Alfred.

"It appears your friend has ascended," Alfred declared solemnly. "In the grand scheme of life and beyond, the form of a dog is often the last form one takes before one ascends to a higher state of existence. It seems your friend has earned his place in the afterlife."

The statement hit them like a bolt of lightning, leaving them in a stunned silence.

"So then who—?" Ralph began, his voice tinged with disbelief.

"My last memory was of strong winds and blinding rain," the black Poodle spoke, his eyes uncertain. "And then, a collision. I was a bird, you see, a bird named Wreck because I had a habit of flying into things. I think I hit a glass pane."

For a moment, the group took this in, the weight of the revelation pressing heavily on them.

"Your real name is Pierre," Pippa declared after a pause. "It is the name our friend Alex is called by his owner, Beatrice."

Though a sense of loss hung in the air, there was also a sense of acceptance, a subtle acknowledgment that life, with all its unpredictable turns, was also full of moments to be celebrated. And so, with heavy hearts but lifted spirits, they began their walk back towards the Alice statue, the sun breaking through the clouds as if nodding to the cyclical nature of existence.

As they made their way, each member of the group took turns telling Pierre about Alex, about his struggles and triumphs, his love for Beatrice, and the incredible journey that had led him to this fateful day.

"You must go to Beatrice," said Ralph. "You may not have his memories, but you now have his form, and she must not be left wondering. She will be worried."

"I'll escort you," Spike volunteered, "We've got a lot to discuss, and you've got a lot to learn."

And as they moved forward, a sense of communal melancholy and joy intertwined, coexisting in the strange but beautiful way that only life's most profound moments can muster. They mourned Alex, yet they also celebrated him. His spirit, they knew, would linger in the friendships he'd nurtured, in the lives he'd touched, and in the park, he'd called home.

The sky, now clearing up, seemed to agree. After all, in the circle of life, there were ends, but there were also new beginnings. As for Pierre, he had an array of new experiences waiting, and a group of friends eager to help him navigate through them. And so, the Alice Gang moved on, but not without carrying a piece of Alex in their hearts, forever.

Sally wondered, would he remember them where he was. She hoped that someday she might see him again. Their budding friendship was evolving into something more. He gave his life to save her, and she would be forever grateful and vowed that she would be worthy of his sacrifice in her actions and love of her friends.

# heavenly bound

Alex stood at the edge of the lake, watching the friends he had come to love and respect so deeply gather around the lifeless form of his former earthly vessel. He felt lighter than air, a sensation unlike anything he had ever known before, yet indescribably comforting. Transparent, ethereal, and insubstantial, he knew that he was no longer a part of the corporeal world. Still, he felt a profound connection to it, especially as he witnessed the anxious faces of the Alice Gang trying to revive the body he had left behind.

"He's not breathing!" Pippa's cry broke through the air, a desperate note hanging on each syllable.

He watched with a mixture of fascination and relief as Pippa pressed her paws rhythmically on his chest, forcing out water, bringing forth that miraculous, shuddering breath in the dog that was no longer him. Alex felt neither sorrow nor bitterness, only a sense of completeness, as if some cosmic narrative had reached its fulfilling end.

At that moment, Alfred, the majestic grey Irish Wolfhound, spoke in his deep, resonant voice. "It appears your friend has ascended."

To the astonishment of Alex, Alfred turned his gaze upwards, locking eyes with him. It was as if he was peering into another plane of existence. Alfred was the only one who could see him, acknowledging his new spiritual form, a bridge between two realms.

"Who are you?" the Poodle—now named Pierre—asked, his voice tinged with confusion.

Alex looked at Pierre and felt nothing but warmth and acceptance. His former shell would serve as the vessel for another soul's journey; it was the nature of life's cyclical path.

"As the form of a dog is the last form you take before ascension, it appears he has earned his place in the afterlife," Alfred continued, still locking eyes with Alex. "This is not Alex."

Alex sensed the melancholy that settled over the group, saw the genuine grief in their eyes. Yet, a sense of peace washed over him as he realized his friends would continue their lives, fostering the same unity and friendship that had once included him.

"Sally," he whispered, even though he knew she couldn't hear him. "You'll always have a part of me."

He watched as they all started the journey back towards the Alice statue, the physical manifestation of their daily rendezvous, a symbol of community and shared experiences. Alfred cast him one final, acknowledging glance before himself, disappearing into an ethereal form, then into nothing.

"Thank you, Alfred," Alex thought, grateful for the Wolfhound's celestial awareness, "and goodbye, my friends. Carry on, live well, and never forget the love we shared."

The daylight that had previously illuminated the storm-beaten landscape of Central Park began to fade from Alex's vision. Instead, a celestial luminance diffused the space around him, softening the borders between the earthly and the ethereal. Behind him, a blue ring of light materialized on the ground, its edges shimmering like the surface of a tranquil lake bathed in moonlight.

"Alex, it's time. Step into the circle," the voice of Max intoned, resounding with both authority and comforting familiarity. It was a voice imbued with the weight of eons, yet tinged with an intangible warmth, a paternal gentleness that made the words more inviting than commanding.

Taking one last look at his friends who were now starting to disperse from the lake's edge, he whispered to himself, "Be well, my friends. Until we meet again." With that, he stepped into the glowing blue circle.

No sooner had he done so than the circle lifted him off the ground, whirling him into a vortex of light and color. He was catapulted through an unidentifiable medium that was neither space nor time. An array of memories, emotions, and perceptions unfurled before him, each one a part of his human, insect, and canine lives, each one a thread in the intricate weave of his soul.

As quickly as the journey had begun, it ended. Alex found himself back in a familiar setting. He was in the Recycling Center, stepping out of what Max had called the Soul Recycling Generator. The walls, adorned with a myriad of monitors and control panels, were a familiar setting.

Max was there, looking just as Alex remembered, an enigmatic blend of divine steward and congenial mentor. His eyes glinted with a knowing spark as he said, "Welcome back, Alex. Your journey has come full circle, but as you know, circles have no end."

Alex felt a myriad of emotions. "I witnessed them, my friends, the park, all that happened after... after I couldn't be there anymore. It was both beautiful and heartbreaking."

Max moved toward one of the control panels and gestured for Alex to follow. "The duality of existence, the blend of joy and sorrow, love and loss, it's all part of the grand design. Your recent sojourn on Earth, as a human, insect, and a dog, adds new threads to that ever-expanding story."

"And what happens now?" Alex inquired, still reeling from the metaphysical whirlwind that had been his life, or should he say lives?

"Now," Max began, his fingers dancing across the control panel as a new set of coordinates were entered, "we prepare you for your next chapter. Each life is a unique story, yet all are chapters in the same grand book of existence."

"Will I remember any of this, the park, my friends, Beatrice, Sally?" Alex's voice tinged with longing and curiosity. "What of Beatrice? I am worried for her."

Max pointed to a monitor and pushed a button showing the live scene of Spike returning Pierre to Beatrice and her giving him the warm broth and settling in under her chair.

"That's comforting," he said. "She is a good soul."

Max paused and looked at Alex, his eyes softening. "You will remember everything now. You may not always remember every detail, but you will always feel it, in the recesses of your soul, like an everlasting imprint."

A new circle started forming on the ground, this one glowing with a hue Alex could not name, a color not of the Earth but of someplace far more extraordinary.

"Are you ready for your next adventure, Alex?" Max's voice filled the room, as another set of coordinates blinked into existence on the control panel.

"Wait," Alex said. "What is happening next?"

"You will enter this next circle and be transported to the receiving center to enter the afterlife, for you, that would be Heaven," explained Max.

Alex looked at the circle, then back at Max. The myriad threads of his existence, his love for Beatrice, his friendship with Sally and the Alice Gang, his human life, his canine life, all seemed to blend into a single, luminous strand.

"Yes," he replied, his voice echoing with newfound resolve. "I am ready."

And with that affirmation, Alex stepped into the glowing circle. No sooner had Alex's ethereal form solidified in a new dimension than he was enveloped in an atmosphere of inexplicable familiarity. It was as if he'd arrived in a place that was both completely new and agelessly known to him. He stood in what looked like a receiving center, an area both grand and serene, defined by archways of luminous, flowing energy and floors that seemed to be woven from threads of celestial light.

As his eyes adjusted to this celestial setting, a sight even more astonishing unfurled before him. Waiting there, draped in human forms yet unmistakably recognizable, were Sally, Pippa, Ralph, and Spike.

"Sally! Ralph! Pippa! Spike!" he cried out, unable to restrain the jubilance that welled up within him. They all turned, their faces lighting up with joy and amazement, eyes widening in disbelief yet also in recognition.

"Alex!" they chorused, as if orchestrated by some divine maestro.

"How is this possible? How can we recognize each other in these forms?" Alex wondered aloud, bewildered yet elated.

Ralph answered, his voice imbued with the same calm rationality he'd always had, "Alfred showed us visions in the cavern, remember? Visions of our human selves. It seems that wisdom stayed with us, even through ascension."

Alex nodded, understanding dawning upon him. "Ah, Alfred and his celestial visions. He was there, at the lake. He saw me."

Pippa interjected, her eyes twinkling with a mischievous delight. "We've all ascended at the same time., well except for Dale. Hopefully, he can continue to guide Pierre."

"What? When? How?" The questions tumbled from Alex's lips.

Sally took a step forward, her eyes meeting Alex's with a depth of emotion he'd only felt in glimpses during their time in the park. "The day after you... after the lake, we went back to the Alice statue to pay our respects, to honor your memory."

"And while we were there," Ralph continued, "each of us, one by one, began to ascend. I ascended for hearing and spotting Sally in the lake, for alerting everyone that she was in trouble."

Pippa chimed in, her words flowing with a newfound gravitas, "I ascended for saving Pierre's life, for bringing him back from the brink of death."

Spike, who'd always been a beacon of quiet strength, added, "And I, for lending my strength to pull Sally to safety and escorting Pierre home to Beatrice so she would not have to mourn the loss of her beloved Mon Cheri."

Last to speak was Sally, her voice suffused with a tender solemnity. "And I ascended for you, Alex, for turning a lost soul into a model of redemption, for showing me the way even when you were struggling to find it yourself."

Alex looked around at his friends, his eternal friends, as it now seemed. He was struck by the gravity of it all, the poignancy of these multiple narratives culminating in a single point of celestial convergence.

"It's overwhelming, isn't it?" Sally said, sensing Alex's emotional tumult.

Alex nodded, taking a deep, spiritual breath. "To think that our actions, our lives, have rippled through the fabric of existence in ways we could never comprehend, it's humbling."

"And it's only the beginning," Ralph reminded him, pointing toward another radiant circle that began to form at the edge of the receiving center. "Who knows what adventures lie ahead of us?"

Sally took Alex's hand and gave it a reassuring squeeze. "What I do know is that we'll face them together, as we always have."

"And so," Alex said, "our journey continues."

Together, they stepped into the new circle of light, their forms dissolving into a radiant mist, as if they were made of stardust. The circle lifted, and the group was swept away into the next chapter of their boundless journey. But as they left, their laughter and voices echoed back in the receiving center, a timeless testament to their friendship and to the mysterious realm of existence.

www.ingramcontent.com/pod-product-compliance
Lightning Source LLC
Chambersburg PA
CBHW060907140726
47996CB00001B/156